The Christmas Town

A Time Travel Novel

Elyse Douglas

COPYRIGHT

Time is, time was, but time shall be no more.

—James Joyce

For Julia, who lives in the time of play.

.

The Christmas Town

CHAPTER 1

The twin engine airbus pitched and bucked in the snowstorm. The *fasten your seat belt* light had been on for 5 minutes, and anxious passengers were hunched over their phones, laptops and tablets, struggling to ignore the erratic motion. Megan Jennings glanced about and thought that everyone she saw was tense and jumpy. She tightened her seatbelt and swallowed hard, feeling her stomach sink and rise with the movement of the airplane. She was not an easy flyer, anyway, and the snowstorm was unnerving her. *Can't they fly above these things?* she thought.

The captain came on, his smooth voice calm and reassuring. "Ladies and gentlemen, sorry for the bumpy ride. We're trying to swing around the main part of the storm, but the winds are pretty strong, as you can feel. Unfortunately, the Portland International Airport has just closed down and they are diverting us over to the Montpelier area, to the Burlington International Airport."

There was a chorus of sighs and groans.

The captain continued. "The storm has blanketed Portland, but it has temporarily thinned out over the

Montpelier area, so we shouldn't have any problems landing in Burlington. The center of Montpelier is only about 37 miles away. My apologies for this sudden change, especially since it's only five days before Christmas, and I'm sure many of you will have to make alternate travel plans in order to get home. However, there's not much we can do about this except to get you safely on the ground. We appreciate your bearing with us and we thank you for your patience. We should be landing in Burlington in about 30 minutes. If there's anything the flight attendants can do to make you more comfortable, please let them know."

Megan sighed, heavily. Montpelier? Burlington? How was she going to get to Portland? It had to be at least 200 miles away. There would be a mad dash of passengers charging the car rental agencies as soon as they were allowed off the plane, and all the rentals would probably be gone, anyway.

She could call her father, but she didn't want him driving in the storm, especially with his high blood pressure and his classic case-study of impatience and worry. Megan laid her head back against the seat and closed her eyes. Maybe she'd just have to spend the night at some hotel and try to find a ride in the morning. A burst of wind punched the airplane, and it shuddered. Megan's eyes popped wide open. She was terrified.

Near the rear of the plane, in window seat 23A, Jackie Young had just shut down her tablet, fighting irritation and wishing she'd just stayed in New York. Her gut had told her this would not be an easy flight. She'd been watching the weather reports, constantly, for days. The storm was predicted, although it wasn't supposed to be severe over New York and Boston; it was supposed to be moving away. But weather always had a way of fooling the weather people and, this time, the storm had stalled and was dumping heavy snow over a wide swath of 800 miles. She was lucky to be on one of the last planes to leave LaGuardia, before they shut down all but one runway. Lucky or unlucky?

Jackie and Eric had planned for her to spend Christmas with his family, since they had spent Thanksgiving with her family in Chicago. The truth was, she was dreading it and *had* been dreading it for weeks. Eric's parents were nice enough, but in an effusive and strained kind of way. Whenever she was around them she had the feeling they just didn't think she was the right match for their son. Maybe it was because she and Eric had met on one of those online dating sites. Maybe it was because they had always wanted Eric to marry, literally, the girl next door, Molly Ferguson. She didn't live next door to them now, but she had during high school and through most of Eric's college years. Molly was pretty, quiet and simple. Jackie was perky, a little too aggressive sometimes, and complicated, or so Eric sometimes told her. Yes, she could admit to all those things because they had helped her move up the ladder to become the senior graphics manager for Lotus Design Corp., where she also was the coordinator and Line Producer for Meetings & Corporate Events. It hadn't been easy climbing that ladder, and she had worked hard, ever since graduating four years ago from Northwestern.

She was jarred from her thoughts by another gust of wind and she turned to the window, grimly, seeing a mass of snow fleeing by. God, she'd be relieved when they were finally on the ground. Her stomach growled. She hadn't eaten since breakfast, and it was after 7pm. Where was Montpelier anyway, and how far was it from Portland? She'd have to find a way to get there. Managing expectations, deadlines, budgets and stress was her specialty. She did it all day long, so she was confident that she'd be able to find a car rental with a GPS and, after some wretched airport food, she'd be on her way.

The captain came back over the intercom. "Ladies and gentlemen, please stay in your seats, with your seatbelts fastened tightly around you. We're about to make our final approach into Burlington. Flight attendants, please prepare the cabin for arrival. Again, ladies and gentlemen, our apologies for diverting the flight and we hope you will think of us again, when making any future flying plans. We'll be on the ground shortly."

It can't be shortly enough, Megan thought, especially since the guy next to her was a giant and taking up all of his seat and a third of hers.

Her parents would be so disappointed when she called to tell them. They'd surely have an argument over it, especially since Megan's father had wanted her to come two days before when the weather was bright and sunny. Megan's mother had supported Megan's decision, because she had an audition for a new Broadway show and her agent said she was perfect for the role. Well, the audition went okay. She'd danced better than she'd sung. Still, she was hopeful she'd get the part. She hadn't been in a show since she'd played Nellie Forbush in the road production of *South Pacific*, and that show had closed back in late October. Her savings were dwindling, and she needed the work. Also, she'd foolishly loaned her ex-boyfriend two thousand dollars back in September and he still hadn't paid it back, even though he'd promised to pay her by the first of November. Okay, well, that was another reason he was her *ex*-boyfriend.

The airplane descended from low clouds like a gray

ghost, a frenzy of snow spinning in its landing lights. It hovered for seconds above the runway and then its wheels touched down, squealing, snow spurting beneath them. The plane roared down the runway, braking, snow rising in a cloud around it as it came to a stop.

After the plane had taxied to the gate and the airway tunnel was securely attached, passengers stood, feverishly tapping out texts and emails. Many had phones to their ears, delivering the bad news to friends and family who were waiting all over southern Maine.

Megan waited until she had come through the tunnel before she called her parents, hearing placid Christmas carols from overhead speakers. She'd already put on her slim, dark-blue down coat, and a white wool scarf around her neck. Her eyes darted about frantically, as she dragged her cream-colored carry-on suitcase, searching for the signs to the rent-a-car stands or kiosks. Passengers poured out of the tunnel into the quiet terminal, eyes wide and searching, bodies springing into action.

Just as her father picked up, Megan saw a woman about her own age shoot by, walking briskly toward the signs announcing the location of the rent-a-car desk, her violet leather suitcase in tow, its wheels growling across the tiles. She wore dark woolen pants, heels and an elegant cashmere coat.

"Dad? Megan. Look I have to be fast here. Our flight was diverted to Burlington, near Montpelier."

"I know, dammit!" he said, sharply. "I'm still at the airport, trying to figure out what to do. We got the word a half hour ago. You should have come two days ago! Now, I'm going to have to come and get you."

"No, Dad. No! You are not driving in this snowstorm. I will rent a car and drive myself. If I can't get a car tonight, I'll stay in a hotel or get a car or plane out in the morning."

"Megan, you have trouble driving in good weather, let alone in a dammed snowstorm."

"Dad, I'm not going there right now. I have to hurry to the rent-a-car place or there won't be any cars left. I'll call you later, okay? Mom alright?"

"Yeah, yeah. Why don't the two of you ever listen to me? If you had come two days ago, this wouldn't have happened."

"Dad, I'm hanging up! Go home. I'll call you when I know something. Bye."

"Wait... I..."

But Megan had hung up. She was clicking across the tile in her two-inch heels. Why the hell hadn't she just put her flats on before she boarded the plane?

She rounded a corner, following the signs, and when she saw the line at the car-rental desk, she cursed. It was five deep. The stressed male service agent wore a red blazer and black tie. His stiff blond hair had wilted and his eyes were downcast. He was on the phone while holding up a hand like a stop sign, trying to hold off the attractive dark-haired woman who had zoomed past Megan earlier.

Megan got in the line, feeling her pulse race. Finally, the hassled service agent turned back to the impatient woman.

He shrugged. "Like I said, I don't have any more cars. It's just that simple."

"You've got to have one. Just one car. You're a rent-a-car agency, aren't you? Don't you plan for things like this? Surely, you or your bosses watch the Weather Channel and know that when a storm is coming you put more cars in the garage or wherever?"

The weary agent heaved out a deep sigh and averted

his eyes. "All I can tell you is that there are no cars here or at any other agency here at the airport. Maybe we'll have one or two of them in the morning. If you want, I'll put you on the list."

The girl was undaunted. She leaned forward, her elbows on the counter. "I'm sorry, what is your name?"

"Steve," he said, pointing to his gold bar name tag.

The woman softened her tone. "Steve, my name is Jackie. It's nice to meet you. Now, Steve, you must, must have one little car. One single car for me."

Megan watched Jackie, admiring her persistence, but impatient with her lack of ingenuity. Megan had an idea. She broke the line and stepped up to the rental desk, standing next to Jackie.

Megan focused on Steve's name tag. "Sir, I have an emergency. My mother is sick. Very sick, and she is expecting me to show up with her medication. She is out of her medication and she didn't order more because it's very expensive and I was coming to Portland, anyway. So I bought her medication in New York. Now, it is vital, a matter of life and death, that I get to Portland tonight. Do you have any kind of vehicle, anything at all that I could have, so I can get this medication to my sick mother?"

Jackie looked at Megan, incredulous. "Excuse me? I was here first."

Megan nodded, the actress in her producing a soft, humble expression. "Yes, you were, and I am so sorry, but I'll do anything for my mother. You only have one mother, after all."

The service agent closed his eyes for a long moment.

A heavy-set man behind the woman stepped forward. He was about 45, dressed in a smart business suit, clutching a brief case. "Excuse me," he said. "Maybe I can help."

Steve was pleading now. "Sir, I don't have any more cars. I really don't, and we're closing now. There's nothing more I can do."

"Yes, son, I understand. But you have a reservation for Harold Dodge, do you not?"

Steve's eyes searched the computer monitor. He typed in the name and waited. He glanced up, attentively, refusing to look at the women.

"Yes. It's the last car. We saved it for you."

Jackie was about to speak, but Harold cut her off. "I couldn't help but overhear. Both of you ladies are going to Portland, aren't you?"

Jackie glowered at Megan, who smiled pitifully at Jackie. Megan then turned that same pitiful smile on Harold Dodge. "Yes, sir, I believe we are both going to Portland. Is there anything you can do to help us?"

Jackie rolled her eyes.

"Yes, ladies. You can have my car and, this way, both of you will be able to get to Portland for Christmas." He looked at Megan. "I would feel awfully bad if your mother had to be in the hospital on Christmas Day. And anyway, during the Christmas season, aren't we supposed to be generous?"

Jackie lifted her chin, suddenly hopeful. Megan paused, feeling a sudden pang of guilt. She let out a little sigh, remembering what her mother had always told her. "Remember, Megan, God is always watching you, so always do the right thing."

"Excuse me?" Jackie said, hoping to jar Megan from her guilty daydream.

Megan took in a bracing breath and faced Harold Dodge. She swallowed. "Sir, I can't take your car."

"What?" Jackie snapped.

"I can't. But thank you. It was very kind of you."

"I don't understand," Mr. Dodge said. "Don't you need to get your mother her medication?"

Megan looked away, struggling for dignity. "No, sir. I lied to you because I wanted a car. Any car. The truth is my mother is not sick, and I lied. You keep your car and you and your family have a very merry Christmas."

Jackie's mouth was open. Her face a blank, eyes blinking.

Harold Dodge studied the girls, carefully. He pursed up his lips in thought. "I tell you what. You take the car anyway."

Megan snapped a look at him. "But I lied, and…"

Mr. Dodge cut her off. "… Honesty is its own reward. No, you take the car. I want you to. I want both of you ladies to have it. I have friends I can stay with tonight. I'll get a car in the morning."

Megan was contrite, her eyes staring down at the floor. She reached out, took Harold's hand and shook it firmly. "Mr. Dodge, that is a very nice thing to do. Thank you."

"And your name is?" Harold Dodge asked.

"Megan Jennings."

They shook hands. "Well, Ms. Jennings, I hope you and your family have a very merry Christmas."

Jackie had barely recovered from the emotional roller coaster ride.

Harold took Jackie's hand. "I hope you'll have a merry Christmas too, young lady. And what is your name?"

Jackie managed a smile. "I'm Jackie Young. Thank you, Mr. Dodge, and Merry Christmas."

"Ladies, may you both have the merriest of Christmases. Now please be careful driving in this storm. May you have a great adventure as you both make your way home to your families."

Mr. Dodge turned and strode away, whistling the carol *We Wish You a Merry Christmas.*

The other weary, resigned travelers left the line, some wandering to the nearest chairs, slumping down, while others reached for their phones to find over-night accommodations.

Steve handed Megan the paperwork, as Jackie watched Megan fill out the forms.

"Did you know that would happen?" Jackie asked.

Megan continued scribbling. "Of course not."

"I feel guilty taking his car," Jackie said. "I hope nothing bad happens to us."

Megan stopped writing. She looked at Jackie and through Jackie, with no change of expression. "Well, you don't have to come."

Megan turned back to the form and resumed writing.

"I'm coming," Jackie said. "He wanted both of us to have the car."

Megan completed the forms and handed them to Steve. He took them but didn't move. Megan questioned him with her eyes. "Anything wrong, Steve?"

He stared back, uncomfortably. "Mr. Dodge did want you both to have the car." He indicated toward Jackie. "Shouldn't she sign on as an extra driver?"

Jackie looked at Steve in triumph, and then gave Megan a firm nod. "Yes. Thank you, Steve."

Steve handed Jackie the forms, and she went to work filling them out.

Afterwards, Steve processed, stapled and punched the forms, and would not allow his eyes or his countenance to go anywhere near the two girls.

Steve exited through a back door to a glass-enclosed office. A minute later he returned and slapped the keys down on the counter. Before Megan could pick them up,

Jackie snatched them.

"I'll drive," Jackie said. "I'm a careful, efficient and fast driver."

"Have you looked outside lately? It's pouring snow again. Fast is not a word I would use driving in a snow storm."

Jackie smiled, weakly. "I also said I'm careful."

"I'll be back with the GPS in a sec," Steve said.

While they waited, Megan studied Jackie, curiously. She thought her to be about 25 or 26 years old. She had a killer figure, with steady dark blue eyes and a pouty mouth. Her haircut suited her perfectly: a princely cut, with black bangs that came almost to her full black eye-brows. Megan had the impression that Jackie was a will-ful woman, who was ambitious and linear, and didn't al-low much of anything to get in the way of her definite energy, pretty face and urgent purpose.

The women stared, eye to eye.

Jackie looked Megan over for the first time. She saw Megan's shining, dramatic shoulder-length reddish-blonde hair, friendly green eyes and pretty face. Her cheek bones were high, lips sensual—and the scattered freckles on her cheeks and nose added a touch of girlish whimsy. Jackie figured Megan was not more than 25, and probably had a restless, emotional nature and a practiced charm that most men surely found attractive, and most women cer-tainly found irritating. Jackie found her irritating.

"I always get nervous whenever I go back home," Me-gan said. "Especially during the holidays."

"Then why go?" Jackie asked.

"Let me put it this way. My father and mother are waiting for me. My brother's coming from Florida to-morrow. It's not the happiest family on the planet, and it will not be the merriest of Christmases on the planet, because my father shouts a lot and my mother pushes all but one of my buttons. My father pushes that last button. Nonetheless, it will be Christmas with my family, and I'd like to be there with them."

Steve returned with the receipt, a map and the GPS. The girls snatched their travel bags and started for the rental lot.

Outside, Jackie and Megan fought a sharp frigid wind and driving snow as they navigated the parking lot, searching for the car. It was Megan who found it, shouting out in triumph. It was a late model red Ford Fusion sedan. They quickly swung their carry-on luggage into the trunk, slammed it shut and piled into the car. Jackie started the engine and found the heat, allowing the vents to blast hot air at their upper bodies.

"It is wild out there!" Jackie said, buckling up. "I thought this storm was moving away East."

"There must be 7 inches of snow on the ground," Megan said. "Maybe we should find a place to stay for the night and get out of this. The storm's not going to let up any time soon."

"Storm or no storm, we're going to Portland," Jackie said, her voice strong, her face determined. The wipers came on, slapping the splashing snowflakes, clearing a brief patch of windshield.

Megan felt a ball of tension build in her stomach. "I'm hungry."

Jackie dropped the car into gear and drove away, squinting looks for the exit sign. "I was going to get something at the airport, but there wasn't time. I haven't eaten since breakfast."

"Maybe we'll find something on the way," Megan said.

"No time for that. I'm going straight through to Portland. According to the GPS, it's two hundred and twenty-two miles. We should get there in about 3 hours and 20 minutes."

Megan gave a little irritated shake of her head. "Were you in the military?" Megan asked.

"No, but my father is. He's a general."

Megan gave a sharp nod, and mumbled under her breath, "Of course."

Minutes later, they were swallowed up by the swarm of snow, buffeted by puffs of a driving wind.

Both women were silent as they searched for signs and markers. To relax, Megan reached into the glove compartment and drew out the operator's manual. She switched on the overhead dome light and read.

"Hey, listen to this. This car gets an EPA-estimated rating of 47 miles per gallon in the city and on the highway, or a combination of both. It says that this Fusion Hybrid can travel up to 62 miles per hour on electric power alone. Well, it won't cost us a lot of gas, anyway."

Jackie checked the GPS. "Let's make sure we find I-89 South/White River Junction and merge onto I-89-South."

But they had already missed the turn off, turning instead onto a seldom traveled road that led northwest.

"How did we miss that turnoff?" Jackie asked.

"I don't know, I was watching."

"Okay, so we have to get back. Check the map."

"What does the GPS say?" Megan asked.

Jackie slapped it. "It's Jacked! All messed up. It's not working. It says we're somewhere in New Mexico."

They were traveling down a snow-covered, two-lane road, that curved and twisted and meandered through dark moving trees.

Jackie began to perspire. "Where the hell are we?"

Megan was pouring over the map, but she had no idea where they were. "I don't know. I'll use my phone. I'll pull up a map and see where we are."

They stared out into the infinite wild stormy night, growing increasingly anxious.

"I can't connect," Megan said, trying to keep the mild panic from her voice.

"Try mine," Jackie said.

Megan did, but Jackie's phone was dead.

"It can't be dead. What happened!?" Jackie exclaimed. "It was charged. I haven't used it since the airport."

Megan lay Jackie's phone aside and tried hers again. The screen went black. She stared in astonishment and dismay. "That's weird. Why are they both dead?"

Jackie took a couple of deep breaths. "Okay, we'll stop at the next town or restaurant or whatever. Help me look. Somebody has to be out there."

"Have you seen a car pass?" Megan asked, knowing the answer.

"No."

"That's odd, isn't it?"

They craned their necks and strained their eyes, but saw nothing but hectic snow exploding across the headlight beams, and desolation all about them.

"What now?" Megan asked. "What do we do now?"

For the first time, Jackie had lost some of her confidence, and Megan could see that she was frightened. "I don't know... We're lost, Megan."

CHAPTER 2

They crept along, eye-weary, back-weary and bone-weary. They'd been driving for over an hour and they had not seen another car, road sign, house or town.

"Okay, I'm freakin' out," Megan said. "I mean, if we don't see some sign of life in the next few minutes, I am going to freak out!"

"Let's try to stay calm," Jackie said, feeling jittery, her uncertain eyes daring about.

Megan shut her eyes and took deep breaths.

Minutes later they were still struggling to relax, squinting into the relentless storm.

"I can't see anything but blinding snow," Megan said.

The wind howled like a wild animal, and snow blew across the road, piling into drifts against the base of trees.

"How far have we gone so far?" Megan asked.

"I don't know. Maybe 40 or 50 miles."

Megan blew out an audible sigh. "I feel like I'm in a snow globe and some crazy kid just keeps shaking it."

"Dramatic," Jackie said.

"Scared," Megan said.

Megan thought she saw a sign ahead, caked in snow and leaning precariously to the right, as if a burst of wind would blow it down.

"Jackie, stop! Look. I think there's a sign over there. See it?"

Jackie slowed, saw the sign and stopped. "God, I hope it tells us where we are."

Megan struggled into her coat and gloves and pulled on her hat. She shoved the door open, braced against the wind, and got out. Snow lashed at her face and she turned away, protecting her face with her hand. She trudged through nearly a foot of snow until she reached the sign, illuminated by the car beams. With her right hand, she brushed snow from the sign, little by little, until she was able to read HOLLY and then GROVE 1 MILE. A little black arrow pointed right. Megan looked right, shading her eyes, and peered into the distance. She saw something. She saw the shadow of a covered bridge, looming out in the blur of snow. That must be it. The town was across the bridge. Energized, she whirled, stomped back to the car and got in.

She was breathing rapidly. "It's wild out there," she said, shivering. "There's a bridge just ahead. Holly Grove is about a mile away."

"Sounds quaint," Jackie said. "I hope they have a mo-tel and an all-night restaurant."

Jackie drove toward the bridge, the narrow road to the bridge looking dark and foreboding.

"Wait a minute, Jackie."

Jackie paused before making the turn. "What's the matter?" she asked.

"I don't know. I just hate to leave the main road."

"Megan, across that bridge is a town. We have passed absolutely nothing on this 'so-called' main road. Please, let's just get across the bridge and spend the night in Holly Grove."

Megan nodded, still reluctant. "Okay..."

Jackie made the turn. But at the threshold of the bridge, Megan called out again.

"Stop!"

Jackie hit the brakes again, irritated. "Megan, what?"

Megan stared at the bridge. It wasn't a large bridge, probably no more than 90 feet across a rocky stream, but something gnawed away at her, some ineffable feeling of danger that she couldn't put her finger on.

"Megan?" Jackie said, seeing a far-away look in Megan's eyes. "What are we waiting for?"

"Okay, okay... It's just that..."

"What?"

"Forget it."

Jackie nudged the car forward and it rattled across the bridge. The two girls held their breath in the cave-like interior, darkness swallowing them, the wind screaming through the cracks all around them.

When they finally exited on the other side, they released trapped air from their lungs.

"Wow, that gave me the creeps," Megan said.

Jackie looked about uneasily. "What a freaky night this is."

They passed through a gray and white shroud of blowing snow. Suddenly, as if a curtain were being drawn from both sides of a stage, a gust of wind passed over the car and blew the snow away.

Jackie stopped the car. The girls looked at each other, then blinked around in astonished wonder.

"What happened?" Megan asked.

Jackie was speechless.

There was snow on the ground, but only two or three

inches. There was no sound of wind, no blowing snow, just a few gentle flurries. The whispering sound of the windshield wipers was loud in the sudden silence and Jackie switched them off. They sat there, staring. Jackie rolled down the window and felt a cool, intoxicating breeze on her face. She looked up into the sky and saw a few stars and a ghostly near-full moon swimming over the top of a distant shadowy mountain.

Megan opened the door and stepped out, without hat or gloves. She turned in a circle, smelling fresh pine, hearing the splashing stream they'd just crossed. It was quiet, a deep satisfying quiet that relaxed her. She took an easy breath and smiled.

"Jackie... it's beautiful," she said, as she held out her hand to catch a few random snowflakes.

Jackie stepped out. It was still cold, but not a punishing cold. There was a softness in the air. Megan looked at Jackie, her brows raised in a query. She shrugged. Jackie shrugged. It was as though they were suddenly watching the world at a slower movie projector speed.

Jackie saw a glow, just ahead, advancing toward them. She pointed, excited. "Megan, look! A light or something, up ahead."

Megan turned. "Yes! What is it?"

Through the smoky cloud of fog, two glowing headlights slowly approached.

"It's a car! Megan, it's a car. Let's wave it down. Hurry!"

Framed in the headlights, the girls walked to the front of the car, and waved, using both arms. The car began to slow to a stop.

Megan gave Jackie the thumb's up. Jackie stayed back, but Megan moved toward the stopped car as the driver's window rolled half way down. Megan drew up alongside and looked in to see an elderly man, with wary, watery eyes peering up at her.

White vapor puffed from her mouth as she spoke. "Hi there. Thank God you came by. We're lost and we haven't seen anything or anybody for miles."

The man didn't blink. He just stared. He stared at Megan. He stared at Jackie. He stared at their car.

Megan noticed his car. It was old—a very old black car—dusted with snow. She noticed the running board and heavy fenders. It looked like something out of the *Bonnie and Clyde* movie her father repeatedly watched.

Megan was actually looking at a 1934 Ford Tudor Sedan, two-door body.

"Can you help us?" Megan asked.

"Well, what do you want me to do?" he barked.

"We were trying to get to Portland and we must have missed the turnoff somewhere back."

"I'll say you did. You're a good 30 miles away from it. You're going in the wrong direction."

"We haven't seen a motel or anything. Is there somewhere we can spend the night?"

He kept looking at her strangely, then he stared at Jackie again, and then at their car. "What is that?"

Megan followed his eyes. "What? Our car?"

"Yeah. What is that?"

"It's our car."

He shook his head. "Dang, I ain't never seen a car like that before. What is it?"

"It's a Ford. A Ford Fusion Hybrid."

"A what!?" he asked, pinching up his face and cupping his ear with his hand. "What did you say it was?"

"It's a Ford. Can you please tell me where the nearest town or motel is?"

He couldn't pull his eyes from the car. "Ain't never seen anything like that."

"Sir, please! We are very tired and very hungry."

He looked at her again and jerked a thumb behind him. "Holly Grove is about a mile up the road."

He rolled up his window, threw the car in gear and plodded off. Jackie waved. As he passed the Ford Fusion, his eyes bulged wildly, face blank with shock. He pressed down on the accelerator, hurrying off into the night.

Megan strolled back to Jackie.

"What did he say?" Jackie asked.

"Well, I guess he's never seen a hybrid before."

They got back into the car and continued on into the uncertain night, straining every muscle to see the town. Moments later, they came to some railroad tracks, bumped across them and saw a white sign with black letters that read

WELCOME TO HOLLY GROVE VERMONT
POP 5,400

"That's what I call a small town," Megan said.

"What time is it?" Jackie asked.

Megan checked her phone. It was still dead. She looked at her watch. "Nine forty."

They crested a little hill and entered the quiet town along Main Street. The first thing they saw was a billboard sign. It loomed large over a low dark warehouse. There was a large picture of a white pack of Wrigley's Spearmint gum over a bright green mint leaf. The advertisement read: SPEARMINT HAS GONE TO WAR.

Jackie said, "What's that all about?"

They passed 19th century brick storefronts, a post office, a pawn shop and a barber shop, with a Christmas wreath hanging inside its window. All the signs were turned off. They saw Dandy's Market and Dot's Café. Plastered on the red brick face of Dandy's Market were soda signs: Coca-Cola, Orange Crush and Royal Crown Cola. They also noticed a large poster with the photograph of a cute boy about 5 years old, with ruffled brown hair and a pleading, sorrowful expression. He wore a white shirt and had a little blue ribbon and medal around his neck. He was holding a toy car. Below the photo it read:

HE KNOWS WHY THIS CHRISTMAS ALL OF US SHOULD GIVE WAR BONDS

That struck the girls as odd, but their attention was drawn to the deserted streets. *The town must have shut down for the night*, they thought. What struck them as particularly strange were the cars parked at an angle by the curb. They were all old, as old as the one that had stopped back up the road, and they looked bulky, blocky and heavy.

"I've seen cars like this in those silent movies. Those Charlie Chaplin movies," Megan said.

"Those two pickup trucks are definitely vintage. This town must be poor," Jackie said.

Jackie and Megan were processing this as they drove by the town square, with its tall stately Christmas tree, elaborate manger scene, and old redbrick courthouse with a white-faced Roman numeral clock tower.

At the Gulf gas station, Jackie slowed down as they took in the two obelisk-type antique looking pumps. They saw a sign that said GAS 14 CENTS A GALLON. Next to that was another sign written by hand. NO GAS.

The pump on the left had rolling type numbers, and the one on the right had a clock face, showing a dial-type gas meter.

Megan read a stand-alone sign near the entrance.

GET IN THE SCRAP
OFFICIAL RUBBER COLLECTION DEPOT

Jackie's face fell into perplexity. "What's going on here? A gallon of gas for 14 cents?"

"The whole town looks like some kind of old movie or something," Megan said. "And there's nobody around. This place is giving me the creeps."

"We've got to find a place to stay," Jackie said. "I am absolutely exhausted."

"I'm *so* hungry," Megan said, hearing her stomach growl. "I'd love a Katz's Corned Beef sandwich."

"Oh, God, they are so good, aren't they? How much are those now?"

"15.95."

"Really?"

"It's worth it."

They saw Green's Drugstore and John's General Store, with a 6-foot Christmas tree outside. Just then, a young man about 15 or 16 stepped out of Green's Drugstore, carrying several little brown bags. When he saw them, he froze in utter shock, his eyes bulging, mouth open. He actually did a double-take.

Jackie stopped, and Megan rolled down her window and waved at him.

"Hello there," Megan said.

The boy was rigid. Then he trembled.

"Is there a hotel or motel or Bed & Breakfast nearby?" Megan asked.

The boy swallowed, whipped his head about, as if calculating the best route for escape, and then bolted away right. He found a narrow alley, skidded on his heels, and disappeared.

Megan turned in a slow confusion, facing Jackie. Jackie lifted a puzzled eyebrow. "What was that all about?"

Megan lowered the sun visor and examined herself in the little mirror. "I know I'm tired, but do I look that bad?"

Jackie massaged her temples. "This has been the strangest trip I have ever taken. Let's just try to find someplace to eat and sleep and forget this crazy little excursion ever happened."

They drove on toward the outskirts of town, passing THE GROVE movie theater. The movie marquis displayed GIRL CRAZY, starring Judy Garland and Mickey Rooney.

"I saw that on TCM a few months ago," Megan said.

Jackie stared, darkly. "There is something going on, Megan. Something... weird."

After the movie theater, they spotted The Grove Hotel, but it was closed. Fighting fatigue and despair, they turned off Main Street onto Maple Street, a quiet tree-lined street with neat framed houses, and the occasional vintage automobile parked in the driveway or along the deserted street.

"I just can't get over all these old cars," Megan said. "They look like something out of those old gangster movies."

"Yeah... it's weird. We have got to find someplace to stay. If our stupid phones worked, we could have found something by now. What the hell is the matter with this place? I am going to go out of my mind if we don't find some place to stay, and soon."

"Okay, okay, calm down. Let's stay positive," Megan said.

"Okay, positive," Jackie repeated, fighting for calm. "Positive. Yes. I just need something to eat, and everything will be cool."

"Do you want me to drive?"

"No! Find us a place to eat."

Megan spotted something. "Jackie! Stop. Look over there."

Jackie slammed on the brakes and they rocked forward, Megan's hands braced against the dashboard.

Jackie followed Megan's pointing finger to a modest two-story house, with a white fence surrounding a little yard. Above the porch, hanging by two thin chains, was a sign that said BOARDING HOUSE. It was swinging easily in the modest breeze.

"The sign on the porch says boarding house," Megan said, excited.

Jackie crouched and looked. "Are there any lights on?"

"I don't care. Let's try it."

Jackie parked at the curb, killed the engine, and the two girls snatched their coats and got out. Jackie led the way, with energy and purpose. She crossed the sidewalk, released the latch on the white gate and marched up the walkway, mounting the three concrete stairs to the door, where a Christmas wreath was hanging from inside. Megan arrived, and both shaded their eyes, peering inside through the square glass that was covered by a white lace curtain.

"I see a light on in a back room," Jackie said.

Megan noticed something hanging in the picture window. She stepped over to examine it. It was a blue star on a small red cloth banner. She shrugged and joined Jackie.

Jackie gently pressed the doorbell. They heard a soft DING DONG. They waited, anxiously, taking in the silent neighborhood. There were no lights on anywhere and it was very dark.

"No action in this town," Megan said. "It reminds me of a town in Indiana where I did summer stock a few years ago. Two months there seemed like two years."

The front room light flickered on, not the porch light. The girls inhaled hopeful breaths. They saw an elderly woman draw back the lace curtain and peek out. The girls gave her their friendliest smiles.

A moment later, the door opened, but only a couple of inches.

"Hello," Jackie said, brightly. "Can you help us?"

The door opened a little wider. She was a small, thin woman and a bit stooped. Her white hair was up in a bun and she wore a long gray nightgown. Peering out from the granny spectacles on the end of her nose, she looked at them slowly and carefully. "What do you want?"

"Please..." Jackie said. "We have been traveling for hours and hours and we are so tired and hungry. Do you have room for us?"

The woman hesitated, then opened the door fully. Her eyes widened as she studied them, up and down. "It's late. Why are you out so late?"

"We got lost. We were trying to get to Portland."

"Portland? That's hours away. You would have run out of gas. There's no gas anywhere. Did you get it on the black market? I don't take people who cheat. I've got a grandson fighting in Italy."

Megan and Jackie exchanged mystified glances. Both were thinking, "*Is this woman nuts?*"

Jackie said, "No ma'am, we don't cheat. We just want a room. Please."

"I only have one, with one double bed. The other two rooms are occupied with regulars."

"That's fine," Jackie said. "One room is fine."

The woman was conflicted. "This is very unusual. I

only take in people I know or who are referred to me. How many nights are you wanting to stay?"

"Just tonight," Megan said, twisting her cold hands. "Please. We are so tired."

The woman stepped aside, let them in and then closed the door.

"My name is Aunt Betty. May I know your names?"

"I'm Jackie Young and this is Megan..." Jackie looked at Megan, forgetting her last name.

"Jennings. Megan Jennings."

"Well, that'll be a dollar each for the night and 35 cents each for breakfast. If you want something to eat tonight, that'll cost you 50 cents. I was going off to bed, but I'll put something out for you."

Megan stared into Jackie's uncertain eyes.

"You mean one single dollar each?" Jackie asked.

"That's a fair price," Aunt Betty said, a little defensively.

"Oh, yes, that's very fair," Megan said, quickly. "That's fine, Aunt Betty. And we'd love something to eat. We don't want to put you out. Anything that's easy."

"You get your things then and I'll take out some cold chicken, apple pie and bread. I hope that'll do."

The girls smiled, gratefully. "That sounds wonderful," Jackie said.

After Aunt Betty padded off toward the kitchen, the girls took in the surroundings.

The living room seemed from another world. It was a simple square room, with a mantel, hearth and several seascapes set in gilded frames. The mantel held a manger scene, some holly surrounding it, and a white candle in the center. Next to that were simply framed black and white photos of what must have been a family. There was a meager 3-foot Christmas tree, garlanded, with ornaments but no Christmas lights.

The room was clean enough, but both women noticed that the white paint had yellowed and the rose wallpaper was faded, with some damp spots. They saw floral Victorian antique lamps with opaque glass stems, hand-painted with roses or white and yellow flowers.

They stood on a thin, patterned floral carpet and first heard, and then saw, an old grandfather's clock standing resolutely in the corner. Its tick tock was steady and loud in the muted silence. A solid wood console radio, with a lighted dial, seemed to dominate the room, much as a TV would, but neither Jackie nor Megan saw a TV.

The furniture was simple and heavy, the couch and chair upholstered in solid fabrics, the couch looking worn but comfortable, and the broad arm chair sunken and looking dejected.

Jackie sensed something was wrong, but she was too hungry and tired to care. Megan glanced about, feeling strangely out of place and time. There was a quality of light and energy around them that neither had ever experienced before, and it was unsettling. There was a growing, uncomfortable sensation that they had become lost—very lost.

CHAPTER 3

Megan and Jackie sat in wingback chairs at the formidable mahogany dining room table, covered with a white tablecloth, fringed at the edges. It reminded Megan of her grandmother's dining room table in rural Ohio. The girls ate ravenously. The cold baked chicken was surprisingly good; the home baked bread delicious, even without butter, and the hot drink that Aunt Betty delivered had chicory in it.

"With rationing and shortages, it's hard to get coffee and sugar," she said. "I save the coffee for breakfast."

The ladies nodded, uncertainly, savoring each tasty bite, feeling the food and warm beverage revive them.

"This is so good, Aunt Betty. This is the best tasting chicken I've ever had. Really, it's so flavorful."

Aunt Betty smiled briefly, pleased by the compliment. She eased down in a chair between them, at the head of the table. She still eyed them suspiciously, and both girls were aware of it.

"Where are the two of you from?" Aunt Betty asked.

"New York City," Jackie said.

"Well, I guess that explains your clothes. New York is more stylish than we are here."

Jackie stopped chewing, looking down at herself and then at Megan. "Yes, well, these are sort of our traveling clothes."

"We never dressed like that in my day, but then the war has changed so many things."

"The war?" Jackie asked. "Are there a lot of men in town serving in the military?"

"Yes, of course," Aunt Betty said.

"Do you have family here?" Megan asked.

"My daughter used to live with me. This was her boarding house, but she went off to Newport News, Virginia to help build ships and I'm just helping her out. I just couldn't believe it when she left like that, but these people from the Newport News shipyard came through town recruiting workers. With the men all gone off to war, they started hiring women. There were two of them doing the recruiting, a man and a woman. The man was a foreman, I guess, and the woman was a welder. Anyway, they offered Ruby, that's my daughter, a fifty dollar sign-up bonus and a free train ticket to Norfolk. I was just so surprised when she signed up. She works a 10-hour shift 6 days a week, and sometimes she works 7 days to get the overtime. I don't know how she does it. But the war has changed so many things. So many, many things."

Jackie wiped her mouth with the embroidered white napkin. "You mean the war in Afghanistan?"

Aunt Betty was confused. "Well... yes, I guess it's over there too. I don't really know where all those places are. I have to get the map out sometimes when I read the paper or watch Movietone News about the Pacific Islands and those places in Africa."

Megan smiled, indulgingly. "Geography was never my

best subject in school either."

But Jackie was watching Aunt Betty, with new interest, increasingly aware that something just wasn't quite right.

Aunt Betty continued. "Ruby said that a lot of the men who work with her still haven't accepted the women. I can't say I blame them."

Megan took a bite of the apple pie and her happy eyes rolled back into her head. "Oh, wow, this is so good. This apple pie is so, so good!"

Aunt Betty's pride helped her to sit up a little straighter. Another smile creased her wrinkled face. "I'm glad you like it."

As Megan's hunger abated, her thoughts turned to the audition she'd given the day before. The director and choreographer had told her they'd be making casting decisions before Christmas. Megan was anxious to check email.

"Aunt Betty, do you have Wi-Fi?"

Aunt Betty's face was a blank piece of paper. "Why? Why what?"

Megan tried again. "Wi-Fi? A Wi-Fi connection?"

Aunt Betty's lips started to move, then stopped. "I don't know that."

Jackie spoke up. "Do you have an internet connection?"

Aunt Betty was straining to comprehend. "I don't know. I have a telephone. Do you need to make a call? It's extra."

Megan blinked a look at Jackie, who was staring back at her.

"Aunt Betty, do you have a computer?" Megan asked.

Aunt Betty was growing agitated by her lack of understanding. "A com.... putor? I don't know. I don't know what that is."

"Do you have cable?" Jackie asked.

There was a sudden recognition in Aunt Betty's eyes. "Well, yes. Out in the garage. Earl, that's my husband, keeps a pair out there. Do you need them to start your car?"

Now the girls were confused.

"In the garage?" Megan asked.

"Yes, Earl keeps them in the trunk of the car. He's away too, working in a war plant in Providence, Rhode Island."

Both saw that Aunt Betty was completely flummoxed. They slowly comprehended that she was talking about jumper cables.

"I see," Megan said, finishing the last of her pie. "Yes, well, maybe we'll use them in the morning."

Aunt Betty was scrutinizing them anew. Suddenly, all of them were uncomfortable, sitting in the confusing silence.

Aunt Betty stood up. "Well, I'm way past my bedtime. Why don't I show you to your room?"

Jackie and Megan carried their dishes to the old-fashioned kitchen and placed them into the deep sink. The girls turned in surprise to view a vintage white ice box, and a vintage 1930s white & green porcelain gas stove, with an IN-A-DRAWER-BROILER.

Aunt Betty said her hired housekeeper, Rose, would wash the dishes in the morning.

Megan and Jackie followed Aunt Betty up the creaky staircase to the first room on the second floor. She stared at their carry-ons, peculiarly, especially Jackie's violet leather case, as she ushered them into the first room on the left.

"I've never seen suitcases like that," Aunt Betty said.

She switched on the light and paused at the door,

stepping aside to let them enter.

"There's a bathroom down the hall. Towels and wash cloths are in the bottom drawers. Extra blankets in the clothes closet. Breakfast is from 7 to 8am. Goodnight, ladies."

She closed the door, and they heard her plod away down the hallway.

The girls took in the room. There was a brass frame double bed with a patchwork quilt, a side table with a lamp, and a chest of drawers. The walls were painted an egg shell white, holding a tarnished mirror and a paint-by-number oil painting of kids sledding down a wintry hill, a yapping black dog chasing after them.

Jackie placed her hands on her hips. "I hope you don't snore."

Megan frowned.

After visiting the bathroom and changing into pajamas, the weary girls slipped into the squeaking, moving bed and Megan switched off the light. It was so dark, neither could see a hand before her face. The quiet hurt their ringing ears.

"It's like summer camp," Jackie said.

"Or a slumber party," Megan said, at a whisper.

Jackie said, "This morning, if someone had told me I'd be lying in bed with a complete stranger, in an old town out in the middle of nowhere... well..." her voice drifted into silence.

"Jackie...?"

"Yes."

"Have you noticed that all the old things don't look that old, even though they are old? They look, well, new old."

"Huh?"

"Everything in this town looks vintage, but it looks authentic."

Jackie didn't speak.

"I've done shows... I did a George Gershwin show called *Girl Crazy*, that originally opened in 1930. We wore period clothes and had period furniture and all that, but it all looked, well, you know, staged and made up. This town and this house and the cars, they all look authentic. Old but new."

Jackie breathed in and then let out a sigh. "I'm a graphics designer, Megan. The signs I've seen, the fabrics downstairs, the cars and storefronts... well, I don't know what's going on, but something is definitely going on. Something's off. There's a big disconnect somewhere. My grandmother, who is the least tech savvy person on the planet, knows what a computer is. She loves her TV, and she has an e-Reader."

There were more sighs and more silence.

"Jackie...?"

"Yes."

"Maybe these people are like the Amish people. Maybe they don't believe in the modern world."

Jackie shifted, and the bed bounced and squeaked. "I don't know, but I do know that I'm exhausted and I'm going to sleep. First thing tomorrow, after we eat breakfast, we are leaving this town and I, for one, will never, ever look back."

"Jackie?"

"Yes, Megan," she said, yawning.

"Did you see the calendar hanging in the kitchen? The Coca-Cola calendar with the picture of the three Army guys, each drinking a coke from a little bottle?"

"No, I didn't."

Megan remained silent.

"So... what about the calendar, Megan? What did you

see?"

"Just before Aunt Betty turned off the kitchen light, I glanced at it. The calendar said it was Monday, December 20, 1943."

CHAPTER 4

Megan charged into the bedroom, rushed over to the bed and shook Jackie violently. "Jackie! Wake up. Wake up!"

Jackie sat up, startled, eyes blinking into the early morning light. "What!? What!? What time is it?"

"It's almost 6:30. The car's gone! It's gone!"

Jackie's eyes opened wide. "What do you mean it's gone!?"

"It is gone, Jackie! Our car is gone."

Jackie kicked the quilt off and swung her feet to the cold linoleum floor. "No way! No way! It's got to be out there."

"I've looked up the street and down the street. I have searched driveways and peeked into garages. It is gone, Jackie! Gone. What are we going to do?"

Jackie pushed up and rushed over to the window that looked down onto the street. She parted the curtains and yanked the circular pull string on the brown window shade to release it. It shot up, flapping. Jackie peered out. She didn't see the car. She heaved up the window, stuck her head out into the cold, flat gray light and looked up and down the street. It wasn't there. It definitely wasn't there.

She turned, facing Megan, her face worried. "Damn!"

Megan was agitated, her gloved hands twisting. "That's not all."

"Yes? You're going to tell me all, Megan?"

Megan gathered herself, pulling off her blue ski cap, her hair spiked from static electricity. "While I was searching for the car, I began checking license plates. I didn't just look at one. No. I looked at every single license plate on the street."

"And?" Jackie asked, spreading her hands, waiting.

"Okay... take a deep breath."

"I don't need a deep breath, Megan, I'm already hyperventilating. I'm already freaking out. Just tell me!"

"All the license plates say 1943. They all, every one of them, say Vermont 1943. If all the license plates say 1943, and if the calendar downstairs in the kitchen says it's December 1943 then... I don't know, maybe it's just, just, just, maybe it's just 1943!"

The girls stood dead still, thinking, processing, evaluating.

Jackie made a steeple with her hands, bringing them to her lips. "Okay... Okay. Let's not panic. There is no need to freak out and panic."

"Well I'm panicking here, Jackie! I mean, I'm really ready to like go nuts and panic, because I am, *really*, like scared."

"Stop saying, *like*, Megan. I need to think and that's, like, just so distracting."

Jackie looked up, sharply, realizing what she'd said, then she shook it away. She began to pace, suddenly aware that her feet were ice cold. She reached into her suitcase for a pair of socks and bounced down on the bed to pull them on.

"Okay, we know it's not 1943," Jackie said, struggling for calm. "We know that for sure."

"Because?" Megan said, now pacing.

"Because it is impossible, Megan. It's stupid, and it's impossible!"

Megan crossed to the window, running a hand through her thick hair. "Jackie, look at the facts. Just look at them. Everything is old, old, old. You know that. Why did that boy run away when he saw us? It must have been the car. He'd never seen anything like our car before. It scared him half to death, so he ran. And remember the way that man looked when he passed us out on the road? He'd never seen anything like us or like that car either. What about all the references to the war that Aunt Betty made? Building ships, her husband working in a war plant; the gasoline and the black market. It all adds up, Jackie. It all makes sense. I don't know what in the hell is going on, but I can't think of any other explanation."

Jackie sat in a furious concentration, steepling her hands again, bringing them to her lips and nibbling on the nails.

"I can't go there, Megan. I just can't. There's got to be something else. Maybe this is a joke or something. Maybe we stumbled onto a movie set and they're making a movie about World War II. I don't know."

Megan turned away, frustrated. "Yeah, right. You know that makes no sense. Listen to yourself."

"Well listen to you! What, are we in *The Matrix* or *The Twilight Zone* or something? No way, I'm not going there. I can't go there."

Megan threw up her hands in frustration. "Okay then, I don't know."

"Well, I don't know either. When was World War II, anyway?"

"I'm not sure. My brain has locked up."

Instinctively, Jackie reached for her iPhone. Then it occurred to her that it was dead, and she tossed it down. "Why don't these people have an internet connection? How are you supposed to find anything out?"

Megan said, "Wait a minute! World War II began in December of 1941, didn't it, when the Japanese bombed Pearl Harbor?"

Jackie stood up. "Yeah, I think so, and I think it ended in 1945, if I remember my high school history. But, let's not get into all that, because I'm not going there. All I do know is that we have to find our car. Without that car, how are we going to get out of here?"

"I say forget the car and let's get on a train or a bus. Let's just go," Megan said.

They stood frozen, thinking about it.

Jackie began nodding. "Yeah.... Yeah, that's not bad. We should be able to catch a train out of here. We crossed some railroad tracks driving in, and every little town has a train going through it, doesn't it?"

Megan was nibbling on her lower lip, shaking her head, her mind racing. "Oh, God."

"What?" Jackie said, going back to look out the window. "What's wrong?"

"I don't know. We've really got to think about this."

Jackie turned to her. "We are, Megan. That's what we're doing. We're discussing, we're thinking."

They were absorbed, brains working.

"Hold it!" Jackie said. "Just hold it a minute. We're going at this all wrong. What do people do when something is stolen? They call the police. So, let's call the police and tell them that somebody stole our car."

Megan gave her a cold, flat stare. "Are you serious? And when they ask you for the year and the model and the description of the car, what are you going to say?"

"I'll tell them... I guess. I don't know?"

Megan shook her head. "Jackie... Jackie, please just think about this for a minute. Every car in this town has a license plate that says it's 1943."

Jackie opened her mouth to speak, but Megan threw up the flat of her hand to stop her. "Just hear me out. If that is true, then what do you think will happen when you tell this local cop that we have a 21st century Ford Fusion Hybrid? If I recall correctly from the owner's manual I was reading, it can travel up to 62 mph on electric power alone. Wouldn't that be handy in World War II? Oh, also, Mr. Local Cop from 1943, it has an AM/FM stereo with a single-CD player and MP3 capability with audio input jack. It also has a keyless-entry keypad and—drum roll please—a GPS. What was that, sir, you say? You have never heard of a GPS? Well, let me explain it to you, sir. GPS stands for Global Positioning System and it's a network of about 30 satellites that orbit the Earth. Each one transmits information about its position and the current time at regular intervals. This little GPS picks up these little signals, traveling at the speed of light, and are intercepted by your GPS receiver, which then calculates how far away each satellite is, based on how long it took for the messages to arrive."

Jackie narrowed her eyes, fascinated. "How do you know all that?"

"I did a commercial for a GPS device a year ago."

"Well now," Jackie said. "Okay, so you're right. You have definitely impressed me."

Megan grinned. "Well, thank you, ma'am."

"But you're still assuming we are, somehow, living back in 1943. I still say we are not, and that there is a rational explanation for all this."

Megan folded her arms. "Are you willing to gamble by calling the local small-town sheriff? Because if you're wrong, we are both going to wind up in some stuffy, moldy jail or, even worse, some government agency will grab us and send us off to some secret place, because they will suspect we are aliens or spies or something."

Jackie's shoulder lifted, then fell. "Okay... Okay. But now I have a question for you. If what you say is true, and we are back in 1943, then how is getting on a train or bus going to get us back to the 21st century?"

Megan lowered her head. "Yeah, I didn't think about that. Well, look, we won't know until we try. Let's buy a ticket to the next town and see what happens."

"Before we do that, I want to make sure, once and for all, that we are, for certain, back in 1943."

"And how are you going to do that?" Megan asked.

Jackie grinned. "Simple. I'm going to ask."

At 7:10, Jackie and Megan went downstairs for breakfast. Megan's hair was in a pony tail and Jackie's was brushed back, de-accenting her bangs. Both decided to wear slacks and simple, cotton blouses. They did not want to be conspicuous.

Jackie led the way through the living room into the dining room, where a stony-faced man, dressed in overalls, sat at the head of the table, eating a bowl of oatmeal and reading a newspaper. He glanced up over the top of it, regarding them without reaction. He was in his middle 40s, with a strong face, deep set dark eyes, short thin graying hair and a firm mouth. The girls noticed that a metal lunch box sat next to him on the table.

There were three empty chairs on either side of the table. Jackie went around the table and took one. Megan sat opposite her, with the gentleman to her right.

"Good morning," Megan said to the man. "I'm Megan."

"Marnin," he said, barely audible, not giving his name.

Jackie nodded to him. He didn't look at her. She tried to steal a glance at the front page of his paper, but he had folded it.

An attractive teenage girl entered, wearing a blue and white day dress, with a high neckline and square padded shoulders. She wore saddle shoes, with her white socks rolled down to her ankles. Her brown hair included pin curls and perfectly placed finger waves. She carried a basket of freshly baked rolls and placed it in the center of the table.

"Good morning," she said, halfheartedly.

Megan and Jackie introduced themselves.

She regarded them with a teenage apathy. "I'm Rose. Where'd you get clothes like that with a war going on? You must know a general."

Aunt Betty stuck her head out from the kitchen. "Rose, you mind your manners. Pay her no mind. Rose, come in here."

Megan and Jackie looked at their clothes, self-consciously.

A few minutes later, Rose returned with two bowls of oatmeal, two cups of weak coffee, and a little pitcher of milk. When Jackie asked her if it was whole milk or cream, Rose looked at her, disapprovingly, and said it was powdered milk.

"We don't get the milk delivery until Friday morning," she said.

The girls ate, quietly, both glancing over at the paper, searching for a date.

"Any important news?" Jackie asked the man.

He grunted. "About the same."

"Is that the local paper?" Megan asked.

"Yep," he said, reading on.

"Can I read that after you?" Jackie asked.

"Yep," he said.

Aunt Betty came in, wearing a long, light blue dress and chunky dark shoes. "Did you sleep well?"

"Yes, we did," Megan lied.

"What time will you be leaving?" she asked.

Jackie hesitated. "We're not quite sure."

"Well, you let me know so I can send Rose in, to clean the room."

There was the sound of heels clicking down the stairs. Both girls glanced up to see a woman of about 35 enter the dining room. She wore a pink flowered print dress and black, high-heeled shoes with ankle straps. Her long blonde hair was neatly rolled up in a hair net, and she held her black purse in white-gloved hands.

Megan turned and stared, amazed by the woman's outfit. Megan had worn a similar outfit when she'd been a principal dancer in a Broadway musical entitled *Come Back Home, Johnny*, three years before. The musical was set in 1945, right after World War II had ended, and it had closed after only 65 performances. Megan thought of her audition again and felt an urgent frustration.

"Hello, my name is Ann, like Ann Sheridan," she said, offering a gloved hand.

Megan and Jackie stood and took it. Ann was not a beauty, but she had a warm, friendly face and welcoming gray/blue eyes.

"My, my, Ann Palmer," Aunt Betty said. "Look at you

all dressed up. Aren't you going to work today?"

Ann sat down at the other end of the table, opposite the man, who was still engrossed in his newspaper. She peeled off her gloves, one finger at a time. "Of course I'm going to work. Can't a woman dress up a little once in a while without causing a lot of fuss?"

Rose entered with Ann's breakfast and placed the oatmeal before her. "She's meeting Donald Harris for lunch or something," Rose said, dryly.

"You shut up, Rose. You don't know what you are talking about."

Rose shrugged and retreated into the kitchen.

Ann reached for her napkin. "Anyway, what if I am meeting him? So what?"

"Where do you work?" Jackie asked.

"I'm an operator. There are only five of us, working three shifts."

"Telephone operator?" Megan asked, a spoon of oatmeal poised at her lips.

Ann nodded. "Yes."

The man closed the paper and laid it aside. "Well, look at you, all gussied up."

She ignored him, but it was obvious that she was pleased. "Why aren't you down at the railroad yard, Arthur? Aren't you going to be late?"

"Nope. Eight-thirty today. Working a little later."

"So what's going on with the war, Arthur? And don't say 'about the same.'"

Arthur reached for his coffee cup. "The USS Grayling sank the fourth Japanese ship since December 18."

"Good," Ann said. "I hope our boys push those Japs all the way back to Tokyo. I wish General Doolittle would bomb Tokyo again like he did last year and show them we can do it twice."

Jackie stopped eating and looked at Arthur. "Can I see the paper, Arthur?"

He handed it to her, grudgingly. "I want it back."

"Oh, for crying out loud, Arthur, it's not yours. Let the girl read it."

Jackie unfolded it and searched for the front cover. She opened it and looked at the headline, her eyes growing into two large circles.

TUESDAY, DECEMBER 21, 1943
SOVIET FORCES RECONQUER GUMRAK
AIRPORT NEAR STALINGRAD

Jackie lowered the paper and closed her eyes. Megan saw she'd turned pale. Ann noticed too.

"You okay, honey?" Ann asked.

Jackie took a breath and opened her eyes. They were vacant. "Yes... Yes, I'm fine."

Ann turned toward the kitchen. "Rose, hurry up and bring Jackie some water."

Jackie stared straight ahead, seeing nothing. When she spoke, her voice was low and whispery. "So is it really December 21, 1943?"

Ann and Arthur looked at her, peculiarly. Rose came with the water and handed it to Jackie. She took it, as if in a trance, then sipped at it, absently, and swallowed. She looked directly at Ann. "Is it, Ann? Is it December 21, 1943?"

Ann laid her spoon down. "Honey, unless the good Lord has changed the course and time of this Earth, it is definitely Tuesday, December 21, 1943."

CHAPTER 5

Jackie lay on the bed, an arm covering her eyes. Megan stood by the window, staring numbly out onto the street, watching those old cars pass and drift along, white smoke puffing from their tailpipes. She gazed up into the embracing mountains and the wide gray sky, as morning shadows crept down from the hilltops. It was almost 8:30. They were unable to speak for long periods, as their thoughts circled, tangled and plotted until, finally, anxiety completely possessed the room.

"So what are we going to do, Jackie?" Megan asked.

"I don't know. I just don't know."

"We are in some kind of bad dream, Jackie."

"I wish it were a dream. It isn't a dream, Megan. We are here, wherever here is, and we have to figure out how we got here and how we're going to get back home."

"Should we take a bus or train to the next town and see if that gets us back?"

"I don't know."

Megan turned toward her. "Jackie, we can't just sit here. We have to do something."

"I know. I'm trying to think, but my mind's a complete blank. I still can't get my head around this. How could this happen? It can't happen. It doesn't happen! It only happens in movies and novels. It doesn't *actually* happen. People don't *actually* wind up in other times and places."

Megan eased down in the one rickety chair, near the window. "Well, whether we like it or not, or believe it or not, it *has* happened."

They hovered in silence.

"Have you thought about your family?" Megan asked.

"Of course. But if this is 1943, my parents haven't even been born. None of our friends are around, there is no one we can call, no one we can ask for help, and no place for us to go. We are screwed."

Megan's shoulders sagged, as she turned back to look out the window. "No one we can ask for help. Now that's a cheery thought." She stared at the sky. "It looks like it could snow again."

"I wonder if back in our world, far into the future, we've just disappeared. I wonder if our parents and friends are trying to find us," Megan said.

"Megan?"

Megan turned. "What?"

"We really have to think this through. If we are living in 1943, we'll have to hide our phones, tablets and e-Readers. Bury them in our suitcases. No one can see them. That includes all our shampoos, makeup, everything. Second, where did our car go? How could it just disappear?"

"Maybe it disappeared back into the 21st century."

"That makes no sense. If we haven't disappeared, then it hasn't disappeared. Someone has taken it, but why?"

Megan turned back to Jackie, who still had an arm

over her eyes, lying flat on the bed.

"It must have looked like something from outer space in the morning light. Maybe the police took it."

"Or the military."

"That's scary."

"Yes... They could come looking for us."

Megan straightened up. "That's *real* scary. What would we tell them?"

"I don't know. Anyway, we can't let Aunt Betty, or anybody else, know that the car is missing. And then there's money. Obviously, we can't use our credit cards. How much money do you have?"

Megan thought. "I'd say a little over a hundred."

"I have about the same."

Suddenly, Jackie sat up, eyes focused ahead. "Wait, a minute. We can't use that money."

Megan licked her lower lip, also realizing the truth. "Of course... It's from the future. The look, the paper, the serial numbers would all be wrong."

"Yes. A big red flag would go up at the local shop or bank."

"How are we going to pay Aunt Betty then?"

Jackie looked worried. "I don't know. I've got to think."

"Jackie, we'll have to tell her we want to stay on for a couple of days."

Jackie flopped back on the bed, bouncing. She swung her arm over her eyes again. "Good Golly, Miss Molly."

"What?"

"My brother's expression. It helped him to stop cursing so much."

Megan stood. "Well, I feel like cursing! The hell with Good Golly Miss Molly! We are in the middle of some shit, Jackie."

"Curse away then."

"God, I'm so tense! I wish I could go to a yoga class. Did they do yoga in 1943?"

"I doubt it, Megan. No internet, no yoga, no modern conveniences. I don't think they did much of anything in 1943."

"Jackie, we have to figure something out. We have to get out of here."

"I know, I know. I'm thinking. I'm a good problem solver. Just let me think."

"I've got nothing, Jackie. Nothing."

"Okay, let's rewind here. Rewind us all the way back to last night in that snowstorm. When did we first notice something weird had happened?"

"When we got lost and didn't see a car, a house or a town. Nothing."

"Yes, but remember when we crossed that covered bridge? Remember how the snow suddenly stopped falling, and the wind died down? Remember how soft and clean the air felt? How different everything seemed?"

Megan paced. "Yeah... that was strange. Maybe that was it. Maybe we have to back up and cross the bridge again. Maybe that's the time portal."

"Those time travel movies always freaked me out," Jackie said.

Megan pinched the bridge of her nose, concentrating. "In all those sci-fi movies, whenever the astronauts wind up in another time, they always try to get back to the black hole or time warp or time portal where it all began. That makes sense."

"I tell you, I don't like sci-fi movies," Jackie said.

That stopped Megan's train of thought. "Really? What kind of movies do you like?"

Jackie sat up again, annoyed. "Megan, does it matter?

We've got to stay focused."

Megan stopped pacing, folding her arms. "I am focused and I tell you I've got nothing."

Jackie fell back again, staring up at the ceiling. "So maybe we should go back to that covered bridge and cross over to the other side. Maybe you're right. Maybe that's the portal or whatever."

"How? We don't have a car."

"So we take a taxi. Every town has a taxi or two."

"Does the taxi driver drive us across, or do we get out and walk across? I mean, if he drives us across, will he wind up in the 21st century along with us? Or will we just disappear from the cab, on the other side, and wind up in the 21st century, while he stays back here? Or will we wind up in an entirely different time and place, like the Middle Ages or Ancient Egypt or the Old West or something?"

Jackie raised up, looking at Megan in utter amazement. "Damn, but you have one crazy imagination, girl."

Megan continued. "Or, maybe we have to have *our* car to recreate the events, backwards, so that we can get back. Maybe without the car that brought us here, we will never get back, and we'll be stuck here for the rest of our lives. But then, what if, after we get our car, if we can get our car and cross that bridge, nothing happens and we're still stuck here, in 1943?"

Jackie fell back again, her dizzy head rolling from side to side. "Megan, you're exhausting me. We're getting nowhere."

Megan went back to her chair and sat, with a heavy sigh. "I say we have to adapt to this place until we can find our car and figure out how to get back home. We can't stick out like aliens."

Megan pointed to Jackie's arm. "And I'm sure women

didn't have tattoos in 1943, so you're going to have to hide that little red rose bud tattoo on your upper arm."

"I'll wear long sleeves. Don't worry about that. I just don't know how we can pull this off. We don't know anything about their expressions or figures of speech. We don't know about their products, their culture, and we don't even know that much about World War II."

"The Japanese bombed Pearl Harbor on December 7, 1941."

"I knew that," Jackie said. "Who were we fighting against?"

Megan shut her eyes to think. "Okay, let's see: the Japanese, the Germans and, I think, the Italians?"

"No way," Jackie said. "Not the Italians. I love the Italians. Why would we fight against a great culture like that?"

"Because they were pals with the Germans, Jackie. Remember Benito Mussolini? He was a bad guy. After he was killed, I think the Italians joined us."

Jackie waved a hand. "Okay, okay, whatever. We're not getting anywhere here. Enough about World War II. We know it began in 1941 and ended sometime in 1945. Since nobody in this time knows when the war ended, we don't have to worry about that. So, let's move on. We're going to need money. Do you have any jewelry?"

"A ring, some earrings and a watch."

"The watch is probably out. It's too high tech for this time. I have a diamond necklace that Eric bought me. I was going to wear it on Christmas Day. That should bring us a lot of money for this time, at least enough until we can figure out what to do. Next, we should buy some clothes and find the nearest beauty shop. We don't want to look out of place."

"I like that idea," Megan said, brightening. "Now that

sounds fun. My hair was losing its shape, anyway."

Jackie sat up again, stuffed a pillow behind her back and leaned against it. "Okay, we have a plan. We'll find the nearest pawn shop and hock my necklace." She heaved out a deep sigh. "I guess, Megan, we're going to find out if the good old days really *were* good old days."

Megan turned toward the window to see a car approach, coast to the curb, and stop in front of the house. Two doors opened and two soldiers emerged from the car, looking toward the house. Megan shot up and ducked away behind the curtains.

"Whoa!"

Jackie turned, shooting her a glance. "Whoa, what?"

"Two guys. Two guys in some kind of military hats and overcoats. Two hot looking guys, looking at the house. They're coming in!"

Jackie sprang off the bed and rushed to the window. She caught a glimpse of them as they walked smartly up the walkway to the stairs. Then they disappeared from view. Jackie's eyes were large and fixed. Megan's moved left and right.

"Are they coming for us?" Jackie asked.

"I don't know. Why?"

"I don't know. Maybe Aunt Betty called them. Maybe Ann. You saw the way she looked at us when I asked her if this was 1943. Like I was out of my mind."

They heard the front door open and close.

At the same moment, they heard a knock on their door. Both girls jumped.

"Yes," Jackie called.

"It's Rose. I need to clean your room. What time will you be leaving?"

Jackie and Megan exchanged nervous glances.

"Hello?" Rose called.

Jackie spoke up. "Umm... Rose, tell Aunt Betty that we'll be staying on for a couple more nights. Don't worry about cleaning the room. We'll do it."

"Whatever you say," Rose said.

Both girls summoned an inner reserve of strength as they prepared for what was to come.

Five minutes later, they stood at the door, ears pressed against it.

"Can you hear anything?" Megan asked.

"Nothing, just muffled voices."

Jackie backed away. "This is ridiculous. Let's go down there. I'd rather face them than hide up here like a scared rabbit."

Megan pulled her ear away. "I vote for the scared rabbit."

"We've got to face it sooner or later."

"Later," Megan said, checking her face in the tarnished mirror. "I look so tired and pale."

"Well, I'm going," Jackie said.

Megan seized her arm. "Wait! What's our plan?"

"What plan?"

"What are we going to say down there?"

"I'm going to put on my coat, walk down the front stairs, and tell Aunt Betty that I am going out to do some shopping. That's my plan."

As Jackie reached for her cashmere coat, Megan indicated toward it.

"You saw how Aunt Betty looked at us when she saw our coats and carry-ons, and you heard what Rose said about our clothes and how we must know a general. What are those soldiers going to think when they see us?"

Jackie looked her over. "Okay, we've both got jeans on, designer jeans, yes, but jeans nonetheless. Let's put on sweaters. You brought one, didn't you?"

"Of course, a red one."

"I have a white one."

"We'll look like Christmas," Megan said, grinning.

Jackie ignored her. "Let's tuck our coats under our arms until we get outside, so they won't get a good look at them. Then we'll quickly leave the house, walk into town and find a pawn shop."

"If we get outside."

"Stop being so negative. We can do this."

Jackie opened the door, cautiously, peering up and down the hallway. She heard men's voices coming from the dining room.

"Let's go," she whispered.

They strolled lightly across the hallway to the top of the stairs. They picked up fragments of conversation coming from the living room.

A baritone voice said, "We keep hearing that an invasion of Europe is going to happen soon..."

Aunt Betty said, "I wish this war would hurry up and get over with. I'm just so worried all the time about all our boys. And now you two are going over there. I just hope it gets over soon."

"Once Jeff and I get over there, we'll hurry things along. We'll kick the Krauts back into Germany."

"Now, don't go bragging like you do, Danny Crawford," Aunt Betty said. "Bragging does not bring good luck."

Megan and Jackie took a courageous breath, nodded to each other, and started down the stairs, each step creaking under their feet. At the base, they started for the front door, but Aunt Betty called to them.

"So you're staying another night?" she asked.

They stiffened, cringing a little. The girls turned to see

Aunt Betty seated in the broad arm chair, knitting what appeared to be a blue woolen sweater. Two men in military uniforms, who obviously had been seated on the couch, shot up. Soft gray morning light seemed to frame them. Megan's eyes fell on the man with short black hair and sea-blue eyes. Jackie focused on the man with the boot-camp short, risky red hair.

The two men sorted the two girls out, carefully, with their eyes. Then they looked at them individually, and their eyes filled with easy pleasure. The red-headed boy tightened his shoulders back and puffed out his chest, standing at attention.

The black-haired soldier spoke to the redhead out of the side of his mouth.

"At ease, Danny Boy, they're not generals, they're girls."

But Danny Crawford was stunned to silence by Jackie's pretty, heart-shaped face, pouty mouth and sexy body. She was the most stylish and sophisticated girl he'd ever seen.

Jackie was staring back at him, noticing the impressive uniform, as well as the broad shoulders and slim waist that were inside that uniform. His chin was square, eyes a bold greenish gray, face devilishly handsome. He gave her the impression of a tough audacious kid, who could always find some delightful mischief to get into: just her type, and the kind of guy who turned her on. Yes, Danny Crawford was just the kind of guy she found troubling, disconcerting and, unfortunately, irresistible, especially in that sexy uniform.

He wore a tan shirt, with a brown tie tucked neatly into it. His trousers were bloused into spit-shined brown jump boots.

Her eyes settled on his Airborne Jump Wings, a silver

metal badge in the shape of a fully deployed parachute, with the shroud lines forming a V. Powerful eagle-like wings emanated from the base and curved upward to touch the sides of the canopy with their wing tips. Danny was clutching a Garrison cap and, on the left side of it, was a circular patch of a white parachute on a field of infantry blue.

"That's Corporal Danny Boy Crawford," the other guy said. "Girls still scare him a little, but he'll jump out of a C-47 at 1000 feet and won't even hesitate. At least, that's what his buddies tell me."

Megan's eyes wandered pleasurably over Jeff Grant, the other guy.

"Hello, ladies, I'm First Lieutenant Jeff Grant," he said, with a little courtly bow.

Megan looked into Jeff's splendidly handsome face and, immediately, she wanted to dive deeply into his warm blue eyes. He smiled broadly, showing perfectly white teeth and full generous lips. He was over six feet tall and had the bearing of a man who was intelligent, humorous and confident. Megan loved his strong aristocratic chin, long eyelashes and broad face. His uniform was a perfect fit, and this one looked authentic, compared to the uniforms the men wore in the musical *Come Back Home, Johnny*.

Jeff wore a U.S. Army Air Corps officer's dress uniform, jacket and pants. In his right hand, he held his Army Air Corps Officer visor cap, with the eagle badge on its front. The uniform was made of olive drab wool, with a four pocket belted coat and a four button front. There was an embroidered Army Air Corps patch on the left sleeve, and an officer's Air Corps insignia on the lapels. The silver USAAC pilot's wings over the left breast pocket were impressive, but looked different from Danny's.

The room was silent, while Jeff and Danny stared inquisitively at the girls. It was Jeff who approached the girls, hand extended for a hand shake.

"So, I'm Jeff, and you are?"

"Megan."

They shook.

"Jackie."

They shook.

Jeff glanced back over his shoulder. "Danny Boy, come forth and meet Megan and Jackie."

Danny was twisting his cap. He swallowed, went to the girls and shook their hands, making sure his eyes didn't meet Jackie's. She did not look at him either. Already, their attraction was electrifying and obvious.

Aunt Betty glanced up over her glasses, her eyes evaluating the couples with sudden interest.

"Jeff, Danny, why don't you offer Megan and Jackie some refreshments?"

"Oh, yes," Jeff said, looking toward the kitchen. "Would you like something, ladies?"

Jeff turned back toward Aunt Betty. "What do you have, Aunt Betty?"

"Well I don't have what Green's Drugstore has," she said, coyly, going back to her knitting.

Megan and Jackie exchanged a fast confused glance.

Jeff straightened in recognition. "Oh, yes, well, that's true, Aunt Betty."

Danny was still twisting his cap, standing awkwardly. Jackie's eyes wandered.

"Would you two ladies like to accompany me and Danny Boy down to Green's Drugstore? They have some of the best floats in all of Holly Grove, if not Vermont. Well, actually, because of the war, they don't have floats, but they do have sodas. How about it?"

Danny's cheeks were flushed.

Megan spoke up. "Well, that sounds like it would be fun..."

Jackie interrupted. "... Fun, yes, but we have some errands to do, don't we, Megan?"

Jeff spoke up. "Danny and I will be glad to act as tour guides, won't we, Danny?"

Danny nodded rapidly. "Yeah, sure."

"Well, they're kind of girl errands," Jackie said.

Jeff brightened. "Girl errands!? That's our specialty, right, Danny Boy? We are known to be the best darn tour guides for girl errands in the entire town of Holly Grove and beyond. Why, Danny Boy was just telling me this morning how much he loves to accompany attractive young women, such as yourselves, on girl errands."

Jackie opened her mouth to protest, but Megan cut her off.

"Then it's settled. We accept."

Jackie mumbled something under her breath, but no one could hear it. She had mumbled, "How are we ever going to get back home?"

CHAPTER 6

Outside on the porch, Jeff and Danny slipped into their long winter overcoats, pulled on their caps and politely waited, as the girls hesitated, then self-consciously shouldered into their 21st century coats. They noticed the guys studying them.

"We found these cheap," Megan said. "In the wardrobe department of an old theater."

Jackie lifted an impressed eyebrow at Megan's creative improvisation, as they started down the walkway toward the street.

"You could make a fortune on the black market with those kinds of coats," Danny said.

"Are you an actress?" Jeff asked Megan.

Megan nodded. "Yes, a minor one."

"Aunt Betty said you're both from New York City. Do you act on Broadway?"

"I've done some Broadway shows," Megan said, with a tinge of pride in her voice.

Jeff elbowed Danny in the ribs. "How about that, Danny?"

They paused at the curb.

"Where's your car?" Jeff asked.

The girls stumbled over their words. Megan spoke up. "Oh, well, it needed some work done."

"Oh, is Herman Deckler working on it?" Danny asked.

Megan looked at Jackie for support, but her face was a blank.

"Yeah, well, yeah... Well, he didn't really say what his name was," Megan said. "He just said he'd work on it."

"I used to work with Herman," Danny said, enthusiastically. "I can fix anything."

"Danny Boy's a genius with anything mechanical," Jeff chimed in. "Sometimes old Danny Boy here will tear something down just to see how it works, and when he puts it back together, it works better than if it was brand new."

Danny grinned, shyly. "Well, anyway, a little later I'll go over to Herman's and see how your car is."

Megan's and Jackie's smiles were thin and strained. But both felt some relief that the boys weren't going to drag them away to some jail, to interrogate them about why they had a 21st century car.

"Well isn't that nice, Megan?" Jackie said.

"Oh, yes, so very thoughtful," Megan said, worried.

"Okay, shall we take my car or walk and save gas?" Jeff asked. "The drugstore's only about three blocks away."

As they strolled toward town along quiet streets, snow flurries fell, and there was a chilly draft of wind coming down from the north. Jeff led the way with Megan, and Danny and Jackie were walking behind, together, although they were a good two feet apart. Jackie was feeling desire and despair as she strolled, hands deep in her coat pockets. She looked about, and in the distance surrounding the town, she saw farmland and forests, all with a spectacular mountain backdrop of the majestic Green Mountains, an extended gray mass rising skyward, the mountain peaks shrouded in low-moving clouds and falling snow.

Danny followed her eyes. "Many peaks rise above 3,000 feet."

Jackie still avoided his eyes. "Really? Impressive."

"Yeah, they're part of the Appalachian Mountain system."

"Were you born and raised here?" Jackie asked.

"Yes, I was. It's a small town, but a good town. Good people."

"How did you and Jeff get to be good friends?" Jackie asked.

"Airplanes. Jeff flies airplanes, and I used to help repair the engines. We kind of got close doing that. He's like a big brother to me."

As they strolled past houses, Jackie noticed there were little blue star flags in some windows, and a gold star flag hanging in another.

"What are the flags with the stars all about?" she asked.

Danny gave her a passing glance of surprise. "Are you serious?"

Jackie turned away, realizing from his shocked expression that she'd made an obvious mistake. She struggled to recover. "Oh, yeah. Well we don't have them in New York."

Danny scratched the side of his face. "Really? I thought they were everywhere." He pointed to the gold star house. "That's the Alderson house. Mike was killed in Italy back in September. We had a paper route together when we were 12 years old. He was a smart guy. He wanted to go to college and become a science teacher."

Jackie lowered her head, sadness showing on her face. "I'm sorry. Are a lot of your friends serving in the war?"

"Sure. Almost everybody. That's why there are so many of the blue star flags."

Danny adjusted his cap and stole a quick look at her face. It was a lovely face. There was something about her that stirred up his emotions, a polished elegance and a sexy sophistication that made him weak in the knees.

Jackie was distracted by everything around her, and stimulated by Danny. Distracted because she was still struggling to adjust to the impossibility of her and Megan's situation; worried about being discovered as some kind of alien; worried about their missing car and, if all that wasn't enough, she'd felt an instant, agonizing attraction to Danny. He was simply a sexy guy, and she didn't want any part of him. She had no time for it. There was no future in it.

That's when the thought struck, and it struck her hard, just like a slap across the face. Why hadn't she or Megan thought of it earlier!? They were facing the same problem that all time travelers faced. In college, she'd taken an *Intro to Physics* course. They'd spent an entire class discussing the time traveler dilemma. Could a person from the future, who traveled back to the past, alter the course of history by one act, one word or one thought? Most of the class believed that history would be altered in some way, even if the change was small or insignificant.

Jackie stopped, abruptly, cold with fear.

Danny was two steps ahead when he stopped. He turned back, looking at her curiously.

Jeff and Megan were still walking ahead of them, lost

in an easy attraction and conversation.

"So why did you come to Holly Grove?" Jeff asked.

"We were just passing through."

"To where?"

"Oh... to Portland. We're going there for Christmas."

"Really? Do you qualify for extra gasoline? You two must be involved in the war in some important way to be able to get that much gas."

Megan's eyes moved around, as she strained to understand. "Well, we want to be involved... I mean, we are involved, you know, like most people."

"Do you have a 'B' sticker?"

Megan's mind was scanning her brain database for any kind of match to the question. She came up empty. "A 'B' sticker?"

"Yeah on your windshield. So the service attendants can sell you three or four gallons of gas more a week."

"Oh, you mean a 'B' sticker? Well, yes, sure... I mean, of course, we definitely have a 'B' sticker. Sure."

"So what do you do for the war effort?"

Searching for an answer, Megan glanced back in a delaying tactic. She saw Jackie had stopped, and then she noticed Jackie's troubled face. Danny, standing next her, looked puzzled.

"Well, they seem to be getting along," Megan said, smiling her best smile, hoping that Jeff would see it and change the subject.

Jeff turned. "Is she okay?"

"Oh, yeah, sure, she's fine," Megan said, uneasily.

Green's Drugstore was a two-story building on Main Street. Its exterior was a cheerful yellow and green. Large glass windows had the bold green decaled letters GREEN'S DRUGSTORE displayed in an arch across each window, and there were Army and Navy recruitment posters displayed in the right window. The neon sign had been removed to meet blackout regulations. A placard on the door read:

Green's Drugstore is authorized by the Office of Civilian Defense as a pharmaceutical unit.

This meant that the store would provide a kit of medications and supplies for the casualty station in case of enemy attack.

Jeff opened the door, and a bell jangled. The group streamed in behind him and he closed the door, rubbing his ungloved hands together vigorously.

As Jackie passed a barrel by the door, she looked in to see layers of tin cans. They had been washed and flattened, their labels removed and their tops and bottoms cut off.

"It's getting cold out there," Jeff said. "More snow on the way, I think."

Inside, Megan thought the place smelled a lot like her grandmother's attic, a dry wood smoky scent. From a radio behind the soda fountain a Bing Crosby song was featured. He was singing *I'll Be Seeing You.* Megan recognized the song immediately as a song from *Come Back Home, Johnny.* The song had been sung by the female lead and, as her understudy, Megan had fervently hoped that somehow the lead would have to take a night or two off, so Megan would get the chance to play the part and sing the song. But it never happened. Megan never got to sing *I'll Be Seeing You*, and she thought it was one of the most beautiful, heart-wrenching songs she'd ever heard. A song about love and separation, and seeing one's lover *"in all the old familiar places."*

Danny and Jeff waved to a middle-aged man standing

behind the counter. He wore wire-rimmed glasses and had a bald dome, with wisps of salt and pepper hair on the sides. He was short and round, with a pleasant face and lively eyes. He wore a white apron over a white shirt and dark pants.

"Merry Christmas, Mr. Green," Jeff said, hand raised.

"Hello, boys. Merry Christmas."

Mr. Green's eyes enlarged when he saw Megan and Jackie.

"We're here for some of your famous sodas, since we know you don't have those delicious floats," Danny said.

They saw a thin, serious-looking woman, about 30 years old, behind the prescription counter. She glanced up but didn't wave, because she was the new pharmacist, and Danny and Jeff had been away and didn't know her. Her name was Sarah Teal. The old pharmacist, Bob Mackey, was in the Army serving in the Pacific.

The group moved through the aisle toward the soda fountain, past clean shelves with depleted stocks. Proprietary medications, cosmetics, toiletries, and medical supplies were abundant, but rubber hot water bottles, silk and nylon stockings, hair pins, curlers, candy, and cigarettes were all in short stock—or unavailable. Metal tins had been replaced by glass jars and cardboard boxes.

Jackie noticed particular items, her graphics eye trained and focused on artwork and packaging. She saw Alka-Seltzer, Brylcreem, Dorothy Gray beauty products, and Pepsodent Toothpaste, with a photo of Bob Hope endorsing it.

On the wall, she noticed a red, white and blue poster of a sinking ship engulfed in black smoke. It read: LOOSE LIPS MIGHT SINK SHIPS.

They went to the soda fountain and sat on green vinyl stools, resting their elbows on the marble top, noticing the solid steel soda fountains. Mr. Green went behind the counter to meet them, just as the front door rang and two elderly women entered. He excused himself and rounded the counter to wait on them, giving Jackie and Megan more time to look around.

On the back wall, beside the mounted plastic head of Elsie the Cow advertising Borden's milk, was yet another poster of three little children playing in a sandbox in the shadow of a Nazi swastika. The poster read: DON'T LET THAT SHADOW TOUCH THEM. BUY WAR BONDS. They also saw a Pepsi Cola motorboat stainless steel fountain dispenser, next to a red Coca-Cola dispenser.

"Do you know what you want, ladies?" Jeff asked, turning to the girls. "We can't get too fancy. There's not much sugar, syrup or chocolate."

"So we'll all have a Coca-Cola or 7-up," Danny said, answering for the three of them.

Mr. Green returned and slipped behind the counter. "Okay, what'll it be, folks?"

"You're wearing many hats, Mr. Green," Jeff said.

Mr. Green made a sad, resigned face. "Yes, well, as you know, Charlie was the best soda jerk we ever had."

"Have you heard from him?" Danny asked.

"One letter. He was somewhere in England, flying a P-47 Thunderbolt. So what about you boys? How long is your leave?"

"We both have to be back on December 26th," Jeff said.

"It's a shame you can't stay until after the New Year," Mr. Green said.

"Well, you know how it is, Mr. Green," Danny said. "Jeff and I have got to get over there and win this war."

"Don't be so eager, Danny Boy," Mr. Green said. "I

want you back here all in one piece. I want you *all* back here in one piece. We've lost too many boys in this town as it is. Okay, well, enough about the war. Are you going to introduce me to these pretty girls?"

Jeff did so, and both girls saw him studying their coats and hair with a cautious curiosity.

"They're from New York," Jeff explained, seeing the questions in Mr. Green's eyes.

"Oh, well, you're welcome here. Visiting relatives?"

Jackie spoke up. "No, we're going east to work at a war plant."

The three men looked at them, admirably.

Mr. Green leaned in close. "I don't mind women taking over some of the work, since the men are all gone off to war, but there are a lot of people in this town who are not too thrilled to have a 'girl pharmacist.'"

"She can do the work, can't she?" Jackie said, with a bit of a challenge. "I mean, she's competent, isn't she?"

Mr. Green nodded. "Yes, Sarah knows her stuff all right, and she works real good. And she doesn't cost me as much as Bob Mackey used to cost me, so it's okay with me. But she's still a woman."

Jackie bristled, ready for an argument, but Megan kicked her gently in the lower leg. When Jackie turned in surprise and then irritation, Megan grinned, sweetly. "Well, that's nice, isn't it, Jackie?"

Jackie regarded her darkly, but closed her tight lips.

Mr. Green placed white doilies down and waited for their orders, his left hand resting on the tap of a soda fountain.

Jackie and Megan ordered Cokes, Jeff a Dr. Pepper and Danny a 7-up, receiving it in a forest green 7-up glass.

After Mr. Green went back into the store to wait on customers, both couples turned to face their partners, seeking privacy. They lowered their voices into intimate conversation.

"Why did you come to Aunt Betty's today?" Megan asked Jeff.

"Truth?"

"Always," Megan said, realizing she could never tell him the truth.

"Aunt Betty called my mother and told her she had two very pretty and very mysterious girls at her place, and she wanted me to come over to check them out. You see, Aunt Betty's daughter and my Mom are best friends. Anyway, being the curious pilot that I am, I called Danny , and we hurried over."

"I didn't realize we were so mysterious," Megan said, liking the sound of it.

"Oh, yes, you are *very* mysterious. This is a small town, even smaller since the war has taken so many young people away, so when two young and very pretty women appear, dressed... well, dressed in an unusual way, that is mysterious."

Jeff pushed the bill of his cap back, studying her up and down. "I'd say you're about the most mysterious girl I've ever seen."

Megan grew self-conscious. Her eyes moved down and away. "I don't know why. We're like any other two girls."

"No, Megan, you're not. There's something different about the both of you. I can't quite put my finger on it, but the second I saw you, I thought 'Where did they drop in from?'"

Megan glanced back over her shoulder, wondering what Jackie and Danny were talking about.

Jackie sipped her Coke, allowing her bold eyes to stare into Danny's. His eyes held hers for just a minute before he felt a rush of heat flush his cheeks red, and he turned to stare at the plastic mounted head of Elsie the Cow.

"So you jump out of airplanes, Danny?" Jackie asked.

"Yeah."

"And then what do you do?"

"We find the enemy and kill them. What else?"

His direct approach was both jarring and attractive.

"We're the best fighting men that ever was. We're going to win this war next year. We're going to kick their butts back into Japan and Germany."

"And then what?" Jackie asked.

Danny shrugged. "I don't know. I think I'll go to school, and maybe I'll become a teacher or something. I don't know, maybe I'll just throw in with Herman and work on cars. Maybe I'll race cars or work on airplanes. I don't know. We've got to win the war first."

"Have you already been over there?"

He stared into the marble countertop. "No. They wouldn't let me because I'd crashed my car back in January 1942, right when I was ready to enlist. I was in the hospital for a while and the doctor said I had seeing and circulatory ailments. They classified me IV-F. Do you know what people call you when you're a IV-F? 'F-Fers.'"

Danny looked at Jackie, apologetically. "Sorry, but that's the truth. Well, I couldn't stand that, so I started working out—every day—I worked out, strengthening my body and doing these eye exercises that a doctor told me to do. I went back for a physical in late 1942, and the bastards turned me down again. So I kept up my exercise regime, hiking 20, 30 and 40 miles, with a heavy pack, also doing calisthenics and my eye exercises. Finally this year in February, I passed, and I enlisted in the Army. Then I got accepted into the Airborne."

Jackie felt the thrill of sexual energy boost her pulse.

What was it about this boy that turned her on so wildly? she thought. Had she ever felt the electricity of desire singe her so swiftly, so excessively?

She batted her smoky eyes. "You're incredibly persistent, Danny. Girls must find you irresistible," and she heard the low sexy tone of her voice, and saw a little fire of desire dance in Danny's eyes. She sat up a little straighter, allowing her breasts to lift and press against her sweater.

Danny faced her, his full daring eyes taking her in. She felt him study her face, lips and breasts. The moment expanded into imagined rapture, as they leaned in closer, staring, mute with enjoyment and possibility.

CHAPTER 7

Megan and Jackie were standing outside Pearl's Beauty Shop, anxious and worried. Snow was falling, dusting the tops of cars and the sidewalks. There was no wind and the heavy sky was white and gray, with shadows creeping across the mountains.

Jeff and Danny had separated from them only minutes before, and then, only because the girls agreed to meet them for dinner that night.

"I'm losing it," Jackie said. "I mean I'm really losing it. That guy really turns me on, and we don't have the time for me to be turned on."

Megan turned her back on people as they walked by, glancing over their shoulders with inquisitive stares.

Jackie looked about. "Don't people know that it's rude to stare? We must look like freaks or something, Megan. Why are we here? Why?"

"I don't know why. This whole thing is just, well I don't know, confusing. I look around and I feel like I'm in some kind of old movie, and Bette Davis is going to come walking by, arm in arm with Humphrey Bogart.

We have got to find our car and get out of here."

"I will say one thing," Jackie said. "Those guys are hot. I mean, what is it with them? The uniform? I always did like a good uniform. Maybe it's the clean air."

"I don't know, Jackie, but I think Jeff is on to us. He keeps looking at me as if he's trying to figure me out or something. And then there's you and Danny. You were like coming on to him. I could hear you."

Jackie waved her hand, dismissively. "What is it with me? Here we are, lost, in another time and place, completely confused and freaked out, and I look at this guy and I'm in love. I'm losing my focus and I don't like it."

"Jeff wants me to take an airplane ride with him."

"Really?"

"Yes, in one of those airplanes that have two wings and two open seats. He says it's from the First World War. He says it's as safe as riding in a car."

"The First World War?" Jackie asked. "When the hell was that?"

"I'm not sure. And..." Megan said, with a sigh. "I told him I would."

"Well, Danny wants me to go skiing with him. I love skiing, but I don't want to get distracted from trying to figure out how we're going to get out of here." She looked up into the mountains, captivated. "I bet the skiing is spectacular up there."

Jackie massaged her forehead. "Okay, we have got to focus. I can't even think straight anymore. We have got to find that pawn shop we passed when we drove into town, get some money, buy some period clothes and get our hair done. I'm tired of everybody looking at us like we're aliens from another planet. Then we have to find that damned car and get back home."

"Did you bring the necklace?" Megan asked.

"Of course. It's in my pocket. Let's go."

Burt's Pawn Shop was a dark narrow building that sat on the edge of town, literally, on the other side of the railroad tracks. To the right of the building were wooden bins, stuffed with old stuff. A scruffy-looking black and white cat was perched on one, his glowing yellow marble eyes narrowed, sinisterly, as he watched the two girls approach.

To the left of the building lay a rickety old one-car garage, the two doors shut and padlocked.

The grimy looking front window said BURT'S PAWN SHOP, but many of the letters on PAWN and SHOP were worn away, and Burt never bothered to repair or change them, because everybody knew where his shop was and, if they didn't know, Burt didn't particularly care.

Burt Skall made out all right. He dealt in the black market, hoarding and selling commodities such as sugar, chocolate and cigarettes. He traded straight pins, radio tubes, cooking utensils, garbage can lids, and used vacuum cleaners. Wrist watches sold for as much as $50 above ceiling prices. Occasionally, he even managed to sell gasoline. Burt was known to have connections to shady types far and wide. Burt had been the black sheep of the town, ever since he'd arrived 10 years before. He was proud of it. He reveled in it.

Jackie and Megan looked at the building, warily, then at each other, and then at the building again. Snow lay on their shoulders and on their dark ski caps. They stood there, thoughtful and doubtful.

"It looks spooky," Megan said.

"It looks like a good place for a crime," Jackie said. "But we have to do this."

They shrugged, went to the door and opened it. It creaked and moaned, as if it were insulted by their entry.

Inside, it was a place of shadows. Both girls squinted about, smelling stale, musty old things and dust. The room was separated by a wall. There was a narrow counter, and a square window with a wooden grill and a little metal scoop tray, used to slide items under the grilled window. A dim light glowed from the back and they heard the rustle of papers and a man's peevish groan.

"Who's there?" a gruff male voice asked.

"Hello?" Megan said, meekly.

Jackie marched up to the grill and peered between its bars. "We want to pawn something."

They heard the squeak of a chair and shuffling footsteps. A moment later, Burt's face appeared, half in shadow and half in light. It was an underachieving face, with craggy features, an aquiline nose, dark crafty eyes and long, thinning hair hanging well over his ears. He cocked a suspicious eye toward them, like it was the barrel of a gun.

"What are you wanting with me then?" he barked.

He had a strange accent, perhaps Irish or British. He wore dark pants and a dingy white shirt, with a frayed gray shawl wrapped about his thin shoulders.

Jackie backed away, intimidated by his menacing eyes and harsh manner. She drew the necklace out of her coat and held it up. "I want to pawn this."

Burt straightened up a little, his hard eyes suddenly changing when he saw it. Now they twinkled with avarice. "Are you now?"

He peered out at them, and then he made a little sound of surprise. "Oh, well, I see. Two ladies, is it? Two pretty young ladies come to sell the jewels in order to buy some other pretty little thing to enhance desire, or perhaps to pay for that one sinful night with a soldier before he left for the war?"

Jackie recoiled, insulted. "No, nothing like that. I just want to pawn this. How much will you give me for it?" Jackie asked, now assaulted by the man's appalling body odor.

"How can I tell you that if I can't get a good look at it? Huh? Bring it closer," he said, summoning her with wiggling fingers.

Jackie hesitated, then stepped nearer, but still out of his reach. "They're real diamonds."

"Sure they are. They're always real diamonds, aren't they, Love? What good would a necklace like that be without real diamonds? Sadly, that's what the war has done. They bring out the real diamonds, don't they, because the man is gone, and the gift is old and it needs to be, now let me see, what is the phrase? It needs to be *discreetly* removed, and all traces eradicated. Well, that's fine, isn't it? You came to the right place, Love."

"Just tell me how much," Jackie insisted.

Megan drifted back to the door. She had the impulse to pull the thing open and run for it.

"I know what it's worth," Jackie said, trying to sound confident.

"Do you now? Well, then what do you need me for, huh? What do you need from the likes of me, young pretty girl?"

Megan shivered. Burt gave her the creeps. Megan's right fingers were reaching for the doorknob.

"Just tell me," Jackie said, wanting to run from the place too.

Burt's face fell into resentment. "I don't want it. Go away! Take the damned thing and get out of my sight."

He turned and shambled away.

"Wait, a minute!" Jackie said. "What do you mean you don't want it? They're real diamonds. It's a beautiful necklace."

He turned, a hunched and sneering man. "Did you steal it?"

"Of course not! It's mine. Just tell me how much you'll give me for it. Please. I need the money."

Burt hesitated, liking the sound of her desperation. He always played the game of disinterest, until he heard the quivering sound of desperation in his customer's voice. He wiped his forehead with a dirty handkerchief and shuffled slowly back to the window. "Okay, hand it over, so I can examine it."

Jackie jerked it back. "You can see it from here."

"If you want to sell the blessed thing, then I have to examine it. I can't tell anything about it with you holding it back there in the dark. If you want to sell it, then give it to me or get out!"

Jackie turned to Megan for support. Megan had her hand wrapped tightly around the doorknob. She weighed choice against importance. They needed money. Without money, they'd be finished. Reluctantly, she nodded.

Jackie lifted her shoulders, inhaling a breath to bolster her courage. She stepped forward and gently dropped the necklace into the scoop tray, closing her eyes, whispering a little prayer. If Burt took the necklace and refused to pay her for it or to give it back, there'd be nothing she could do. She couldn't call the police. She couldn't call anybody.

Burt made little mumbles of interest as he grasped the necklace in a shaky hand and held it up into the weak light. He lay it down on a white cloth and pondered it, his eyes opening a little wider, as the possibility of prosperity filled him with wary excitement. Burt used a 10X triplet magnifying loupe, with black framing around the lens, to grade the diamonds and chain. His right eye zeroed in on the diamonds and focused.

"Well?" Jackie asked, impatiently.

"Patience, girl. Have some patience. Nothing worthwhile is achieved in this world by being impulsive."

Burt worked, grunted and pondered.

Megan had released the doorknob and had moved to the center between the door and Jackie. Both girls waited in an agitated silence.

Finally Burt lifted his head. He lay the loupe aside and pursed his lips, as he made mental calculations.

"How much?" Jackie persisted.

He faced her, his face mostly in a gray shadow. "Where did you get this?"

"What does it matter?" Jackie asked. "How much?"

"Where did you get it, girl?! Answer me!" he demanded.

"My boyfriend gave it to me!"

He coughed out a hoarse, mirthless laugh. "Boyfriend. I've never seen this kind of work before. It's strange. Very strange."

Jackie stepped forward, boldly. "How much?"

Megan screwed up her courage by moving the strap of her purse from her left shoulder to her right.

"One hundred, and no more!"

"A hundred?" Jackie exclaimed. "It's worth at least four times that!"

"And how would you know that, Love?"

"I looked it up online," Jackie said.

"Online what?" he asked, suspiciously.

Jackie stammered. "I mean... I looked it up in a catalog. It's worth at least three hundred."

"Maybe, girl. Maybe it's worth three hundred, if you can get three hundred. But can you?"

Jackie stood, seething.

Megan cursed.

"I don't have all day, girls, take it or leave it."

He grinned, darkly, showing dirty jagged teeth.

Dispirited, Jackie and Megan ambled down Main Street, past the post office, the town square, and Dot's Café, where they were going to have dinner with the boys that evening at 6:30. They stopped at John's General Store, and as they passed the Douglas Fir Christmas tree and entered through the single glass door, they saw yet another black and white poster hanging from a back wall.

USE IT UP-WEAR IT OUT-MAKE IT DO!

They were grateful for the heat as they stomped the snow off their boots and peeled off their caps. Hanging in the air was the pungent odor of a pipe, but they didn't see anyone. It was a square space, with a cast iron, pot-bellied coal stove in the center of the room, and one wall lined with wooden shelves, sparsely stocked with Life-buoy Soap, Colgate Chlorophyll Toothpaste, Chase & Sanborn Coffee, canisters of dried milk, brown packages of dried fruit, Woodbury Cold Cream and nylon-bristle hairbrushes. At the end of one shelf was a big, heavy, white scale. There was a red sign advertising Robin Starch and a blue sign advertising Concentrated Beef.

In another area, the girls strolled past brass lanterns, wooden ladders, flower pots, ornately carved pipes and pipe racks, and cartons of cigarettes: Lucky Strike, Chesterfield, Regent and Camels. Toward the back of the store, the toys were displayed: old stuffed bears and dolls, miniature figurines, metal trains, Mickey Mouse riding a little bicycle, and wooden toy guns.

Near the front counter was a barrel filled with potatoes. A handwritten sign tacked on its front announced:

Potatoes 10 lbs, 69c. Manor House coffee was 49c/lb and Gold Medal Flour (25 lb bag) was $1.85. There were six glass bottles of Coca Cola in a wooden carrying case going for a quarter.

Jackie immediately became lost in the products, nosing toward the vintage packaging and prices, mesmerized by the colors, design and workmanship of the toys. Megan was distracted by the charming chaos of the place.

Behind the counter, in a rocking chair and smoking a pipe, sat John Howard. He was watching the girls with bland interest. He was 60, with white thinning hair and Benjamin Franklin spectacles. He was wearing a pair of blue overalls and a white shirt.

"Can I help you girls with anything at all?" he asked, in a thick Vermont accent.

The girls turned, gently startled. They had not seen John, because he was tucked behind a tall, cigar store Indian statue. It was a wooden, hand-carved figure standing on a pedestal. The broad, bare-chested Indian had a beaded headband with a feather, and a red, white and blue loin cloth tied about his waist. His hand was shading his eyes, and he was looking out yonder at something in the distance.

"We're looking for clothes," Megan said.

John stood. He was tall and thin and his voice was high and reedy. He pointed to the clothes department with the stem of his pipe.

"Well, what you see there are bits and grabs that were collected by my daughter before she left. She's not around anymore. She volunteered for service early this year and was assigned to the U.S. Army Hospital Ship Shamrock last July. So, I don't know much about those women's articles. Don't sell that much of them. Girls like to go ride the train to the cities to get their clothes.

They don't shop here much."

"This is quite a place," Jackie said, still taking it in.

"It'll do. You'll be from out of town, I guess?"

"Yes, we're just passing through. We're going to Portland to work in a war plant."

"Yes, well, I guess that's what all the women are doing these days. It don't seem quite right, but then, with the way things are, it don't seem quite wrong either."

John sat back down and rocked, the chair creaking the old floor. Jackie joined Megan. There was only one rack of clothes, with a sparse selection. A wooden table alongside offered folded blouses, overalls, socks and sweaters. The girls picked through the rack, examining skirts and dresses. The shelf behind the rack held shoes. Megan checked them out, disappointed by what she saw.

Jackie found a dress, held it up, checked the size and thought it might fit. It was blue, with puffy padded shoulders and puffy sleeves, a white collar and white buttons down the front.

"Not bad," Megan said, glancing up.

The "fitting room" was a women's washroom in the back corner, so Jackie went there to try the dress on, while Megan continued her search. After Jackie returned, Megan went to try her choices on. A half hour later, they'd both managed to find a few things to buy.

"Should we put these clothes on now, so we don't keep standing out like sore thumbs?" Megan asked.

Jackie paused. "Shouldn't we wash them first? They smell like they've been here awhile, and we don't know where they came from."

"Have you seen a Laundromat?" Megan asked.

"I don't think they had those then," Jackie said, and then she corrected herself. "I mean, have those things *now*. Anyway, I haven't seen one."

"Let's just put the clothes on. That way, when we go to pay and we don't have ration stamps, he'll be less likely to make us take the clothes off and come back later with our ration stamps."

"Good idea, since we don't have any ration stamps to begin with," Jackie said, smelling the musty dress again. "Maybe Aunt Betty has a washer."

After taking turns in the ladies room, they walked toward the counter wearing the 1940s clothes, carrying their 21st century clothes as well as a few additional finds. Jackie was wearing the blue dress, and was carrying dark slacks, a yellow cotton blouse with padded shoulders, and wedge shoes made of mesh, with cork soles and one-inch heels. She later learned that the style was dictated by United States Rationing Rules.

Megan wore a brown knee-length skirt, light brown wool sweater, a white collared shirt and loafer-type shoes. She'd also found a cotton blouse and black slacks, not a perfect fit, but good enough.

As they approached, John heaved himself up from his creaking rocker and stepped to the counter. He stared at them, scratching his head. "You're wearing them? Well, that's unusual. Never had anybody wear clothes out of the store before."

Both girls smiled, brightly. "We just couldn't wait. We really like them."

"Surprised you found all that," he said, flatly. "And you want these others too, here on the counter?"

"Yes, all of it."

John scratched the back of his neck with the pipe stem. "Yeah, it's all pretty unusual, isn't it? But most things is pretty unusual these days, and my daughter said I'd better get used to it."

Jackie presented the money she'd received from Burt. "How much?" she asked.

John lifted his chin and adjusted his glasses. "You have your ration stamps?"

Jackie looked at Megan. The two girls had learned by now that Megan was the best liar. "Well, sir, you see, we lost them."

His little eyes enlarged. "You lost them? You lost your ration books?"

Megan made a sad, sorrowful face. "Yes, sir. We were so upset. But we have money and do want to get to the war plant as soon as we can. And we love our new clothes. Be sure to thank your daughter."

John just kept scratching his head and making little whistling sounds of bewilderment.

CHAPTER 8

Jackie and Megan crossed Main Street in their "new" clothes, clutching brown paper bags under their arms, already feeling more like 1940s women. They pushed into Pearl's Beauty Shop and were met at the white gleaming desk by Pearl herself, a matronly woman in her 50s with a remote and impassive face. Her smile seemed calculated. Megan thought it must have taken great effort for Pearl's tight mouth to smile at all. But then surely, in this small town, she'd heard about them and was suspicious. Pearl's hair was a soft gray, with permed curls packed tightly against her head. It did not look like a 1940s hair style, Megan thought. According to her acting and makeup experience, she'd guess 1930s.

"Hello, ladies," Pearl said, in a precise and affected manner that made her sound half British and half 1930s drawing room comedy. "How can I help you?"

She reminded Megan of Margaret Dumont, the actress who'd co-stared in many of the Marx Brothers movies her father loved so much. She'd grown up watching them and loving them.

Pearl's Shop had plenty of Christmas wreaths, pine garlands with red bows, mirrors, and glass display cases exhibiting hats, purses and jewelry. A cosmetics counter with makeup and creams stood in the corner. Two teenage girls were browsing the shop, along with a twitchy elderly woman, dressed all in black, including her silk hat with a veil and feather. The teenagers wore skirts, sweaters, loafers and socks rolled up at the ankles. All turned, warily, to view Megan and Jackie.

Jackie was staring at a poster ad propped on one of the glass cases. It pictured a profile sketch of a regal, elegant woman, with sharp features and a red button mouth. Her eyes were half closed, as if in rapture, revealing extravagant eyelashes. Pink bottles of makeup were artistically sketched at the bottom of the drawing. The advertisement read: *"Women are expected to keep busy... and keep beautiful."*

Pearl ushered the girls into the back room where the sinks and dryers were. She introduced them to her "girl" and they sat for a consultation.

The "girl" was Sue Peters, a tall, lanky 19-year-old who wore a white lab coat, and had a blonde peek-a-boo haircut in the style of the 1940s popular actress, Veronica Lake, whose 1942 movie hits were *This Gun for Hire* and *The Glass Key*. It was sexy, sweeping hair with finger waves, and a wisp of blonde falling mysteriously over one eye.

Sue appraised their faces and current hairstyles from out behind the wisp of hair that covered her right eye. She twisted up her lips in dissatisfaction, folded her arms and shook her head, blowing the hair from her right eye.

"Whoever did your hair the last time really did a number on you, sister," she proclaimed to Jackie. "And you too," she added to Megan.

Megan's last cut had cost well over a hundred dollars. Jackie's, about the same. They stared up at Sue in aloof annoyance, while Bing Crosby sang *White Christmas.*

But they gave her the go-ahead and so she went to work on Megan first, studying her face, then washing, conditioning and trimming her hair. While she worked, the radio played a commercial with an enthusiastic baritone proclaiming, *"... And for all you wives out there, take PEP Vitamins for pep. Remember, the harder a wife works, the cuter she looks."*

Megan and Jackie narrowed their eyes into irritated slits.

"You've got good, thick hair like Rita Hayworth," Sue said to Megan. "You'd look great in Victory Rolls. We'll keep the rest of it flat to your head, with finger rolls at the ends. Don't worry, you'll look like a movie star when I'm finished."

Jackie waited patiently in the next chair, gazing at a *Ladies' Home Journal* magazine, reading an article that explained the principles behind sugar rationing. Evidently, sugarcane could be used to make explosives. There was a second article about the conservation of animal waste fat, which could be used to make glycerine for explosives. The article encouraged people to bring all waste fat back to their neighborhood butcher.

When Sue had finished with Megan, she stood back and examined her work. "Okay, get under the dryer." She led Megan to a helmet, dome-shaped dryer hovering above a comfortable chair. "You'll need a couple hours with hair that thick."

"Two hours?!" Megan asked, but Sue had already begun her scrutiny of Jackie's face and hair.

"For you, I think a Vivien Leigh look, since you already have thin eyebrows. Your hair needs some curl, though. I'll put pin curls on the sides, and when it's dry, we'll pin the hair up in layers, with a few bobby pins. We'll keep the bangs, but do something with them."

Sue washed Jackie's hair, and then twirled strands of it in pin curls on both sides of the center part. She put clips on the bangs to give them waves, and then placed Jackie next to Megan, under another dryer. For over an hour, both girls sat in the heavy, padded chairs under twin dryer cone helmets, feeling like the original Cone Heads from the old *Saturday Night Live* TV show.

Jackie found another *Ladies Home Journal*, while Megan leafed through an old copy of *Parade Magazine*. Her eye was drawn to an article that offered dating tips for single women. She laughed out loud a few times, elbowing Jackie so she could share her amusement.

The article listed dos and don'ts:

1. Don't be sentimental or try to get him to say something he doesn't want to by working on his emotions. Men don't like tears, especially in public places.

2. Don't use the car mirror to fix your makeup. The man needs it to drive, and it annoys him very much to have to turn around to see what's behind him.

3. Men don't like girls who borrow their handkerchiefs and smudge them with lipstick. Do your makeup in private, not where he sees you.

4. If you need a brassiere, wear one. Don't tug at your girdle, and be careful your stockings are not wrinkled.

5. Don't be conspicuous and talk to other men. The last straw is to pass out from too much liquor. Chances are your date will never call you again.

When Sue had finished, both girls stood staring into the mirror, impressed and captivated. They actually looked like women from the 1940s. The top of Megan's hair was swept back into two Victory rolls, exposing her forehead and giving her height. The sides of her face were framed with long and lavish reddish-blond finger curls. In the back, her hair was pressed more tightly to her head, a little straighter, but ending with casual curls. Jackie's black hair was piled in luxurious curly layers, with wavy bangs gently covering her forehead.

"What do you think?" Sue asked, obviously pleased with her work.

The girls nodded approval, confident now that they would blend into the fabric of 1943.

A light snow was still falling as the girls started back to the house, their hair wrapped in white scarves they'd purchased on the way out of Pearl's. They'd also bought some makeup and perfume. They wanted to look and smell as authentic as possible.

"This dress is too loose," Jackie said. "It needs a belt or something."

"This skirt is too tight in the waist," Megan said, "and these loafers are pinching my feet."

They left Main Street and turned right, starting down a deserted sidewalk, past a small apartment complex.

Megan stopped, took the loafers off and put her boots back on.

"Megan, I say we take a cab to the covered bridge, first thing tomorrow morning, and we walk across it. What do you think?"

Megan looked up into the gray quilted sky, feeling the cold flakes strike her in the face. "Yes. Yes, we've got to try."

They walked on in silence, deep in thought. "What do we do if nothing happens?" Megan finally asked.

Jackie gave a little shake of her head. "I don't know."

"What are we going to tell Danny tonight when he tells us that Herman doesn't have our car, and that Herman has never seen us or heard of us?"

Jackie gave another little shake of her head. "I don't know. You're the liar, can't you come up with something?"

"The only thing I can think of is this: let's act mysterious. Let's be mysterious. I mean, we *are* mysterious, so why not act the part completely?"

"I'm not an actress, Megan. I like the real world. The honest world. Not a world of make believe."

"All right, then just do what I do. Just nod your head or something."

"I wish Harold Dodge would have taken that damned car and left us at the airport. None of this would have happened."

"Oh, God, don't bring that up," Megan said. "If I'd just kept my big mouth shut, we wouldn't be in this mess."

"I wonder what happened to him, to Harold Dodge. He's probably home right now with his family sitting next to a warm fire."

"I've been thinking about that," Megan said. "What if, somehow, Harold Dodge was like a wizard or something and he?"

Jackie cut her off. "Don't even go there, Megan. That is just too crazy for me and, anyway, so what? He's in an entirely different century. I mean, it just doesn't matter."

They arrived at the house by mid afternoon to find Aunt Betty still in the living room, knitting. She glanced up over her glasses, just as the girls pulled off their scarves and revealed their new hairdos.

"Well, what a change!" Aunt Betty said. "Quite a change. I'm afraid you missed lunch, but there's some cold chicken and bread if you want a snack."

The girls declined, climbing the stairs to their room.

As soon as they entered, they froze. The bed had been made, the room tidied up and their suitcases had been moved, so that they lay on the floor side by side.

The girls passed each other a look of alarm. They closed the door and hurried to their carry-ons.

"We told Rose not to clean the room," Jackie said, in a panic.

They dropped to their knees, unzipped the top flap and looked inside. Jackie's face went pale. Megan sighed.

"Rose has been in here," Megan said.

"Yeah. She's probably seen my tablet, phone and e-Reader," Jackie said.

"I hope she didn't see my novel," Megan said, rifling through her suitcase.

Jackie shot her a glance. "What novel?"

"*Left for Dead*, by Percy Towne."

"What is it?"

"A thriller. I love thrillers."

"Don't you have an e-Reader?" Jackie asked, upset. "Novels must look different in 1943. Novels have copyrights in them."

"I like to read real books. I bought it at LaGuardia before we left."

Jackie got up, turned in place and then sat on the edge of the bed. "Okay... so Rose probably looked at the copyright."

"Maybe not," Megan said, standing, unable to stop herself from walking to the mirror to look at her new hairdo. "I mean, how many people pick up a book and look at the copyright? I'm sure she didn't."

"And I'm sure she did. How old is the book?"

"I don't know. It's been out awhile. Maybe 2012."

"Rose is a teenager, and like all girl teenagers, she's a curious little bitch!"

Megan was still admiring her new hairdo.

"Megan, can you please focus on this and stop looking at your hair? This is serious."

Megan turned. "So what do we do? Aunt Betty seemed normal enough, so Rose probably didn't tell her."

Jackie stood, biting her nails. "I bet Rose told Jeff and Danny Boy. They'll probably ask us about it tonight."

"Jackie, we don't know if Rose actually searched our bags. We're just guessing. Let's not jump to conclusions here."

"Things are closing in on us, Megan. I tell you, things are closing in and this is just our first day. We are in big trouble."

CHAPTER 9

Jeff and Danny arrived at Aunt Betty's at 6:15. Since the entire country was on "War Time" or Daylight Savings Time, night had fallen. The girls descended the stairs, poised and smiling, hoping their new hairdos, rich red lipstick and second-hand attire would impress the boys.

Jeff and Danny were grasping their caps, staring with delight.

"Hello, ladies," Jeff said.

"Evening, ladies," Danny said.

Their voices were steady and unemotional, but their eyes held a kind of drowsy fascination. All four stood like nervous, anxious teenagers on prom night.

Outside, they climbed into the 1937 Ford V8 Fordor Sedan, Megan in front with Jeff, and Danny in back with Jackie.

Jeff started the car, shifted into first gear and drove off. "These are double adjustable seats," Jeff added. "This is my father's car. I sold mine when I went off to flying school in South Carolina. He stills loves this car, the rounded look, the horizontal bars and the hood-side grilles. You should see all the photos we have of him standing next to it."

Jeff was blabbering on because he was nervous. He found Megan's perfume thrilling and intoxicating, and her new hairdo reminded him of Rita Hayworth, his favorite actress.

In the backseat, Danny turned to Jackie. "How was your day?"

Jackie sat stiffly, feeling a swelling of unwanted desire. "Oh, just fine. Really fine."

Dot's Café had a gray, worn, tile floor, burgundy colored booths along one wall, a lunch counter with burgundy padded swivel stools running along the opposite wall, and wooden tables and chairs in the center. The quartet found an empty booth near the back, close to the jukebox, with its beautiful light show and color animation. It was playing Bing Crosby and The Andrews Sisters singing *Jingle Bells*. The café was half full, with older couples seated at the tables, and families with kids at the booths. A man in overalls was at the counter having The Blue Plate Special, and a sailor and his girl were having pie and coffee, staring longingly into each other's eyes.

A sign on the wall said, DON'T ASK FOR BUTTER OR FOR A REFILL OF COFFEE. Just below that was a handwritten comment: *"My nephew is fighting the Japs!"*

There was a Christmas tree near the cash register where Dot sat like a monument, flipping through movie magazines and sipping something from a red, white and blue mug. Dot was heavy, friendly and watchful.

"The club steak is good," Jeff said.

"Meatloaf too," Danny said.

When Jackie and Megan saw Rose approach in her

white and blue uniform, they almost did a double-take. She had a pad and pen in hand, was chewing bubblegum and had a no-nonsense manner.

"What'll it be?" she asked, ignoring Megan's and Jackie's inquiring eyes.

Then she looked the girls over, coolly. "Where'd you get those clothes? At the General Store? First a general and now the General Store." She smiled weakly at her own joke.

Megan blushed. Jackie bristled.

Danny laughed. "Ladies, Rose has been a sassy girl ever since she was a little bitty thing."

"I am not sassy, Danny."

"She's a sassy lassie," Jeff said, "and I think that Jackie and Megan are beautiful, and they are dressed beautifully."

Danny held up an empty water glass. "I'd drink to that, if Rose had remembered to fill it."

"You know what rudeness gets you, Danny?" She stuck her tongue out at him. "Nothing."

Danny laughed, then reached for the paper menus propped between the sugar dispenser and the salt and pepper shakers. He handed them to the others. "Well, Rosy Rose, what's good tonight?"

"Everything and nothing."

"Helpful, as always," Danny said.

Jeff spoke up, looking at Megan and Jackie. "Rose is only happy when I put money in the juke box and play *All or Nothing at All*, so she can swoon over Frank Sinatra."

"Shut up, Jeff. You think you're so smart because you can fly an airplane."

"Not just any airplane, Rose. It's a B-17, with four 1200-horsepower Wright Cyclone Engines, and a cruising speed of 170 miles per hour. And it can fly all the way up to 30,000 feet."

Rose made an ugly face. "You're just trying to impress the girls, Jeff, and you and I know it."

"Well, of course I'm trying to impress them," Jeff said, turning to Megan. "Megan, are you impressed?"

Megan nodded, searching Rose's face for a sign that she knew their secret, based on her deliberate exploration of their suitcases. But Rose's face was empty.

"You're not impressed, Megan?" Jeff repeated.

"Oh, yes, yes, I'm very impressed," Megan said. "Is that the plane you're going to take me flying in?"

Rose rolled her eyes and turned away. "Oh, brother. She doesn't know the difference between a B-17, 4 engine bomber, and a little World War I biplane."

"Rose, be nice," Jeff said. He looked at Megan. "We won't be flying a B-17 Flying Fortress, Megan. We'll fly my Jenny, my single engine girl, and she's much smaller and a bit slower."

Danny leaned forward, "Megan, don't let him take you up in that rickety old biplane. He suckered me into taking a ride a couple of days ago and he nearly crashed the thing into old man Moore's barn. And he thinks I'm a risk taker. I'd rather jump out of a C-47 at 600 feet than get into that thing again."

"Maybe we should all just go on a sleigh ride instead," Jackie said.

Rose inhaled an irritated breath. "Are you all going to order, or do you want me to come back in five or twenty minutes or three days?"

Megan and Jackie quickly perused the menu. Above the menu items they read:

Due to Rationing and Shortage of Foods, These Menus Are Subject To Change Without Notice

The World's Best Hamburger was 25 cents. The Fried Chicken Dinner was $1.00. The Extra Fine Western Tenderloin Beef Steak Plate was 75 Cents. The Club Sirloin Steak was $1.20. The Fish Plate was 60 cents. The Blue Plate Special, meatloaf, peas and mashed potatoes, was 75 cents. Coffee, tea, milk and buttermilk were 10 cents.

Megan ate the meatloaf and Jackie the fried chicken, while the boys devoured the Club Sirloin Steak, with French fries and salad.

"I went over to see Herman today," Danny said, nonchalantly, cutting into his steak.

"I bet our car wasn't there," Megan said.

Jackie stopped eating.

Danny looked up. "No, it wasn't. He said he never got your car."

"That's because we didn't give it to him," Megan said.

Jeff turned to her. "I thought you did."

"I thought you did, too," Danny said.

"It was all just a misunderstanding," Megan said, blithely.

Jackie was waiting for Megan's lie, shrinking a little.

"We never actually had a car. We got a ride from the train station. It was actually that person's car that needed to be worked on."

Jackie's eyes shifted, uncomfortably.

"I don't understand," Jeff said. "I thought you said it was your car."

Megan made a little wave of her hand. "Yes, well, it's all just a misunderstanding."

Jeff spoke up. "But wait a minute. Didn't you say you were driving to Portland? Didn't you say you had a 'B' sticker so you could buy extra gasoline?"

"Sure I did, but my car is at home in New York. That's what I meant. No, Jackie and I are going to take the train to Portland. Right, Jackie?"

"Sure. We like the train. We always take the train to save gas. And, you know, there's just not much gas around anywhere, is there?"

Jeff and Danny glanced at each other, confused.

"So Aunt Betty saw you come in somebody else's car?" Danny asked.

"Yes, that was definitely somebody else's car," Jackie said.

"Whose car was it?" Jeff asked.

"Who?" Megan asked, swallowing hard. "You mean, who gave us the ride from the train station?"

"Yeah," Jeff asked. "I guess that's what I mean."

"Oh, I don't know, really. Some man I think."

Jackie rolled her eyes.

Jeff and Danny exchanged another baffled glance.

Jeff lay down his fork. "All right, you two. There's a little too much mystery going on here. Things are not adding up. Aunt Betty said you came in around ten o'clock. She said she couldn't see clearly, because it was dark, but she did see a car parked at the curb and you told her it was your car. The last train stops in Holly Grove at six thirty in the evening. Now I'm sure you weren't waiting at the train station all that time, were you?"

Jackie shrugged. "Why don't you answer that one, Megan?"

Megan saw that she was in way over her head. She drew a breath and pulled out the last card she had. She lowered her voice, glancing around, conspiratorially. "Look, I can't tell you everything. Obviously, things don't quite add up, because they're not supposed to add up. Surely, you can understand that."

Danny stopped eating, utterly engrossed and bewildered. Jeff was rapt. Jackie had closed her eyes, tightly.

"The truth is, Jackie and I are involved in something... something secret, and that's really all I can say about it right now."

Megan went back to her dinner, eating casually. Jackie slowly opened her eyes to appraise the expression on the boys' faces. Had they fallen for it? Jeff was circumspect. Danny picked up his fork, tracing the top of his teeth with the tip of his tongue. She found that very sexy.

"So you don't have a car?" Jeff asked.

"Yes and no," Megan said.

Jackie blew out a sigh. "No, Megan," she said, forcefully. "Just say it. We don't have a car."

Jeff and Danny waited.

"Okay, we don't have a car and that's that," Megan concluded.

"Secret?" Jeff said, dryly.

"Yes, very secret," Megan responded.

"Does it have something to do with the military?" Danny asked.

"Secret. All secret," Megan repeated. "That's all I can say."

They ate in silence.

"How long will you be in town?" Jeff asked.

Megan looked to Jackie, who looked to Megan.

"Why don't you answer that one, Jackie?"

Jackie laid her fork down and folded her hands in her

lap. "Well, that depends, of course."

Megan was intrigued. So were the guys.

"What does it depend on?" Jeff asked, uneasily, afraid of the answer.

Jackie's eyes traveled around the room, searching for an answer. "Well, Megan can tell you that."

Megan had meatloaf in her mouth. She chewed vigorously, taking her time, while everyone waited for her answer. She struggled to create yet another lie. She swallowed and glanced up at the ceiling, seeking inspiration. "Well... it all depends on when we get the *word*."

Jackie nodded, pleased. "Yes, that's right. We're waiting for the *word*."

Jeff leaned back, shaking his head, and looked directly at Danny. "Danny Boy, for the first time in my life, I don't know what to say."

Holly Grove was quiet and dark, since most of the lights were out. The population was obeying the blackout regulations in case of an air attack. As the couples strolled, it made the cold night seem cozy and intimate. This time, Danny and Jackie moved ahead while Jeff and Megan lingered back, in silence, each waiting for the other to speak.

"I heard you tell Mr. Green you'll have to go back right after Christmas," Megan said.

"Yes. Danny Boy and I both got 10-day passes. We have to leave the day after Christmas."

"That's only five days from now."

"There's still a lot of fighting to do over there. We're ready to go."

"Where will they send you?"

"I'm surprised at you, Megan. You and all your secrets and waiting for the *word*. Loose lips, sink ships, remember? I can't say. I'll give you a hint though. Shakespeare spent time there."

"You'll be flying?"

"Yes."

"A lot?"

"Well, I hear the brass has just upped the mission count from 25 to 30 and even higher. I don't know. We'll see when I get there. My crew and I will be a replacement crew. A lot of planes have been shot down. It's been rough over there. The Nazis are fierce fighters."

"Why didn't you go to war earlier, after Pearl Harbor?" Megan asked, drawing closer to him, wanting him to take her arm, or to hold her and warm her.

"I don't mean to brag, Megan, but I'm a good pilot. They say I'm kind of a natural flyer. I started flying when I was 19. I can land a B-17 so softly that if you're blindfolded, you won't even know you've touched down. Anyway, the Army Air Corps needed flight instructors. I wanted to fly combat missions but my C.O., my commanding officer, pulled me aside and asked me if I'd stay stateside to train other pilots. What could I say? I said okay. So I've been in Columbus, Mississippi for over a year. Finally, a few weeks ago, I went to the Colonel and again requested I be sent into combat."

"Do you want to get into the war that badly?" Megan asked.

Jeff moved closer and she saw the white vapor puff from his mouth and felt the masculine power of him. It excited her. He turned and faced her. "Megan, I want to help win this war. I want to fight for my country. I don't want to stay behind and play it safe, when all the other guys are over there, risking everything to win this awful war. I've got to go. I couldn't live with myself if I didn't go and fight."

After his words fell away, they moved closer, breathing, feeling, staring into each other's face. Megan longed for him to kiss her. She'd never felt as comfortable or as safe with a man as she did with Jeff, even though they'd just met. His eyes revealed tenderness, and there was a down-to-earth strength and sincerity about him, a calm mature confidence.

It struck her then, that in *her* time—the 21st century—Jeff was part of the distant past. He was probably long dead. She shivered, suddenly feeling strange and sad.

"Are you all right?" Jeff asked.

She nodded, struggling for emotional balance.

When he took her hand, she wondered if she and Jackie would ever get back home. She wondered if she could make a life for herself in this time; make a home in this time. Jeff's hand was a strong, masculine hand, a gentle hand. Without hesitation, she squeezed it, and after she did, he raised her hand to his lips and kissed it, looking deeply into her eyes.

"What a mystery you are, Megan."

Jackie and Danny wandered the empty streets in silence. Danny felt the impulsive desire to reach for Jackie and kiss her, but he wouldn't. He wasn't raised that way. He'd never done anything like that in his life. His mother had trained him to be a gentleman, even if he'd resisted her every step of the way. Why was he feeling so impulsive now? Was it the war? The awareness that once overseas and in combat, he could be killed? He didn't think so. He'd been attracted to Jackie from the start, from their first meeting. He felt ringing alarms and impulsive desires banging around inside his body. She unnerved and puzzled him. He loved the way she sashayed, the way she twirled the ends of her hair with those long slender fingers and red polished nails. He knew he'd never forget her—could never forget her.

"What were you like as a kid?" Jackie asked.

"Well, my mother called me a rascal."

"I haven't heard that word used in a long time."

"I was always sneaking up on her and scaring her. I'd loosen her clothes line just before she went to hang out the clothes and her clothes would fall into the dirt. I did rotten things like that. I hid in the woods and scared the girls when they were coming home from school. Boy things. All kinds of things like that."

"So, you *were* a rascal."

"Yeah, I guess I was. My favorite prank was the Sunday Morning Campaign, as I called it. I left the church service one hot summer day, just as Pastor Riley started his sermon. Below one of the windows, I lit some firecrackers. When they went off, you should have seen that congregation scream and jump. They thought the end of the world had come."

Danny laughed. "Boy, did I get in trouble for that one. But it was worth it."

They were near the edge of town and a cold wind surrounded them. Jackie reached into her pocket, took out her scarf and tied it over her head.

"Do you want to start back?" Danny asked.

"No, let's keep walking."

They continued on in silence, kicking along the walk.

"Did you grow up in New York?" Danny asked.

"No, Chicago. Well, all over the place for a while. I was an Army brat."

Danny stopped, surprised. "Really? Your father is old Army?"

Jackie was afraid she'd revealed too much. "Well, yes... I guess you could say old Army."

"Where is he now? Europe? The Pacific?"

"Well... he's in Europe someplace. You know, secret."

Recognition dawned on Danny's face. "Yeah, sure. Of course. I get it. Now it all makes sense."

"It does?" Jackie asked.

"Yes. You and Megan are working with your father, doing some war work for him. That's the secret, and the '*word*' is you're waiting for him or one of his staff to call you so you can continue on."

Jackie seized the idea, gratefully, but she didn't let her expression show it. She looked away, demurely. "Well, yes, I guess you could say that."

"Okay, so it all makes sense then."

Jackie relaxed. She quickly changed the subject. "So what about you, Danny? When you leave here, where will you go?"

"I'll be part of a replacement crew in a parachute infantry regiment, a PIR. I don't have orders yet. I'll get them when I get back to Georgia. We'll ship out soon after that. That's the word, anyway. Everybody's talking about the invasion of Europe. I guess I'll be in the thick of it."

"Do you like jumping out of airplanes?"

He shrugged. "Yeah, I do. But it's more than that. I'm trained in map reading, demolition and communications. But all of us guys work as a team. We're there for each other. We'll take care of each other. All of us just want this war to get over so we can get back home."

They turned and started back through town. They didn't see Jeff and Megan.

Danny pushed his hands deeply into his pockets. "Leonardo da Vinci designed a linen parachute, you know," he said. "And old Ben Franklin thought about the idea of 10,000 men falling from the skies to attack and overwhelm an enemy on the ground, so parachutes aren't a new idea. And the Germans have been successful with their paratroopers since 1935."

Jackie looked at him, and she thought his boyish face was both lovely and resolute. "You'll be careful over there, won't you, Danny?"

"Me? Oh yeah. I know how to duck."

He looked at her. Their eyes had adjusted to the darkness and they stared, fearlessly, desire rising, Jackie feeling a quivering longing to reach for him.

"So, do you think you'll be in town for a while?" Danny asked.

Jackie smiled, warmly. "I don't know, Danny. I really don't know."

CHAPTER 10

Jackie and Megan were wide awake at 6am, lying in the double bed, staring up at the ceiling, deep in thought.

"It's awful, isn't it?" Megan said.

"What?"

"That they have to go off to war."

"...Yeah."

"What are we going to do?" Megan asked.

Jackie sighed. "We're going to that bridge and cross over to the other side. We are going to hope, like we've never hoped before, that we wind up back in our own time. I want my life back. I want all my crazy clients calling and texting me, day and night, because their presentations, logos and magazine covers are late, and because they want to make changes to every single damned design, even though they've already signed off on them. I suddenly love them and I want to hear from them. All of them."

"I wonder if I got that role?" Megan reflected. "It could make me a star, you know. It's a good role. One of those once-in-a-lifetime roles that actresses always dream about."

"Don't actors and actresses always think they're once-in-a-lifetime roles?" Jackie asked.

"Yeah, I guess so."

They lay in silence, absorbed in thought.

"What do we take with us?" Megan asked.

"Just what we're wearing. We'll leave everything else. It won't matter if we get back to our time."

They were quiet again.

"I keep thinking about Eric," Jackie said. "He hasn't even been born yet and we're engaged to be married. And I pawned the diamond necklace he gave me. How am I going to tell him that one? Where is your necklace? Eric will ask. Well, I have a very simple explanation, honey. I had to hock it back in 1943, so I could return to the 21 century."

The quiet relaxed them, and their breathing grew easy and shallow.

"There's something about those guys, isn't there?" Megan asked.

"Yeah."

"How old is Danny?" Megan asked.

"Twenty-two, but he seems a lot older, not that I care one way or the other. How about Jeff?"

"He's my age, twenty five. There's something so mature about them. They're so strong and confident. Jeff can fly a four-engine bomber, for crying out loud."

Jackie pulled the sheet up to her chin. "Yeah. Most of the guys I know can't even fly a kite."

"And Danny seems so confident and assured."

"Yeah, and he is so hot," Jackie said, troubled. "I perspire just being next to him. I've got to get out of here before I do something stupid and, I know me, I'll do something stupid. I have a track record of doing stupid things when it comes to men."

Megan wiped the sleep from her eyes. "Do you really want to go back, Jackie?"

Jackie turned to face her. "Are you kidding? Yes, of course I do. Don't even think about staying here. We're not going to lose our focus, Megan. We don't belong in this time."

"Then why are we here?"

"I don't know why, but I'm going back, one way or the other, because that's where we belong."

Jackie swung her legs out of bed and stood up. "Let's get dressed and call a cab. The sooner we leave here, the better."

A half hour later, they stood by the door, looking back at their suitcases.

"What will happen to history if they find our things?" Megan asked.

"I don't know or care. Let history deal with it. Let's go."

"Wait, a minute. We can't leave without leaving Jeff and Danny a note. We can't."

Jackie waited. "I thought about it, but what can we say? We're going back to the 21st century, sorry you can't come?"

"We have to write something."

They quickly searched the drawers and found an old 9" by 7" spiral notebook and two pencils. Megan tore off a page and handed it to Jackie.

"What?" Jackie asked.

"Write something. Then I'll write something."

Jackie dropped onto the edge of the bed and fell into concentration, finally writing:

Dear Danny:

How wonderful and fun it was spending time together, but Megan and I have to move on. I know you'll understand. Please take good care of yourself over there, and remember me sometimes. I will miss you and never forget you.
Love,
Jackie

Megan went to work writing her own.

Dear Jeff:

Please forgive me for this short and abrupt goodbye, but Jackie and I have been called away. These are strange and difficult times and I'm sure you'll understand. I wish we could have spent more time together. I truly believe we could have been good for each other and we could have had so many happy times.
Take care of yourself and come home safe. I'll never forget you.
Love,
Megan

Megan rummaged through the drawer and found a used envelope. She erased the "RECEIPTS FOR 1941" and wrote: JEFF AND DANNY across the front. She placed the envelope on the bed, then changed her mind, thinking it would be more noticeable on the floor, in front of the door.

Five minutes later, they left the room, wearing their 1940s clothes, their coats and their scarves. They crept down the stairs and over to the front door. They heard stirrings in the kitchen, and the mumble of voices that they recognized as Aunt Betty's and Rose's. Neither Megan nor Jackie wanted to see or talk to Rose. They sensed a disaster waiting to happen.

Jackie gently opened the front door, and the girls stepped out, closing it quietly behind them. There was a sharp chill to the air, but the cloudless sky was a bright blue, and the towering mountains were shining with the glare of new snow.

They walked briskly down the walk and started toward Dot's Café, where they'd seen a public telephone booth. They'd call for a cab there. The streets were quiet and, when a car passed, Megan noticed the MD license plate.

On Main Street they moved purposefully past the Grove Theatre. Megan saw a billboard sign in the movie window announcing coming attractions: *A Guy Named Joe*, starring Spencer Tracy. A sign hanging just below the marquee read, **Latest Newsreels and Shorts**!

The two girls entered Dot's. It had just opened and Dot was already seated behind the cash register, dressed the same and looking the same as the night before. She barely glanced up from her movie magazine as they entered, their cheeks pink from the cold. The counter was filled with early eaters, mostly railroad workers, dressed in overalls.

Jackie saw the narrow oak phone booth, opened the folding doors and entered, shutting them behind her and sitting down on the wooden stool. The interior light clicked on and an overhead fan whirled, bringing down a slight breeze.

Megan waited outside the phone booth, feeling conspicuous, even though, to her surprise, none of the sleepy faces seemed to notice them. Jackie and she were finally blending into 1943, just when they were going to leave.

A minute later, Jackie stepped out of the booth, giving Megan the thumbs up. "The cab should be here in 10 minutes."

The girls went outside and paced to stay warm and calm their nerves.

"What do you think they'll say about us when they find out we left?" Megan asked. "The guys, I mean?"

"They'll know it had something to do with the war. They'll understand."

"That was a brilliant stroke, you telling Danny about your father being in the Army."

"He *is* in the Army. He's a Brigadier General. Just not in 1943."

"Yeah, but now they think we're doing secret work for him. That takes care of a lot of our problems. No more lying."

"It doesn't matter. We're leaving. Oh, here comes the cab."

The dark gray cab approached and drew up to the curb. Oscar, the driver, was in his early 60s, with dull, sleepy eyes and a shadow of beard. He wore a heavy wool sweater and a tweed cap. The girls opened the back door, noticing the broad running board, then they piled in and closed the door.

"Hi, ladies. I'm Oscar. Where to?"

"To the covered bridge, Oscar," Jackie said, leaning forward.

"Which one?"

"There's more than one?"

"Yep. There are three, within four miles."

"The one that leads into town," Jackie said.

"North or south of town."

Jackie pointed. "Straight ahead."

"That's north," Oscar said, slapping the meter handle

down, and they were off.

Jackie settled back into the seat and silently said good-bye to the town and to Danny. Danny said he and Jeff would drop by later in the morning and they'd all go up the mountain to ski. It would have been fun, but then, one more day with Danny and there was no telling what she'd do.

"What are you going to do at the bridge?" Oscar asked. "There's nothing around there."

"We heard it has historical value," Megan said.

"I don't know about that. All I know is, it's been closed for almost a year now."

Jackie leaned forward again. "What do you mean closed?"

"I mean it's been closed since last March or April. It's not safe. No one uses it anymore. There's a road that runs parallel to it about an eighth of a mile away. Everybody uses that now."

"Well, we drove across it," Jackie said.

"Not that bridge. A snowstorm nearly destroyed it last spring. There are barricades up. It's about to fall into the river. With these kinds of bridges, you can't see all the timbers, and you can't see all the damage until it's dismantled."

"Are they going to dismantle it?" Megan asked.

"Yeah. Soon. If it wasn't for the war and all the men being gone, they'd have knocked it down by now. I hear some of the older railroad men are going to take it down soon."

The taxi left town and was climbing a hill that meandered through tall birch and spruce trees. Megan and Jackie stared out, growing increasingly uneasy as they approached the bridge. Both sat up, gazing intently ahead.

The girls didn't retain a clear recollection of the size,

color or construction of the bridge. The night they'd crossed it, they had been too tired and preoccupied.

Drawing near, they saw the bridge, once painted a vivid red, was now faded, bleached by the sun and harsh weather. It was enclosed and had a single lane. The girls were startled by the three sawhorse barricades that blocked the entrance to the bridge. A bright red sign was clearly posted on the center barricade.

DANGER
UNSTABLE BRIDGE
DO NOT CROSS!

Oscar parked on the shoulder of the road and looked back at them. His wintry, saggy face and drooping eyes reminded Megan of a hound dog's.

"Well, is this your bridge?"

Jackie pushed open the door and climbed out, with Megan exiting the other side. They closed their doors and started toward the bridge, inspecting it, eyes unsure and probing. They listened to the hiss and splash of the stream as they drew near the dirt entrance.

"Is this it, Jackie?" Megan asked, tentative.

"I think so. Yes. This is it. It's got to be. We crossed it, and then we drove back the way we just came, into Holly Grove. Yes, this is definitely it."

They heard the car motor shut off and turned to see Oscar emerge from the car. He was built like a big fire plug, sturdy and short. He ambled over.

"So, what do you think?"

"We definitely crossed this bridge the other night," Jackie said. "I'm sure of it."

He took off his cap and scratched his head. "I don't mean to be disrespectful, ma'am, but if you tried to cross that bridge you'd wind up down in that creek. Now this is a timber-truss bridge. It's about 94 feet long. The roof was originally covered with wooden shingles, and it doesn't have any steel reinforcements. I know all this because my father helped rebuild it back about 20 years ago. I spent a few days working with him."

Jackie was unconvinced. "We crossed this bridge, and we did not wind up in the creek."

Oscar shrugged his right shoulder.

Megan turned to him. "What else can you tell us about this bridge?"

"It was used to haul timber from a saw mill up the stream. Years ago, sweethearts used to come out here. There was even one story about how a couple, maybe 50 years ago, came out here to elope, because the girl's father forbade the marriage. And then they just disappeared and were never heard from again."

Jackie pivoted toward him. "They disappeared?"

"Well, it's just a silly story."

"How did they know they just disappeared?" Jackie asked.

"Well, because the girl had another boyfriend, and he got wind of the whole elopement thing. He met them at the bridge to try to talk the girl out of it. He wouldn't take no for an answer. Anyway, according to his story, he said the couple took a one-horse buggy across the bridge, but they never came out the other side. He went looking all over for them, but they had just vanished. They were never heard from again."

Megan's and Jackie's eyes filled with an urgent wonder.

"You said this happened about 50 years ago?" Megan asked.

"Yeah, about that. It's just a silly story, a tall tale. Some of these silly stories go all the way back to the Revolutionary War."

"Were there any other stories like that?" Megan asked.

"One or two, but nobody ever took them that seriously, except for Martha Combs. She collected a lot of stories from around this area and tried to publish some of them, but nothing ever came of it."

"Is she still alive?" Jackie asked.

"Martha? No, she's been dead for years."

Both girls sagged a little.

"Her daughter is alive though."

The girls brightened. "Does she live in town?" Megan asked.

"Yes... well, about two miles out of town. Her name's Hazel. She's a bit strange, like her mother. She married a conductor on the railroad and he and their son went off to war. She's alone now."

"Can you take us to her?" Megan asked.

Jackie nudged her, indicating toward the bridge.

Oscar nodded. "Yeah, I can take you over there."

"Never mind," Megan said. "We'll just hang out here for a little while."

"How much do I owe you?" Jackie asked.

"Are you two going to stay here?" Oscar asked, rubbing his stubby beard.

"Yes, sir. We are. We want to look around."

His curious eyes lingered on them. "Okay, well, if you ever need a ride, I'm usually parked near Green's Drug Store."

After the taxi disappeared around the trees and over the hill, the girls stood there looking at each other with doubt and speculation.

"Shall we?" Jackie asked, making a sweeping gesture toward the bridge.

Megan hesitated. "I don't feel good about this."

"What's there to feel bad about, Megan? We came from the bridge, we're going to return to the bridge, come out the other side of the bridge and be back home. Let's go."

They moved around the barricades toward the entrance, the snow crunching beneath their feet. They paused to peer inside, shading their eyes, squinting into the gray shadowy interior.

"It looks spooky in there," Megan said.

"Megan, there is sunlight on the other side. Come on."

Jackie snatched Megan's arm and pulled her forward. They stepped gingerly onto the warped and springy floor, and it creaked. They stopped, took a deep breath, and disappeared inside.

CHAPTER 11

Jeff and Danny were at Aunt Betty's at 10:30 that morning, sitting on the couch, Jeff patting the cushions absently, while Danny inspected his glossy spit-polished jump boots. When they had asked for Megan and Jackie, Aunt Betty told them the girls hadn't been down for breakfast.

"I haven't heard a peep out of them all morning," she said, wiping her hands on her apron.

Rose had her coat on and, since she'd finished the dishes and cleaning, she was about to hurry over to Dot's for a lunch shift.

"Rose, why don't you go up and knock on their door and let them know we're here," Jeff said.

"And why should I do that?"

"Because it would be a nice thing to do," Danny said.

"Am I nice?" Rose asked, with a crooked sneer. "No, I don't think so."

"Go up there and knock on their door," Aunt Betty said, sharply. "What is the matter with you?"

Grumbling, Rose obeyed.

.

A moment later, she bounded down the stairs, stopping at the front door. "Not there. Not in their room, and if you ask me, they're enemy spies and you should call the police or the Army or something."

"What are you talking about?" Jeff asked.

Rose lifted her head, arrogantly. "They've got things in their suitcases that look like something out of that magazine, *Astounding Stories*."

"And how would you know that?" Jeff asked. "Have you been rifling through their suitcases?"

Aunt Betty was horrified. "Rose! You didn't!"

"I accidentally kicked them when I was making up the bed. All I'm saying is they have these little box-like things with windows and little buttons on them. Things I've never seen except in stories about *The Universe of Future Centuries* in *Planet Magazine* and *Astounding Stories*. And that's not all. I've never seen makeup like they have or those crazy colored sneakers. They look like something from another planet. And I saw a novel, and the cover looked weird and different from any I'd ever seen. So I looked at it and I saw the copyright. It said 2012."

"Oh for Pete's sake," Jeff said. "Get out of here, Rose."

"You'll see," Rose said, with a challenge. "Go upstairs and look for yourselves! You'll see I'm right. Those two are enemy spies from the future."

Rose opened the door, exited, and slammed it shut. She skipped down the front stairs and stopped at the sidewalk. With her back to the front door, she covertly drew an envelope from her left coat pocket. It was the envelope Megan and Jackie had left under the door for Jeff and Danny. She read their printed names, grinning with dark satisfaction. Over her shoulder, she passed a final glance toward the house, and then hurried away up the street.

Aunt Betty shook her head. "I'm going to have to call her mother. She is just so sassy and rebellious. I hate to do it, but I'm going to call her mother and tell her what's going on."

"Rose is obviously jealous of Megan and Jackie," Danny said.

"She's got one heck of an imagination," Jeff said. "I'll give her that."

They sat in the living room sipping coffee until eleven o'clock. Finally, Jeff got up and stepped over to the window.

"We did make a date, didn't we, Danny Boy?"

"Yeah. We said we'd come by between ten and ten thirty. They said they'd be waiting."

"Maybe they got the *word*," Jeff said.

Aunt Betty was back to knitting her sweater, working on the left sleeve. "What do you mean, got the *word*?" she asked.

"Oh nothing, Aunt Betty. Danny and I think the girls are doing some kind of secret war work for Jackie's father. He's in the Army."

"Oh, well, now that makes sense. They do seem rather secretive and a little different. They're nice girls, but just a little different somehow, don't you think?"

Jeff turned to them. "They're from the big city. This is a small town. They're bound to be different."

"I suppose," Aunt Betty said.

Danny stood. "But they don't seem the type not to leave a note or something. Why didn't they tell Aunt Betty that they had to step out? It doesn't seem quite right, does it, Jeff?"

"You've got something there, Danny Boy. It does seem a little odd."

"What kind of secret work could they be doing here in Holly Grove? There's nothing here," Danny said.

Jeff locked his hands behind his back as he wandered over to the front door. He pulled back the lace curtain and looked out onto the quiet street. "I don't know. Steam engines come through here all the time, pulling flatcars loaded with tanks and military vehicles of all types going east to the Atlantic seaports. Maybe they're involved with scheduling or requisitions or something."

The boys said their goodbyes to Aunt Betty and started off on foot toward town. They weren't in a hurry and they were both feeling a little downcast.

"What do you want to do, Danny Boy?"

"I don't know. Is there a double feature at the movie house?"

"I don't know. Maybe a Tarzan movie. Maybe Tom Mix or a double feature."

"I like *The Miracle Rider*," Danny said.

"Yeah, but Ted has shown that thing so many times, I'm just tired of it. It's an old movie, anyway. I'm ready for something new, or at least something else."

On Main Street they stopped near The General Store, both looking lost.

"Where do you think they went?" Danny asked.

"The bigger question is, why did they leave their suitcases? If they left their suitcases, they must be coming back, Danny Boy."

Danny lit up. "Yeah. You're right."

Jeff saw Oscar's taxi drift slowly into town. He lifted a hand of hello and Oscar pulled his cab over to the curb near the boys.

"Hello, Jeff. Hello, Danny. You look bored."

"Just hanging around, Oscar. We might go catch a movie later. How's business?"

Oscar twisted up his face in discontent. "Tell you the truth, I think the town's drying up. There's no life in it anymore, with all the boys gone and the gals off working in the war plants."

"That bad, huh?" Danny asked.

"Well, since about seven o'clock I've only had three fares. Old man Moore, because he doesn't have any gas and his car's no good, anyway. Mary Morgan and her brat of a kid, and then two pretty girls I'd never seen before. They went off on a fool trip to the Holly Grove Bridge."

Jeff and Danny came to attention, pulling their hands from their pockets. "What? Two girls? Where did they go?"

"Out to that old broken down bridge north of town."

"Why did they want to go there?" Danny asked.

"I don't know. They were asking me about its history, so I told them some stories."

"How long ago, Oscar?" Jeff asked.

"It was early this morning, about seven o'clock, maybe seven thirty."

Jeff glanced at his watch. It was almost noon. "Oscar, can you take us out there?"

"To the bridge?"

"Yeah."

"That was over four hours ago," Oscar said.

"I don't care. Let's go, Danny Boy."

The boys scrambled into the back seat and Oscar made a U-turn and motored up the road.

Jeff and Danny sat in the back seat talking and thinking. Jeff pushed the bill of his cap back. "What are these two girls up to, Danny?"

Danny was staring out his window, watching the trees go by. "It's funny how they just suddenly appeared in town. Nobody ever comes to this town, even before the war, and certainly not pretty girls like Jackie and Megan."

"Well, everything's changed, Danny Boy. Just look around. Women are doing men's work, while men are fighting all over the world. Before the war, you and me had never even left the State of Vermont. In the next few months, you'll probably be in Rome and Paris and I'll be flying missions over France and Germany, going to London when we can't fly because of bad weather. No, Danny Boy, the big wide world is getting smaller and crazier and more mysterious every day."

Danny looked at his friend in amazement. "You're sounding like some kind of philosopher, Jeff."

Jeff looked at Danny soberly. "That's what war has done to me, Danny. I don't know what I'm going to meet over there. We've lost a lot of good soldiers. I've seen so many good men crash their planes and die, and that was just while they were learning to fly. There's no guarantee any of us will make it back, Danny."

"You're depressing me," Danny said.

Jeff reached over and slapped him on the shoulder. "I think too much sometimes, Danny Boy, forgive me."

"There's the bridge," Oscar said, pointing.

Oscar parked the car beside the road and the two soldiers climbed out. Dark clouds hovered over the mountains, and the sun was being snuffed out by clouds sweeping in from the north. Danny and Jeff pocketed their bare hands as they shuffled about, searching, but not seeing any sign of the two girls.

Oscar approached. "Like I said, it was over four hours ago."

"Did they say how long they were going to stay, Oscar?" Jeff asked.

"No... well, they talked about me taking them over to

Hazel Comb's place, but then they changed their minds and stayed here."

Danny looked at Oscar. "Why Hazel Combs?"

"They were interested in those silly stories about people who disappeared on this bridge. I told them about how Hazel's mother, Martha, had collected weird stories about the town and they wanted to talk to her about it."

"But they didn't call you later?"

"Nope. I figured they just wandered back to town."

Jeff turned to Danny. "I tell you, Danny, these girls are a mystery to be solved."

CHAPTER 12

Megan and Jackie sat huddled and depressed at Dot's Café counter, sipping coffee and eating lunch. Megan was eating an egg salad sandwich and Jackie a hamburger. They noticed Rose was glaring at them from inside the kitchen, through the round, door window.

"What is her problem?" Megan asked.

"She's a teenager, and she's probably a psycho," Jackie said.

"My feet are still killing me," Megan said.

"Yeah, I wish we could have worn our sneakers. I'm still thawing out from that follow-the-train-tracks hike back to town. Whose idea was that?"

"Yours," Megan said, cupping her still cold hands around the warm coffee cup.

The café was bustling with a lunch crowd, again mostly railroad workers, and whenever Rose wasn't serving, she was tucked behind the kitchen door, watching Megan and Jackie.

Both girls kept their voices at a near whisper, as the diners next to them snapped out papers or discussed the latest war news. The jukebox was playing *Paper Doll* by The Mills Brothers.

"Do you know what I miss?" Megan said. "That Christmas song *Rockin' Around the Christmas Tree*. But it won't be written until the 1950s."

"Do you know what I miss?" Jackie said. "My cell phone. We could have just called Oscar instead of taking that long, hard, cold hike. When he left us at the bridge, I was thinking we were still in the modern world. If worse comes to worst, I thought, I'll call him on my cell phone and tell him to come pick us up. What a ding bat I am."

"Do you know what I miss? My emails and text messages. I think I'm having withdrawal or something. I just feel this constant urge to reach for my phone and text somebody."

"Do you know what I miss?" Jackie said, longingly. "My cat, Eaton."

"Ahhh. I didn't know you had a cat."

"He's all black, and soft, and affectionate and he sleeps with me."

"Do you know what I miss?" Megan asked. "Sleeping in my own bed. No offense, but that bed is small and you snore."

"So do you," Jackie tossed back.

"No, I don't," Megan said, defensively.

"Yes, you do."

"No one has ever told me that."

"Well, I'm telling you. You snore like a bear."

"No way!"

"Way!"

The portly man in overalls, on the stool next to Jackie, glanced over.

The girls lowered their heads and voices. They reached for their food and went silent.

Rose swept through the café, expertly cradling three plates. She gave them a look of disapproval as she passed.

"I'd like to slap her silly," Jackie said. "It's the Army brat in me."

"If we don't find some way to get home, you may get a lot of opportunities to do just that, and I'll help you."

Both stopped eating, slumping, staring numbly.

"Well, Army brat's daughter, what's our next action plan?"

"I don't know. I thought for sure once we got to the other side of that bridge, we'd somehow be back... well, home. But nothing happened. Nothing. Why?"

"I never believed it," Megan said.

"You never said that. You believed," Jackie said. "You believed, all right, otherwise, why did you go?"

"No, I didn't believe, and I'll tell you why. I believe, and I am sure, that we have to go back the same way we came. That is, we have to have *our* car, *our* suitcases— everything we brought with us. If we don't, we are stuck here and we will be very old women by the time we finally reach the 21st century. If we live that long."

Jackie considered it. "Okay, the only way we're going to know for sure is if we try it, right? That means we have to find our car."

"And how do we do that?"

"Let's ask ourselves some important questions. Number one, who could have taken the car and why? Second, where could they have taken it to? Third, are they interested in it because of its futuristic look, in other words for strictly scientific reasons, or are they more mercenary, and they want to sell it to the highest bidder?"

Megan drained her coffee and almost asked the older waitress behind the counter for more, when she noticed the sign: DON'T ASK FOR BUTTER OR FOR A REFILL OF COFFEE.

"Do you know what else I miss?" Megan asked, raising her coffee cup. "A big cup of coffee. These little cups are like something from Alice in Wonderland."

"And that's just where we are, Megan my friend," Jackie said. "We are in some kind of crazy Alice in Wonderland."

Outside, they started back to Aunt Betty's, both lost in thought, their spirits low. Some snow had melted, but as they looked skyward, heavy gray clouds were forming, with the promise of more snow on the way.

"The sky was so blue this morning," Jackie said.

"So were our hopes," Megan responded. "What are we going to tell the boys? Our note said we were clearing out of town."

"That's the fifth time you've asked me, Megan."

"And you haven't come up with an answer," Megan said.

"You're the liar, the actress, not me."

Megan thought for a minute. "Okay, so we'll tell them we thought we got the *word*, but it turned out that we didn't get the *word*."

Jackie frowned, staring doubtfully. "I've got a word for that explanation. Think 'big bull with horns, going to the bathroom,'" Jackie said.

"If you have something better, I'm all ears."

Jackie sighed. "I've got nothing. I just want to go to our room, crawl into that narrow, bouncing, squeaky bed and go to sleep."

They passed the movie theater and Megan was seized with an idea. "Jackie! Should we go talk to Hazel? Martha Comb's daughter?"

"What for?" Jackie answered. "She's just going to show us her mother's stories. How's that going to help? Let's not waste more time. We need to somehow get the word out about our car. Somebody in this town knows where that car is. I'm sure of it."

"Jackie, maybe, just maybe, one of those stories will give us an idea we haven't thought about. I think we should go talk to the woman. What have we got to lose?"

Jackie stopped walking. "It's a fantasy, Megan. It's all just fantasy. You heard Oscar. They're all just silly stories. I'm sick of fantasy land. I want to get back to reality."

"So do I. But I think we have to explore everything. Every possibility. Those old stories might give us a clue. After all, if we told our story, wouldn't most people think we were silly or crazy or both?"

Jackie's eyes narrowed and her jaw jutted as she struggled to decide. "Okay, okay. Let's get it over with, but I still say it's a waste of time."

They looked up and down the street and then over toward Green's Drug Store. "There it is!" Megan exclaimed. "There's Oscar's cab."

They hurried over to the cab, but found it empty. They threw darting looks up and down the street and then peeked through Green's Drug Store window. Oscar was just exiting the store, candy bar in hand, chewing vigorously.

"Hello, girls. I thought you two disappeared inside that bridge like all the other ghosts."

Jackie smiled, weakly. "No such luck."

Oscar laughed at his own joke, as he walked over. "Jeff and Danny were looking for you two. They had me drive them out to the bridge."

"Oh really?" Megan said, fretfully.

"They're around somewhere. Maybe they went to the movies."

"Can you take us to see Hazel?" Megan asked.

"Sure. Why not? Get in."

They left Main Street and bumped along a back road, marred with puddles and chug holes. The girls gripped the seats tightly to keep their heads from hitting the ceiling.

"The winter plays hell with this road and there's nobody around to repair it since the war. Where'd you two go after I left you this morning?"

Megan spoke up. "We hiked around, followed the railroad tracks and wound up at the train station. We rested there for a while, looked around and then finally made our way back to town."

"So you still want to read about those old tall tales, huh?"

"It's local color, isn't it?" Jackie said. "We like exploring local culture."

"I don't think we have all that much culture, but we do have some tall tales that people used to tell. I guess they didn't have much else to do in those old days."

About fifteen minutes later, they came upon a single, unprosperous, two-story gray house, looming out from between a line of trees. It was weather-beaten and needed paint, and the porch seemed to lean precariously to one side. The entire area looked barren and forgotten, with cords of wood stacked carelessly, and an old Model T Ford, looking dejected, parked near a garage.

"Hazel lives here alone?" Megan asked.

"Yeah. See the two blue star flags? Her husband and son are serving. Last time I talked to her, she hadn't heard from her son in over a month. She's real worried."

Oscar pulled into the sparsely covered gravel driveway

and stopped. "Should I wait?"

"Can you come back in an hour or so?" Jackie asked.

"Sure."

Jackie paid him, and he drove away. As the two girls started up the risky steps to the unstable porch, the door opened five or six inches, and a rail-thin middle-aged woman, with careless gray hair and a cautious, tight rigid face, looked back at them with distress in her eyes.

"What do you want?" she asked, in a quivering voice.

"Are you Hazel?"

"Yes. What do you want? You're not with the War Office are you, bringing me bad news about my husband or my son?"

"No, ma'am, we're not from the War Office. I'm Megan and this is Jackie. We're just passing through town. Oscar told us about your mother's writings, you know, the stories she collected about some of the mysterious things that have happened around here through the years."

Hazel searched their faces. "What do you want with them? Are you with the military or something?"

Jackie said, "No, ma'am, we're not. We would like to see some of the stories your mother collected. Maybe read a few."

"Why?"

"Because they sound fascinating. And didn't your mother want people to read them? Didn't she want to publish a book about the stories?" Megan asked.

Hazel made a sad face. "People around here thought she was touched in the head. She wasn't. She was a God-fearing Christian woman. She was a good woman."

"We don't think she was touched in the head, Hazel," Megan said. "We'd love to read some of them, that is, if you don't mind. We don't want to intrude."

Some of the tension went out of her. She stood back and opened the door.

The house inside didn't mirror the house outside. The living room was clean, with simple furniture, and a blue patterned carpet. In the corner stood a 6 foot Christmas tree, decorated with holly and several Victorian-type figurines. A stone fireplace offered a pleasant glow to the room and, on the mantel above, were black and white photos of her two men, dressed in their military uniforms. The father looked into the lens with a weathered, resigned face. The son had the firm, resolute face of a warrior. Jackie was surprised by the quality of several landscape oil paintings hanging in the living and dining rooms.

"My son paints," Hazel said, as she watched Jackie study them. "He wanted to go to art school, but then this evil war pulled him away. He's in the Pacific somewhere with the Marines. It was so hard for me to picture him in the Marines, because he was always a sensitive boy. But he took to soldiering, and he wanted to fight for his country."

Jackie and Megan shrugged out of their coats and sat on a soft, olive green couch. Despite the girls' protests, Hazel insisted on bringing cups of coffee and biscuits she had baked that morning.

"I still bake every day. It's a pleasure and a habit I can't break and, in a little way, it brings me closer to my men, because they loved my biscuits so much."

Hazel talked of better times and about her husband and son and their lives. She said they'd barely struggled through the depression when the war hit them. Hazel's weary expression and solemn eyes said it all.

"I pray every night for my men to come home safe. Sometimes at night, when I look up at the swirl of so many stars, I wonder if our enemies' mothers are praying for their sons the same way I'm praying for mine, and then I struggle with my faith. But now I'm just blabbering on, and you didn't come here to listen to an old lonely woman go on so."

Megan and Jackie had listened, patiently, admiring Hazel's courage and endurance, aware that she was terribly alone and frightened.

Megan thought Hazel must be like a lot of mothers, pacing the floor at night, praying for strength and guidance; praying unceasingly for God to bring their men safely back home. When she'd performed in *Come Back Home, Johnny*, the reality of the war was the reality of a musical. There was singing and dancing, along with some tender scenes between parting lovers and families. But it was, after all, just the enjoyable reality of a Broadway show, and not the sober reality of frightful anxious hours, emotional roller coaster rides of hope and despair, and the sharp agony of sacrifice, when the awful news comes that a loved one has been killed.

Jackie thought of Danny, who would be jumping out of airplanes, and she thought of Jeff, who would be flying bombing missions. What were their mothers going through? This was a time in American history of great loss and sacrifice, and she'd never known much about it. World War II had been a subject she'd barely studied in high school and college. She'd never fully appreciated that the entire world was at war and that the entire episode had ended with the dropping of two atomic bombs.

Hazel entered the living room, carrying the 3-ring spiral-bound notebook in both hands, like it was a priceless silver platter. Her expression was reverent. She laid it on a coffee table before Jackie and Megan, and then she stood there, looking down at it with pride and respect.

"My mother spent years finding these stories, traveling as far as a hundred miles. She talked to a lot of the old timers. Some wrote down the strange things that had happened to them or things they'd heard about from family and friends."

The girls stared at the 3½ inch, 3-ring blue jean-textured notebook. The corners were frayed, and there were a few water spots on the cover, but, overall, it was in remarkably good shape. Hazel indicated her consent to both girls, and so Jackie reached over, gently picked up the notebook, and laid it in her lap. She opened it to read the title page:

TRUE WEIRD AND UNEXPLAINED
STORIES OF VERMONT
by Martha Combs

Jackie turned the yellowed page and read the Table of Contents. There were ghost stories, UFO stories and alien abduction stories. There was a story about a little boy with ESP, who could move objects just by concentrating on them. But the story that caught both Jackie's and Megan's eyes was the story entitled *The Man from the Future*.

The girls exchanged a knowing glance. Hazel noticed.

"Now that's a real interesting story. It was one of my mother's favorites and it happened right here in this town."

Jackie flipped the binding tab to the story. The girls began to read.

"It happened about 1890," Hazel said. "The story goes that this man just appeared in town one day, enclosed in a bright red chariot. My mother determined it was actually a car. When he got out, people fled, screaming, running for their lives because they thought they were being invaded by outer space beings."

Hazel leaned over and pointed at a drawing. "Do you see that little pencil drawing on the next page? That's an exact copy my mother made from an old diary she found. You see the guy, he has a kind of short-sleeve shirt on, like an undershirt or something. And on the breast pocket is a little horse and rider, and the rider is swinging what looks to be a polo stick."

Megan glanced over at Jackie. She whispered, "A Ralph Lauren polo shirt?"

Jackie shrugged.

"Do you recognize it?" Hazel asked, turning her hands.

"No, no..." Jackie said. "It's just so interesting."

The girls read as Hazel spoke. "So, anyway when the men of the town came at him with rifles and knives, shooting at him, he got back into that vehicle and sped away.

"The story goes that the Man from the Future wound up about 10 miles away, at the Parker Farm, which isn't around anymore. He hid the car somewhere and went to work as a farm hand. Well, as often happens, he fell in love with the Parkers' only daughter, a pretty little 16-year-old, named Mercy Parker. She fell head-over-heels in love with him. Old man Parker was having none of it, especially when some people from town came by, saw the Future Man, and told him he had a farm hand who was some kind of an alien from another world."

Jackie and Megan stopped reading and leaned back to listen to Hazel, who was completely engrossed in the story telling. She was acting it out, entranced.

"Well, then the Future Man fled, but he promised Mercy he'd return for her and take her away into his world. He had her spellbound with stories about rockets and rocket men going to the moon and about tall, tall buildings and little windows that you carried around in your pocket, that allowed you to send photographs and messages to places all over the world."

Hazel swallowed and licked her lips. "So, sure enough, the Future Man came back for her. But Mercy had another boyfriend, named Harlan, who was madly in love with her. Mercy told Harlan all the things the Future Man had told her. Well, you know how it is, when people don't understand something they always think it's evil. So Harlan thought the Future Man was the devil himself. Harlan was waiting at the Holly Grove Bridge when the red vehicle arrived, with Mercy inside. Harlan stood at the bridge's entrance, blocking their way. He told Mercy not to leave him, but she told him she loved the Future Man, and she was going."

Jackie and Megan waited, while Hazel readied herself for the climax, patting strands of loose hair in place. "So, the two men wrestled and fought. Future Man managed to shove Harlan out of the way long enough to get back into his vehicle and drive away across the bridge."

Jackie leaned forward. "So what happened to them?"

"Well, Harlan stated that he never saw the car exit the bridge. He searched everywhere, and he never saw the vehicle, Future Man or Mercy ever again. They had just vanished."

Megan and Jackie exchanged nods. "Oscar told us they took a one-horse buggy across the bridge," Jackie said.

"Some of the old folks in town got the story all mixed up. Many of them just couldn't understand or comprehend what that vehicle was, so they changed it. Anyway, according to my mother's research, Future Man and Mercy went across the bridge in some kind of future car, at least that's what my mother called it."

Hazel reached for the notebook. "Here, let me find a drawing of it. Harlan drew a crude picture of the car, and my son sketched it from that. Here it is."

Hazel handed the notebook back, and the girls studied the impressive sketch. Jackie was a fair artist herself and she appreciated the skill and technique. The car was a sleek, modern style, with big tires, clean lines and a low-to-the ground purring sexiness. Hazel's son had shaded the body with a bright red pencil and darkened the tires with black charcoal. You could almost hear the hum of the tires and the smooth snarl of the engine as you shifted the gears.

Jackie looked at Megan, whispering, "A Corvette Grand Sport Coupe?"

Megan's eyes widened.

Hazel looked first at Megan and then at Jackie. Her expression turned curious. "Why did you come? Why does this story interest you so much?"

Jackie carefully closed the notebook. "Do you believe the story, Hazel?"

She folded her arms and sat down in an old cushioned chair. "My mother did. She said she'd heard it from more than one person, and all followed the same general story line, which, to her, meant that the story had some truth behind it. Anyway, it makes for a good story and I wish Mom could have published the book."

"I wonder if Future Man got back home?" Megan asked, reflectively.

The girls were standing at the front door, offering their thanks to Hazel, when Oscar's cab turned into the driveway and came to a stop.

As Megan and Jackie ventured out onto the unstable porch, Jeff and Danny emerged from the cab. They waved and smiled.

"Hello, girls. Did you miss us? Danny Boy and I want to invite you to a dance tonight."

CHAPTER 13

"What day is this?" Megan asked.

"Wednesday, December 22, 1943," Jackie answered.

They were on their backs, lying on the bed, staring into the dark.

"What time is it?" Megan asked.

"The guys will be here in about an hour," Jackie said.

"Then it's about six o'clock."

"If you say so."

"We should get dressed," Megan said.

"Yes, we should."

"Why do I feel depressed?" Megan asked.

"Because Rose must have taken our notes to the guys, and so now they think we stood them up and lied to them. They also think we're punk-ass bitches."

"They were nice about it. They believed us when we told them we'd left a note in our room."

"Whatever. We also know from the Future Man story that we've got to have our car to get back home, and we don't have a clue as to where that damned car is. That's why I'm depressed."

"Well, it's still only a story. We don't know for sure," Megan said. "I still say we should try the train or a bus."

"That's a waste of time," Jackie said. "And if it doesn't work, I'll be too depressed to even get out of bed. Here's what I say we do. Tomorrow morning, we need to search this town, look in every garage, behind every house and around every building until we find that car, or at least get some clue as to where it might be. We've got to. It's two days before Christmas. We have to be back home for Christmas. And think about our families. They probably think we're dead."

Megan scratched her cheek, straining for a fruitful thought. "Maybe we should be honest with Jeff and Danny? Maybe we should tell them everything? They might be able to help."

"And they might freak out and call the cops or the MPs."

"What's an M.P.?" Megan asked.

"Military Police. We can't risk it. We have to do this on our own. Oh, by the way, do you know how to dance all the dances they danced back in 1943?"

"Yeah, I think so. I've danced most of them in shows or in dance class."

"Can you show me some steps?"

Megan lifted up on her elbows, turning to see Jackie's dim silhouette. "In half an hour? Are you serious?"

"Just a few steps. At least tell me what the dances are, so I won't look like an idiot."

They dressed first, in their dress and skirt. They applied fresh makeup, finishing with bright red lipstick. Megan fastened on a pair of gold drop earrings and Jackie a pair of silver hoop earrings. They were earrings from the 21st century, but they decided to risk it.

The two girls moved into the middle of the room and Megan went into her serious instructor mode, explaining the various popular dances of the 1940s, including The Lindy Hop, The East Coast Swing and The Jitterbug.

"Now, The Jitterbug isn't an actual dance," Megan said. "It's a dancer. It came from a singer in the 1930s named Cab Calloway. It became synonymous with swing dancing."

"You amaze me, Megan. How do you know all this stuff?"

"I love dancing, Jackie, and you're going to love it too. Let's go."

"I have two left feet, Megan."

"Don't worry. Let's just focus on one dance. One single dance. Just a few simple steps."

Jackie looked down at her feet, feeling her throat dry up.

"Okay, we'll do the East Coast Swing," Megan said. "It's simpler than the Lindy Hop. It's a standard 6 count dance out of a foxtrot basic, with Lindy Hop inspired footwork."

"Okay, I don't know what you just said. Just show me," Jackie said.

Megan held out her hands. "Take my hands. This'll be the basic open position, two hand hold."

Jackie took her hands.

Megan continued. "We'll stand about a foot and a half apart. We'll do a triple step left and then a triple step right. Let's try it."

They began, gliding left, then right. "Triple step left, triple step right, back, rock, 1, 2, 3... 4, 5, 6, and a rock step, good."

Jackie stumbled, and they tried it again. Megan broke the steps down one at a time, while Jackie watched, a hand on her chin. They tried again. Jackie lost the count and cursed. They tried again.

"This is hard," Jackie said.

"No, it isn't. You just have to practice. Let's go. Keep moving. Good, good. Triple step left, triple step right, back, rock... good. Good. One more time."

They continued, with Megan leading and counting. Gradually, Jackie began to fall into the rhythm and feel the dance, her feet light and springy, body poised.

"See, it's not that hard, Jackie. You're getting it. You're a fast learner."

"I took ballet when I was a girl," Jackie said, breathing hard, as they danced across the floor.

"You're good, Jackie. Really good."

"You're a good teacher. I'm going to that Broadway show you'll be starring in and I'll take all my friends."

They laughed, kicked and romped into a timeless joy, circling the room, brushing by the bed and the chair, feet thudding into the floor.

"I've got it!" Jackie said, laughing. "By George, I've got it!"

They were startled by a loud knock on the door. They stopped, turning, chests heaving, sweat on their foreheads and upper lips.

"Ladies. Ladies!" It was Aunt Betty. "I thought we were having an earthquake. You are shaking the entire house. And the boys are downstairs waiting for you."

Jackie stood panting for breath. She threw her arms around Megan and gave her a hug. "You, are the best, Megan. *The* best. Thank you."

The girls stood looking at each other and, for the first time, they felt a warm connection.

Megan extended her hand. "We're a team, Jackie."

Jackie shook it. "Yes! The perfect team. We're going

to find away out of this, Megan. We're going to get back home!"

In Jeff's and Danny's eyes, Jackie and Megan seemed to drift down the stairs, like alluring creatures from another world. They moved toward them with an easy confidence and a comfortable sexuality that was rare and exciting. Megan's torso was lifted, her chin tilted up, her luscious blonde hair gently bouncing on her thin shoulders.

Jackie's hips had a rhythmic swaying motion that seized Danny's eyes. He was like a cat hypnotize by shadowy motion. Her lips were puckered red, as if waiting for a kiss, her sparkling eyes steady and alert with possibility, her long legs carrying the sexiest body he'd ever seen.

Jeff opened his hands, as if to welcome them. He took a deep breath, and then puffed his cheeks with a long exhale. "Well, now, what can I say? As they used to say in the old days, you're both Shebas."

Megan looked at Jackie for clarification. Jackie raised her eyebrows. "Shebas?"

Danny spoke up. "Yeah, you know, from the movie *Queen of Sheba*, with Clara Bow. Jeff knows all those corny phrases. I'll just say you're both real honeys."

Jackie looked at Megan. Megan raised her eyebrows.

"Shall we go?" Jeff said.

In the car, sitting in the backseat with Danny, Jackie felt the return of swift desire. Their knees had touched twice, and both times an electric current sent spasms of hot sexual energy pulsing through her, from her feet to the top of her head.

Danny was fit and strong. She knew that every muscle

in his body had to be in peak condition. Wouldn't it be delightful to see that body naked before her, and to test its strength and endurance? She allowed herself the delicious fantasy of watching her slender hand squeeze his hard muscled arms, his legs and his pecks, lavishing kisses on his face and neck. In her vivid imagination, she saw her hand slide inevitably up his hairy muscled leg toward that great forbidden manly Thing, that would surely rise up to meet her, standing at perfect attention, demanding her attention. She would have to salute it, wouldn't she? And it would surely obey her touch. And then she'd attack, because that's what a good soldier always does. Attack. She was about to continue the fantasy, when Danny spoke up.

"It's hard, isn't it?" Danny said.

Jackie shot him a startled glance. "What?"

"I'm mean, to think that we're all going to have to separate in a few days."

"Stop it, Danny Boy," Jeff said. "We're out for a good time. We're going to dance to the Buddy Loren Swing Orchestra, for Pete's sake. Like the song says, for all we know, tomorrow may never come, so let's just live for today."

Megan adjusted her hips closer to Jeff's. He looked over, giving her a warm smile. "That's nice," he said.

Megan looked at Jeff with considerable speculative care. She felt a sudden lift, a kind of lovely "wouldn't Jeff be nice to come home to" feeling. Was that a radical feeling? For her, yes.

Megan had always been attracted to men who presented a mature and calm reassurance, and that's why she often found older men attractive. Most of the men her age were narcissistic and immature, focusing solely on their careers. She'd dated a number of older men, including the wealthy Brian Ellsworth, who was 56. Unfortunately, she found out a few weeks later that he was married and had three kids.

Megan sensed that Jeff Grant was a solid person and, besides being handsome, she also sensed that he could be trusted with anything. His smile was genuine, his eyes were daring and playful, but kind. Megan had also dated older men because she didn't trust long relationships, and most older men had already done the family thing, with kids and dogs, and they weren't interested in repeating it.

Megan's shrink had once suggested that her preferences had much to do with growing up in a house where her contractor father raged about trivialities, and her mother fought back with invectives, banishment to the basement couch, and nights when she refused to cook dinner. It had not been a happy home.

Jeff's energy was soothing and stable. His lips were often slightly parted and sometimes he whistled a little tune. She found that comforting and sexy. She wanted to kiss those lips and silence the tune with her tongue. She wanted to peel off some of his uniform and explore him. She wanted to experience his weight, his soft kisses on her neck. She wanted to go home with him. Would it be lovely?

"What are you thinking about?" Jeff asked. "I hear your brain ticking."

Megan blushed, but she hooked an arm within his and grinned. "I'm looking forward to the dance," she said. "That's all."

"But first, dinner," Jeff said. "Are you hungry?"

Kelly's Restaurant was in Glover, Vermont, 15 miles from Holly Grove, near the high school gym where the dance was to be held. The restaurant was owned and operated by Kip Kelly and his wife Ida, who were originally from Holly Grove, and they knew Jeff's parents.

Ida met the four at the hostess stand, with a clasp of hands and a broad smile. She was a stout, energetic woman, all fuss and fidgets, and she showed them to a table for four in a window corner of the dining room. It looked out on snow-covered pines. The chairs were made of heavy mahogany, and the tables were covered with white table cloths and flickering candles.

The jukebox pumped out a steady stream of Christmas songs, and a twinkling Christmas tree brightened the room. Wreaths on the walls added to the buoyant holiday spirit.

Jackie and Megan ordered the chicken with mashed potatoes and peas, and the guys ordered steaks, baked potatoes and creamed spinach.

Jeff sat close to Megan and Danny next to Jackie. The conversation was light, centering on the weather, Christmas, flying and music. It was Jeff who turned to Megan with an expression of inquiry.

"I still don't know why you went out to that bridge."

"We told you, Jeff," Megan said. "We heard it was historic, and that it was haunted. We thought it would be fun to check it out."

"When I was a kid," Danny said, sipping some water, "I was scared to death to go near that bridge. My grandfather loved to scare the hell out of us with stories about it."

"Yeah, so that's why we went," Jackie said. "Local history. Local color."

"Yeah, yeah, so you said," Jeff said, unconvinced. "But why didn't you have Oscar wait for you? It was cold out there, especially in the morning."

Megan was about to speak up, when Jeff reached into

his coat pocket and drew out the envelope that contained the girls' goodbye messages to the guys. The same envelope and note that Rose had stolen from their room.

Jackie winced. Megan had the urge to snatch it.

"Where did you get that?" Megan asked.

"Danny and I paid a little visit to Rose at her home."

"And why did you do that?" Jackie asked.

Jeff pursed his lips, looking smug. "Well, it seems that Aunt Betty called Rose's mother to tell her that her daughter had been a little too sassy of late; even a little too snoopy around the guests' rooms. Rose's mother then told Aunt Betty that she just happened to have been in Rose's room, and she found an envelope addressed to me and Danny Boy. Rose's mother opened it and well... you can imagine. But then, of course, you don't have to imagine because you, Megan, and you, Jackie, wrote the notes. Right?"

The girls lowered their eyes.

"Well, then, Aunt Betty called and told me what had happened. When Danny and I arrived at Rose's house and confronted her, she denied everything. When her mother slapped her face, promptly presenting the evidence to Rose, Rose finally admitted she'd taken the letter."

Jeff opened the flap, tugged out the letter and unfolded it. "And, here it is, the note that finally found its rightful owners." Jeff sighed, romantically, as he examined the contents, lips moving in whispers as he read.

Megan and Jackie squirmed. Danny's steady eyes were watchful.

A pretty waitress hustled over with their dinners, all four plates balanced across both arms. She delivered them, smiled, pivoted and retreated.

"I'm hungry," Jackie said, nervous eyes lifting on Jeff's

face and then falling onto the baked chicken. She grabbed her fork and knife and sliced the chicken as Megan sat staring at Jeff, whose eyes were still fixed on the page.

"Okay, you want the truth?" Megan asked.

Jackie cringed. Danny stopped chewing.

Jeff looked at Megan over the letter. "No... I don't want to hear the truth, because I know you're not really going to tell me the truth, anyway. You're just going to say that you thought you had gotten the *word,* but it turns out that you didn't get the *word.* Well, I don't care about that *word,* anymore. Danny and I are more interested in another word."

"Well, that's a nasty thing to say," Megan said. "You're calling me a liar."

"No, not really. You see, I don't really care about *that* word or the first part of the note. Danny and I are more interested in the last couple of sentences and the next-to-last *word* on that note. Yes, that is the *word* Danny and I are interested in. Just to refresh your minds I'll read what you wrote to me, Megan. And then I'll read what Jackie wrote to Danny Boy."

> *I wish we could have spent more time together. I truly believe we could have been good for each other and we could have had so many happy times.*
>
> *Take care of yourself and come home safe. I'll never forget you.*
>
> *Love, Megan*

Megan blushed, lowering her eyes.

"Shall I read what Jackie wrote to you, Danny Boy?"

"Sure. Read away," Danny said, chewing again, turning to Jackie, all smiles. Jackie avoided his eyes.

Jeff read: *Please take good care of yourself over there, and remember me sometimes. I will miss you and never forget you.*

Love, Jackie

Jeff looked at both girls, with a triumphant expression. "Now, unless I'm misinterpreting your words here, your very words, I believe you both said you would miss us and never forget us. And, let me see," he said, enjoying himself greatly, as he glanced back at the note, pointing at the words with his finger. "Here at the bottom of each beautifully written note, you both ended with the *word* LOVE." His grin was small at first, and then it grew bigger and wider, until he showed his very white teeth. "Isn't that a nice word? Love?"

Jackie sat up, gently peeved. "You sound like a lawyer."

"Thank you," Jeff said. "That's what I intend to be when this war is over. And, in conclusion, I believe I have proven, without a shadow of a doubt from your very own words, written on this rather soiled but interesting paper, that you, Megan, and you, Jackie, are in love with Danny Boy and me. That is the only *word* I care about. I rest my case."

Megan sat still. Jackie was cutting her chicken into even smaller pieces. Jeff began to eat and Danny was all smiles, pointing at Jeff with his fork. "Isn't Jeff something? I have the best attorney in the entire State of Vermont and, I believe, he just won our case."

Jackie stole a look at Megan. Her face was so low over her plate, her nose almost touched the food.

CHAPTER 14

Jeff led the group inside the Grover's High School gym door and paid the pretty redhead the fee. Then Danny and Jeff ushered the girls into the wide and surging mass of dancers, being served up *Sing, Sing, Sing* by the 16-piece Buddy Loren and his Swing Orchestra. The musicians, dressed in brown suits and ties, sat in two rows on a platform at the far end of the room. They were swaying back and forth to the music, while Buddy Loren was leaning far back on a high, black-leather stool with his clarinet pointed toward the ceiling, as he bounced through a wild improvisation.

The drummer's face was stretched into crazy ecstasy, his arms flailing, his blurring hot licks sounding like bullets, as he drove the orchestra into a high jubilation.

The gym was packed with pretty girls and soldiers in uniforms of all kinds, Navy, Army and Marine. It was a room pulsing with swing dancers, blasting trumpets, those thumping drums and the sliding wail of trombones. Dancers, loose-legged and twisting, heated up the room in wild and acrobatic jumps and slides, some teetering on the edge of spinning out of control. Arms were raised, hands shaking a razzle dazzle as they circled the floor.

Dresses swayed, skirts flipped and brushed the floor, as partners slid the girls under their legs, pulled them through, shouldered them and whirled them about in choreographed chaos. There were shiny grins, laughing snorts, and faces flushed and wet with perspiration, as the dance thundered on.

Megan stared at the scene in utter shock and admiration. She'd seen old black and white clips of these dances, and she'd participated in big band dances for charitable organizations, but she'd never witnessed or experienced anything like this. This was not a carefully choreographed dancing chorus, this was the bizarre and raw abandon of a wild and frenzied frolic. She was captured by it—felt the pull of it, like a big hand was reaching out and shoving her forward into a thrashing, ritualistic storm.

"I've got to dance!" she exclaimed, looking at Jeff, excited.

"Let's go," he said, and he tugged her toward the dance floor.

To Megan's surprise, Jeff was a great dancer. They slipped into the crowd and found the rhythm. They swayed forwards and backwards with a controlled hip movement, while their shoulders remained level and their feet glided along the floor. Jeff's right hand was low on Mcgan's back, and his left hand enclosed hers and was down at her side. They danced off, and Megan was as happy as she'd ever been in her life.

Danny and Jackie moved to the periphery, watching for a moment, Jackie feeling tentative and intimidated by the skill of the dancers. Finally, Danny pointed to the dance floor and gave a thumbs up. When the right moment came, Jackie, caught up by the excitement, took Danny's hands and joined in, following his lead. Within minutes, she and Danny were absorbed in the hectic dance.

When the band fell into the haunting ballad *At Last*, Megan buried her head into Jeff's shoulder and he held her close to him, smelling the jasmine and rose of her perfume. He was falling in love with her by degrees and this was another. If he had started loving her on the top floor of a building, he was now on the first floor. The basement was all that was left. How could he ever let her go? Megan was the girl of his dreams—literally the girl he'd dreamed of whenever he thought of his perfect type. She was that type, that beautiful woman incarnate.

Megan had a strange, dazed look in her eyes. Dancing with Jeff—indeed, dancing with any man—was always an act of giving, of exchange. This exchange, though, had been completely unique and breathtaking. She felt oddly lightheaded. In her mind and in her contented body, she'd just made love to Jeff Grant, and it had nearly overwhelmed her.

They'd danced perfectly together, and she'd come close to tears, an impossibility she'd thought; something that would have never occurred to her. If Jeff's technique was not the skilled technique of a professional Broadway dancer, then his sexy energy, his sly touch and tender gaze were not only skilled, but unequaled. There was simply no denying it: she was in love with Jeff. She was head-over-heels in love with him. How did it happen? How could it happen? What was she going to do?

Jackie and Danny sat in the back of the room, sipping a fruit punch. It was sugary and red, and Jackie would have given anything for a cold beer. She and Danny were quiet. She did not know what Danny was thinking, but she was disturbed and confused. 'Out of place and out of time,' was all she could think about. And yet, she was happy, truly happy, sitting there sipping the awful sugary drink, listening to the band play a ballad she'd never heard, feeling content and tranquil.

Danny looked at her. "It was hot out there."

"Yeah. It's hot here, too."

Danny understand what she meant, and he grinned at her and winked. That really turned her on.

She tilted her head and looked at him, appraising the shape and character of his face. Their eyes met, and she smiled. She got up, took his hand and led him over to a table, where a girl dressed in a WAC uniform was drawing sketches of soldiers and their girlfriends. Jackie asked if she could have a piece of drawing paper and a pencil, and the WAC complied pleasantly.

Jackie led Danny to another wooden table, unoccupied, and sat down in the heavy wooden chair.

"Danny Boy, you sit on the edge of the desk and let me sketch you. I've just got to draw your handsome face."

He shrugged. "Sounds like fun. Just don't give me a pair of horns," he said, grinning.

"Thanks for the idea," Jackie said.

As Jackie was drawing, she heard the band leader, Buddy Loren, ask if anyone would like to come forward to sing *I'll Be Seeing You*. "This music is by Sammy Fain, the lyrics by Irving Kahal," Buddy said, "And I know it has a very special meaning to us all."

Jackie searched for Megan. She spotted her and saw Jeff raising his hand. Megan was shaking her head no, but Jeff nudged her forward. Jackie smiled. Megan might not have had the chance to sing the song in *Come Back*

Home, Johnny, but she could certainly sing it now.

Megan mounted the three stairs to the bandstand, amid thundering applause, and strolled to the microphone. She gave Buddy her name, and he announced her, as the applause crescendoed then died away. Under the lights, she looked ravishing. She was movie-star gorgeous, Jackie thought. Jeff thought so too, picking his way through the crowd, approaching the stage, his worshipping eyes intoxicated by her.

The band played the introduction, the lights dimmed, and Megan began to sing. Her voice was warm, haunting and resonate. The crowd fell into a hush, enthralled by the sound of her voice and by the poignant lyrics that told of seeing the lover in all the familiar places. And then, finally, "I'll be looking at the moon, but I'll be seeing you."

Jeff felt the first floor give way, and he fell hard into the basement. He stood there, and like the rest of the crowd, his eyes were filled with emotion. He knew he'd never let Megan go. He couldn't. She was his perfect girl. He was so in love with her that he ached all over.

Jackie finished the sketch of Danny and handed it to him. He stared at it, wonderingly. When he looked at Jackie, something in his expression had changed. She'd never seen that expression.

"Are you okay, Danny? Don't you like it?"

He nodded, slowly. "Yeah... Yeah, I like it a lot. Yeah. It looks so alive... the eyes look so alive."

Jackie pushed her chair back and got up. She could see he was nearly overcome with emotion.

"Can I keep this?"

"Of course, Danny."

He folded it carefully, opened a shirt button and slid it

inside his shirt, next to his heart.

Jackie took his hand, and they walked to the exit door. She pushed it open and led him outside, away from the lights. It was cold and their breath came fast, white vapor escaping from their noses, as they gazed into each other's warm and inviting eyes.

Jackie waited for him. Danny slipped an arm around her waist and drew her close. He kissed her gently at first. Then it was an urgent kiss, a frightened kiss; a passionate kiss, with mouths nibbling, tongues exploring, wanting.

When they finally disengaged, Danny looked down at his trembling hands. "Look at that," he said, amazed, his voice trembling. "I'm scared."

"Scared? Scared of what?" Jackie asked.

He met her eyes. "Scared of dying. Can you believe that? For the first time in my life, I'm afraid of dying. I'm afraid I'll die and never see you again."

On the way back to Holly Grove, there was little conversation. In the backseat, Danny and Jackie held hands, but they were facing ahead, their expressions distracted and distant. Jeff and Megan sat close, but said little.

When the car entered Holly Grove, it was after eleven and the town was dark, the buildings just clusters of shadows and silhouettes. Jeff drifted along Main Street, so lost in thought that he'd missed the turn off to Maple Street, where Aunt Betty lived.

They were on the other side of town when Jeff realized it. He turned onto Holly Street, made another left and found Maple Street.

He parked in front of the house and switched off the engine. The silence enveloped them like something alive, and time seemed to stretch out into infinity.

Finally, Jeff looked at Megan. "How about that plane ride tomorrow?"

Megan nodded. "Sure."

"How about going skiing with me tomorrow, Jackie?" Danny asked.

"Okay, but can we make it early afternoon? Megan and I have some things to take care of in the morning."

"Another mystery?" Jeff said.

Megan started to speak, but Jeff stopped her with an up-raised hand. "Never mind. I don't need to know. Whatever it is, I'm sure you'll tell me someday."

Megan turned from him, her sad eyes lowered. "Sure. Sure we'll tell you someday."

The four of them left the car and strolled to the house. Jackie and Danny remained below the steps. Megan and Jeff moved up on the porch.

Danny kissed Jackie, pressing her close. Despite the chilly wind, Jackie's temperature rose, and she wrapped her arms around his neck and kissed him deeply.

Megan faced Jeff in the darkness, staring up at him, a deep longing welling up inside her. He gave her a long, lingering kiss, his right arm sliding around her waist. Afterwards, she lay her head against his shoulder.

"Don't go," she said.

"Okay. I won't. I'll stay. I'll stay out here until I freeze to death, as long as we freeze to death together."

"I mean to war. Don't go to war."

He backed away, took her face in his hands and kissed her forehead. "That's the nicest thing you could have said to me. Thank you."

In their room, Jackie and Megan lay on the bed on their backs, in the quiet darkness. They'd been lying there for over an hour. Neither could sleep.

"You awake?" Megan asked.

"Yes."

"It was a wonderful night," Megan said.

"Yes. I'll never forget it."

"Did Danny ask you?"

"Ask me what?"

"If you'd wait for him?"

"No, but he wanted to. He will. Did Jeff ask you?"

"He asked me if I'd write to him."

"Yeah, Danny asked me too."

"What did you say?" Megan asked.

"I didn't know what to say," Jackie said. "I didn't want to lie to him. On the other hand, if we can't get back..." Her voice dissolved into the darkness.

"Maybe it wouldn't be so bad to stay in this time, Jackie. Something happened to me tonight. Something that has never happened to me before."

"Oh God, here it comes."

Megan lifted up on her elbows. "Don't be so negative and cynical."

Jackie turned her head to face her. "Megan, don't you think I'm confused too? Don't you think I'd love to have a relationship with Danny? He's a sexy, good-looking guy, and he's a good guy. A nice guy. A genuine guy. I've never met any man like him before."

Megan dropped back down. "So what are we going to do? We can't say we're not going to write to them. That sounds so cruel."

Jackie inhaled and blew out a long audible sigh. "Megan, you heard Oscar. They're going to knock that bridge down, probably right after Christmas. When the bridge is gone, we'll never get back home. We'll be stuck here for the rest of our lives."

"Is that so bad? I can imagine myself having a life

here with Jeff. I know we've only been here two days, but it seems like two weeks. There's a strange sense of time here, almost like there is no time."

They let the silence stretch out.

"Megan, what if Jeff doesn't come back?"

There was alarm in Megan's voice. "Don't say that. He'll come back. He's got to."

Megan heard Jackie's breathing. "We've got to find that car, Megan. And then we have to cross that bridge and get back to our own time. Then none of this will matter. It will have happened so long ago that all these people will have died, and whatever happened to Danny and Jeff and the war won't matter, because it will all be ancient history."

"It was such a wonderful night," Megan said, wistfully.

"You sang so beautifully tonight, Megan."

"The band leader offered me a job as lead singer. I could be another Doris Day or Rosemary Clooney in this time. I always wanted to sing with a big band like that."

"Megan, I don't want them to go off to war, either. It really bums me out to think about them fighting in a war and maybe never coming home."

"How are we going to do it? How are we going to leave them?" Megan asked.

"I don't know."

Jackie felt the bed move in little spasms, and she knew Megan was crying. Tears were streaming down her own cheeks as well.

CHAPTER 15

On Thursday, December 23, Jackie shook Megan awake at 7 a.m.

"Megan, wake up. I have an idea!"

As Megan peered up at Jackie, her eyes were two slits. She spoke in a hoarse, smoky alto. "What? What time is it?"

"Get up. I have a great idea. It came to me first thing this morning. Come on, get up."

Megan rolled over onto her side and pulled the sheet up over her head. Jackie reached over and snapped the sheet from her face. "Get up. We've got to dress, eat and get over to Green's Drugstore."

Megan moaned and complained. "I didn't get to sleep until after 3 o'clock."

"Yeah, well, I'm lucky if I slept three hours. Come on!"

At breakfast, they had scrambled eggs, baked ham, fresh bread and coffee. Rose ignored them as she deposited their plates and poured the coffee. Megan blew across the little pond of hot coffee, then drank it down in two gulps.

Ann Palmer sat at one end of the table, Arthur at the other. As always, he was engrossed in his morning newspaper, his metal lunchbox nearby.

"So what's going on with the war, Arthur, on this lovely Thursday December 23rd?" Ann asked. "And don't say 'about the same.'"

Megan and Jackie looked at them. Obviously, they had this same conversation every day.

"Well, the manpower shortage extends even to Santa Claus," Arthur said, dryly. "So in Portland, Maine, Mrs. Dorothy Ames will enact the role of St. Nick this Christmas Eve at The Good Hope Presbyterian Church. Now that I'd like to see. Unbelievable. A woman playing Santa Claus. Now I know the whole world's gone crazy."

"That's what I call news," Ann said. "What else, Arthur?"

Arthur looked at her from over the paper. "Why don't you read the paper yourself, Ann? Why do you always want me to tell you what's going on?"

"Because, Arthur, you're so good at it, and you're so warm and willing."

He grumbled and went back to his reading. "The U.S. War Department has disclosed a powerful new air warfare weapon—a 75mm cannon installed in the nose of B-25 Mitchell medium bombers, made possible because of the development of a special type of recoil mechanism, utilizing a secret type of hydro-spring device."

"Okay, enough, you're boring me to tears. You always find the most boring stories, Arthur."

"What time does Green's Drugstore open?" Jackie asked.

"Nine o'clock," Rose said, dropping off more freshly baked rolls. The smell was blissful, and Megan allowed her nose to roam over the basket.

"Did she ask you, Rose?" Ann snapped.

"How did your lunch date go with Donald Harris?" Rose asked, with a smirk.

"I believe that is none of your business."

"I'm just asking."

"And I'm just not telling," Ann said, firmly.

Rose shrugged, and left the room.

"So sassy, that girl. She's going to make some man miserable and gloomy. What are you two girls doing for Christmas?"

Neither Jackie nor Megan looked up from their eggs.

Jackie finally spoke. "Well, we're going to be leaving."

"Where?"

"We both have family in Portland," Megan said. "We'll be taking the train."

"Well, I'm leaving tonight for Montpelier. My mother, sister and little brother, Tommy, are there. Poor Tommy lost an arm fighting on Guadalcanal. He's finished fighting. Thank God he won't have to go back to that awful war."

At 9 o'clock sharp, Megan and Jackie were waiting outside Green's Drugstore when Mr. Green opened the door, and the bell danced to life.

"Good morning, ladies. Come in."

After Mr. Green had closed the door, Megan turned to him. "Mr. Green, on Monday night around 9:30, did a teenage boy come in?"

Mr. Green scratched the side of his head. "Monday night at 9:30? Well, let me think about that. There was a final delivery to make. Mitch left to make the delivery. He's our delivery boy. Do you mean Mitch Spivey? He's the only boy around that time of night."

Jackie brightened. "Yes, that must be him. Do you know where he lives?"

"Yes, he lives on Pearl Street, about a half mile off Main Street as you go out of town."

"Will he be in today?"

"Yes. School's out for Christmas so he'll be here about 10 o'clock. I have a lot of deliveries for him to make. Why?"

"Oh, nothing really. I just want to talk to him," Jackie said.

"Well, he's always on time. A very dependable boy. He'll be here."

The two girls went to Dot's and sat at the counter, ordering coffee and donuts. They managed to talk over the radio blaring war news and Christmas tunes, the rattle of dishes and the clink of silverware.

"Are you going to tell me what this is all about?" Megan asked. "Or are you going to keep putting me off?"

"I don't want you to nix this thing before I've had a chance to talk with this kid."

"Okay, so I won't nix it. Tell me why you want to talk to him."

"Mitch is the same teenage guy who saw us when we first came to town in our car, right?"

"Okay, maybe. Probably. Okay, yes, he probably was."

"No doubt was," Jackie said, emphatically. "No one else saw our car, except that old man out on the road, but he was probably headed out of town. Anyway, he's long gone. Mitch, the teenage boy who delivers prescriptions to people in town, is the only person who actually saw us in our Ford Fusion Hybrid. Right?"

"I'm with you, but I'm not with you, Jackie."

"Think, Megan. Think how he reacted. He ran like he saw green men or, in our case, green women from Mars. That car scared the hell out of him."

Megan's eyes narrowed as she thought about it. "Okay, so if I'm catching on to what you're thinking, you have a hunch he must have told somebody about us and the car."

"It's a possibility. I mean, the car got stolen sometime during the night. Our good friend, Mitch, might have followed us and stolen it, or, he could have told someone else, like a big brother or friend, and they stole it."

"But why? What could they do with it?"

Jackie gave her a knowing look. "Megan, think. They could hide it, sell it, or call the military. There are a hundred things they could do with a car like that. Can you imagine if we saw a spaceship land in Central Park in the middle of the night and no one else was around? What would we do?"

"Run like hell."

"Right, which is what Mitch did. But wouldn't we probably go and find someone to tell them about it?"

"Okay, it's a long shot," Megan said.

"It's the only shot we've got," Jackie said. "So, we're going to be there at 10 o'clock and we're going to surprise Mitch. We'll know if he knows about the car when we see his reaction. You stand by the door and block him from running away, while I interrogate him."

"Why me? Why do I have to be the linebacker on the New York Jets?"

"Okay, Megan, whatever. We'll both block the door. But we have to force him into telling us where that car is."

Megan took a sip of her coffee. "I wish I could wake up and this whole thing would just disappear."

At 10 o'clock, they entered Green's Drugstore. Both girls leaned back against the door, scanning the store with their careful eyes. They saw Sarah Teal behind the Pharmacy Counter, but no one else in the store.

"What if there's a back door?" Megan asked.

"Why don't you go out and swing around back, just in case he sees me and runs for it. Block it with something."

Megan groaned. "All right."

"Megan, this may be the only chance we get to go back home. If Mitch knows where that car is, we can pack up and be out of here before noon."

Megan ran a hand over her face. "Wish me luck. I feel like we're two cops about to make a drug bust."

After Megan was gone, Jackie ventured forward. Sarah looked up from her work and waved. "Merry Christmas."

Jackie waved back. "Merry Christmas."

At that moment, the office door opened and Mr. Green and Mitch appeared. Jackie recognized him immediately. It was the same boy they'd seen on Monday night. She stepped back to the door, blocking it. She swallowed.

"Hi, Mitch," she called.

Mitch was a thin, wiry-built kid, with a mop of dark brown hair and large alert eyes. Those eyes widened in recognition, and then fear, when he saw Jackie. He drew back in astonishment, searching for an exit.

"Mitch, wait!" Jackie called.

Mitch dropped his delivery bags and pushed Mr. Green away, and the man staggered back.

"Mitch," he yelled. "What's the matter with you?"

Sarah watched confused, concerned.

Mitch bolted toward the back door, and hurled his body against it. He bounced off, stunned. He tried again, but the door wouldn't budge. He tried the doorknob, but the door was immovable. Trapped, he licked his lips and looked for a window.

Mr. Green approached. "What's gotten into you, Mitch? Stop this."

"I've got to get out."

"Out where? What's going on?"

"I've got to get away from her," and he pointed at Jackie, who was slowly moving toward him, her hands up, gently waving him down. "Mitch, take it easy. I just want to talk to you."

But his eyes were darting about, plotting an exit.

Mr. Green threw his hands to his hips. "Stop it, Mitch. Just stop it now. Do you hear me? Tell me what is going on!"

Mitch was shaking. He stared at Jackie, eyes nervous with fright. "She's not from here. She's trying to get at me."

"What?" Mr. Green said. He turned to Jackie. "What's this all about?"

Jackie willed herself to be calm. "I don't know, Mr. Green. I just want to talk to Mitch for a couple of minutes. That's all."

"About what?" Mr. Green asked. "It's obvious the boy is scared to death of you."

"Mr. Green, Mitch has misinterpreted something that happened the other night."

Mitch's gaze was moving along the floor. He wouldn't look at her.

"Mitch, just listen to me for a minute," Jackie said. "My friend and I work for the military. My father is a general and we were passing through town on secret military business."

Mr. Green and Sarah both took on interest.

"Secret?" Mr. Green asked.

"Yes. I need to speak with Mitch in private about something that happened on Monday night."

"How do we know you're working with the military? Women don't do that kind of work," Mr. Green said, smugly.

Jackie summoned patience, as she looked at Sarah. "You didn't have a woman pharmacist until the war, did you, Mr. Green? The war has changed many things. Now I need to speak with Mitch for about five minutes. That's all. Please, Mr. Green, can we use your office? Mitch, please. It is very important."

They waited for Mitch. He finally lifted his eyes, but his expression was still cautious. "I want you to stand outside, Mr. Green," Mitch said.

Mr. Green eyed Jackie suspiciously. He turned to Mitch and put a protective arm on his shoulder. "You go on in, son. Nothing's going to happen to you. I'll be right here. You go ahead now."

He lowered his head and stepped into the office. Jackie looked toward the back door, wondering how Megan had managed to block it, and then she joined Mitch inside. She closed the door behind her and took in the room.

The small office held a wooden desk with a heavy black telephone, two wooden file cabinets, an iron safe, and a book shelf stacked with magazines and old medical books. Mitch had his back to her, his hands shoved deeply into his pockets, shoulders hunched for protection.

Jackie lowered her voice to a near whisper. "Mitch, on Monday night you saw my friend and me driving through town, didn't you?"

Mitch didn't respond.

"You saw us driving a car you'd never seen before, didn't you?"

He twisted around. "I saw something like it in *Popular Mechanics*, last year. It was the car of the future."

"That's right, Mitch. It is a car of the future. You're exactly right about that. It is definitely a car from the future and that's why we were here."

He turned slowly, his face filled with questions. "What do you mean?"

"Mitch, my friend and I are from the future, in a sense. We're driving an experimental car that will be built in the future."

"You said it was for the military?"

"That's right. We were testing it for the military."

"They have soldiers that do that. Not women."

"Mitch, my father is a general. I grew up an Army brat. I *am* military."

He considered her explanation.

"Mitch, did you steal that car?"

His eyes bulged again, fear returning. "No. No! I didn't. I didn't take it."

"Did you tell someone about the car, after you ran away down the alley?"

"I didn't take it! Don't call the police. I didn't."

"Okay, Mitch, I believe you. I'm not going to call anybody. I believe you, but did you tell someone else about it?"

He turned away again. "I was scared. I'd never seen anything like that."

"I know, Mitch. I know. Did you tell somebody?"

"I was taking him the delivery, the medicine for his rheumatism."

"Him? Who, Mitch? Who did you take the delivery to? What's his name?"

"I was so scared. I thought you were like spies or aliens or something."

"Yes, Mitch, because you didn't know it was an experimental car of the future. Anybody would have thought that. Who were you taking that last delivery of Monday night to?"

Mitch slowly turned, his face pinched in agony. "To Burt Skall. I told him about the car. I told him all about it."

Jackie closed her eyes, struggling to remember. And then she did. "You mean the pawn broker, Burt?"

He nodded. "Yes. I told him all about it. He was so interested. He sat me down and he had me tell him every detail."

Jackie shivered. Of all people, Burt the pawn broker. He had scared the living hell out of her.

She sagged and sighed. "Damn."

Mitch looked concerned. "Are you okay?"

"No, Mitch, I'm not. I am about to freak out."

"Freak out?" Mitch said, not understanding.

Jackie didn't know when the term had slipped into the English language. Probably sometime in the 1960s.

She folded her hands, her mind racing. "Mitch, did you know he stole the car?"

His eyes dropped to his shoes. "Yes."

"Do you know where it is?"

"Yes. In his garage."

"Do you know what he's going to do with it?"

"He told me not to tell anybody. He said it was our little secret. He gave me 20 dollars not to tell anybody."

Jackie didn't want to lie, but she felt she had no choice. She made her voice sound official and a little threatening. She wasn't the actress Megan was, but she had watched her, and she now hoped she'd learned enough to scare Mitch a little.

"Mitch, that car is owned by the military. Burt could get into a lot of trouble if it's not returned, immediately. You must go and tell him that."

Mitch shook his head, violently. "No, no, he'd beat me. He'd catch me and beat me. He'll kill me. He said he's going to sell it to the highest bidder. He said he's got somebody coming to look at it."

Jackie felt her body go ice cold. She stood there staring and trembling. Now what?

CHAPTER 16

Jackie and Megan were back at Dot's Café for lunch, this time sitting in the same booth they'd sat in with the guys. Megan was chewing the last of her hamburger and Jackie a chicken salad sandwich. They were both feeling deflated, brooding over their options. They'd spent the rest of the morning wandering the town, brainstorming possibilities, and despairing when none of those options seemed viable.

"I say we should just go over there with a crowbar, pry the lock off, dive into the car and make a run for it," Jackie said.

"I know, Jackie, that's the third time you've said it. But I still say, what if Burt has moved the car and then he calls the cops on us? What if he's siphoned all the gas out of the car to stop anyone from stealing it?"

"Why would he do that? How do you even know about siphoning gas from somebody's car?"

"Because I was in a play about a father who stopped his son from stealing his car to elope with the town slut, by siphoning gas from the gas tank."

Jackie stared at Megan in amazement. "Does all your life experience come from some musical, play or commercial you've done?"

Megan thought about it, while she drew a mirror from her purse to check her hair and lipstick. "Yeah, I think so. Hey, it's got me through a lot of stuff, Jackie. Now I say, one more time, that we need to tell the guys everything. I think they would go over to Burt's and beat the shit out of him. Then all us get into the car and drive away across the bridge and live happily ever after."

Jackie shook her head. "And even if they did believe us, which they wouldn't, neither of them would leave with us. This is their time, and their war, and they are responsible, moral, and honorable guys. They are going to participate in this war no matter what. And, finally, if they did believe us, which they wouldn't, they would most certainly destroy the damned car or the bridge or both, to keep us here with them, because you know, as well as I do, that they are in love with us."

Megan took a long drink of water while staring at the Christmas tree. It was garlanded with lights and had a thin, golden haired little angel on top, leaning slightly to the right.

She opened her hands, discouraged. "Okay, so we are right back where we started from, which is nowhere. In one hour I'm going to fly off with Jeff in some crazy World War I airplane and you're going skiing with Danny."

Jackie's face was suddenly set in a determined scowl. "Okay, this is what I'm going to do, with you or without you. Tonight, I'm going to go see Burt Skall."

"Are you crazy?"

"I'm going to tell him that I know everything. I'm going to call his bluff and tell him that the car is owned by the military and that we are on a secret mission."

"God help us," Megan said, leaning back. "He's not going to believe you."

Jackie held up an obstinate hand. "I'm going to charge up that hill and attack. That's what my father would advise me to do. He'd say, Jackie, don't sit around on your ass planning too much. Make your plans, and then attack. Okay, that's what I'm going to do. Attack."

Megan's lips were compressed with concern. "Why don't we just go over there and peek into his garage. It might be that simple, Jackie. If the car is there, then you pry the lock off and we run for it."

Jackie picked up her napkin and wiped her lips, thinking. "Okay, maybe. By the way, how did you stop Mitch from getting through Mr. Green's back door so he couldn't escape?"

"I found some cement blocks lying around. I dragged them over and stacked them against the door."

"You really are something, aren't you?"

Megan shrugged, her chin lifted in pride.

An hour later, the girls met Jeff and Danny back at the house. Jeff was dressed in brown slacks, black boots, and a leather flying jacket with a white scarf wrapped about his neck. Danny wore jeans, boots, a heavy brown woolen sweater, and a knitted cap.

The girls kept their dress simple. Slacks and sweaters.

Jeff took Megan away in the Ford, and Danny drove off with Jackie in a dark green 1934 Plymouth deluxe four-door sedan.

Four miles out of town, Jeff turned onto a dirt road, and they followed it through a cluster of trees, past a pond, until they came to another narrow dirt road. Jeff turned right into a deserted flat field that was an airfield.

It had a single unpaved northeast/southwest runway, an old gray airplane hanger at the far end of the field, and a wind cone—a truncated cloth cone mounted on a mast, used to show the direction of the wind.

Jeff leaned his head out the window and looked skyward. "I see some blue up there."

Megan looked up from the windshield. "It looks pretty cloudy to me."

"You've got to be an optimist, Megan. I saw a patch of blue over those trees over there. It lasted about five seconds. I'll take it. And with this plane, it's all about the wind, anyway. And there isn't much wind yet."

They bumped along the dirt road on the edge of an airfield, drew up to the hangar and came to a stop. A biplane was parked just outside the hangar.

"This is called Wicker's Airfield. My old buddy, Harry Wicker, owns this place. He's the guy that taught me how to fly. He's flying transport planes now somewhere in the Mediterranean. His father looks after everything now."

They got out and Megan quickly began having second thoughts. She advanced to the plane, carefully, as if it might reach out and slap her. It was an open cockpit 2-seater biplane, with a yellow propeller and a silver body, with a red stripe running along the full length of the fuselage. The airplane looked small. It looked old. It looked fragile.

"It's really small, isn't it? And it has two sets of wings," Megan said, uneasily. "Do the extra wings make it a lot safer?"

"Sure, why not," he said, grinning. "This is a great little baby. She's called a 'Jenny.'"

"Named after a girl, no doubt," Megan said.

"Well, actually, its official designation is JN2. It's a

169

post-war surplus girl, and a real honey. I bought my first one for 300 dollars and did some barnstorming in it."

"What's barnstorming?" Megan asked.

"I flew across the Midwest and sold rides to people who'd never been in an airplane before. It was a lot of fun."

"Does this thing go fast?"

"It's a 90 horsepower wonder, with a Curtiss OX-5 V8 engine. Top speed: 75 miles per hour."

"That's not very fast, is it? I mean, can it get off the ground?" Megan asked, twisting her hands nervously.

"Oh sure. And it can fly as high as 6,000 feet, maybe a little more. Old Charlie Lindbergh himself soloed in one back in 1923."

"Who?" Megan asked.

Jeff looked at her, doubtfully. "Charles Lindbergh. Don't tell me you've never heard of Charles Lindbergh?"

Megan struggled to recover, aware that she'd better act like she knew who he was. "Well, of course I've heard of him. Yes, I mean he flew airplanes, didn't he?"

Jeff laughed, helplessly, slapping his knee with his right hand. "Oh, yes, Megan, he certainly flew airplanes. He's the guy who made the first solo nonstop flight across the Atlantic Ocean on May 20-21, 1927. He was the most famous man in the world for a while. Where have you been living? On the moon?"

Megan forced an awkward smile.

"Lindbergh's always been a hero of mine, well, until he snuggled up to the Nazis awhile back, but then that's another story."

They walked to the hangar and Jeff rolled back the hangar door. They stepped inside under a dim overhead light. Megan saw Harry Wicker's all-metal monoplane fighter, the single engine XP-9, originally designed to carry cargo and mail. Beside that was an old car, covered by a tarpaulin.

"That plane looks safer," Megan said, still struggling for courage.

"Yeah, it's a good solid plane. Old Harry used to carry the mail in it in the old days."

"Is that your car?" Megan asked.

"No, that's Harry's old 1932 Chevy Coupe. He left it here before he went off to war. I take it out for exercise now and then and Danny Boy has kept the engine in good order."

Jeff took flying suits from an old wooden locker and handed one to Megan. They pulled them on and then Jeff gave her a flying helmet. He helped her slip it over her head and snap on the glasses.

They walked outside to the Jenny, and Jeff checked the wind direction with a raised moist finger and then stared out at the wind cone. He helped Megan up, and she gingerly pulled herself into the forward cockpit, surprised by the small space. She eased down into the narrow seat, avoiding the joy stick, or control stick, that was between her legs, and she buckled herself in. Before her, on the instrument panel, she saw a compass, a fuel gauge and an altimeter, an instrument that measures altitude.

Jeff scurried up to her, and Megan looked at him with anxiety.

"I'm not going to have to do anything, am I? Like move this stick?"

Jeff laughed. "No, no. The forward seat was for the student flyer. The backseat was for the teacher. Don't worry, I'll fly the plane. You just enjoy the ride. I'm going out to give the propeller a little helpful boost. When I do, you flip that switch, okay?" he said pointing to it. "That should kick the engine over."

171

Megan nodded, her brow furrowed. "Okay." And then she called out to him. "Jeff, I'm not really all that comfortable in airplanes."

He jumped down and went to the propeller. He glanced at her, flashing his confident smile, and gave her the thumbs up. "Don't worry, flying in this plane is as safe as rocking in a baby's cradle. You'll see."

With both hands, Jeff gripped the propeller blade, ready for action. "Okay, Megan, hit the switch!"

Megan did. Jeff gave the propeller a downward thrust. It sputtered, coughed and shuddered to life, gray smoke billowing from the engine. Jeff ducked away and pulled the two wheel chocks from the tires. He climbed up into the cockpit, dropped into the backseat and buckled up. He shouted over the clicking sound of the engine. "Away we go!"

Megan braced herself, as Jeff lowered his glasses and prepared for take off. The Jenny rolled ahead toward the dirt runway. Jeff tied his white scarf around his neck, flinging back its flapping tail. He grinned broadly, as he turned onto the runway, into the wind, and opened up the throttle. The Jenny crept forward, slowly, gathering speed. Megan felt the tail go up, and she gritted her teeth, as the wheels began to skim the ground. Jeff could feel the growl of the engine pulling itself out of the dirt field, every rib, strut and wire vibrating in unison. He checked the wings and saw the fabric rippling, as the Jenny bored her way through the cold air.

Jeff met the lift of the plane with the gentle pressure of the joy stick and he laughed out loud, feeling that rarefied feeling of pure satisfaction and joy, at being one with the little Jenny.

Suddenly, he was barnstorming again, flying wild and free over square patches of green fields, farms, and miniature Midwestern towns.

Megan grabbed both sides of the cockpit, her knuckles white, her eyes squeezed tightly together, sure they were going to crash into the trees that seemed to be racing toward them fast. The plane left the ground, dropped, bounced, surged up again and lifted off, its wheels missing the tops of trees by no more than 10 feet.

They climbed to 2000 feet, into a stiff wind that chilled Megan's face, neck and hands. She felt exposed and vulnerable, sputtering along in the big endless sky, in a little toy-like plane that seemed to have a rubber band engine. The Jenny rolled and pitched, as they pierced stringy white clouds and danced about in the sky. Megan started to feel a little airsick. The last thing she wanted to do was vomit. What a turnoff that would be. She willed herself to forget about it and concentrate, instead, on the way she felt the night before, dancing with Jeff, lost in his strong embrace.

Jeff was ecstatic. He felt the air pressure on the elevators, and the throb of the engine. He felt free, and in harmony with the world. He shouted up at Megan.

"You okay?"

She twisted around and forced a smile. "Yes." She gave him the thumbs up.

"Beautiful, isn't it?"

She nodded, trying not to grimace.

They glided over white shag carpeted fields, frozen lakes and wide slopes of rising pine trees, the mountains looming large to their right, shrouded in mist and snow.

Gradually, Megan began to relax, remembering that Jeff could fly the 4-engine bomber. If he could do that, and teach other pilots how to do it, then surely he could fly this little thing. Surely, she could just relax, let go a little, and enjoy the ride. And so she took in the splendor above, and the gentle slope of the white hills, the narrow twisting roads and graceful farms, and the distant train, puffing smoke, all sliding by underneath the Jenny's fragile butterfly wings. They drifted lazily, passing through low, feathery clouds, lost in a white paradise and a delicious peace.

Megan heard Jeff shout something at her. She twisted around and cupped her hand at her ear. "What? I didn't hear you."

"Will you wait for me?"

She knew what he meant, but she didn't respond. He asked her again.

"Will you wait for me to come back from the war?"

Megan didn't know what to say. She couldn't lie and she couldn't tell him the truth, so she didn't say anything.

The plane nosed over and started down. Megan felt her stomach lift into her throat. She grabbed on tightly, fear rising. The plane slowly came out of the dive, leveled off and banked to starboard, gliding toward the mountains.

"Sorry," Jeff yelled. "We hit a bit of turbulence."

Megan looked down and saw the zigzag pattern of skiers and ski trails. She looked around at Jeff.

"I'll wait for you, if I can, Jeff. I want to wait."

"What?" he said, leaning forward.

"I'll wait for you, Jeff," and as soon as it left her lips, she wanted to cry.

Jeff boosted the throttle, and pulled back on the joy stick. The Jenny surged up. He wiggled the wings and yelled at the top of his lungs. "YA-HOOOOOOO."

Inside the simple and mostly empty ski lodge, Danny and Jackie sat near the blaze of the cobblestone fireplace, in high-backed chairs. Under heavy cross-beams and mounted heads of deer with shiny glass eyes, they pulled on the woolen socks and heavy skiing boots that Danny had brought along.

"This place used to be so busy. Lots of guys from around here joined the Tenth Mountain Division, a branch of the Army that deals with mountaineering tactics. I thought about it, but then decided the Airborne was new and more exciting."

Jackie struggled into the black, fur-lined ski jacket Danny handed her. "You're about the same size as my sister," he said. "This should fit."

Next, Jackie examined the skis Danny had brought for her. They were 6' 9" Montgomery Wards Ridgetop wood skis, with no steel edges. She'd never seen anything like them, and she'd certainly never skied on anything like them.

They left the lodge and crunched through the snow, heading for the tow rope that would take them up into the mountains. A light snow was falling, and some flakes landed on Jackie's lashes. Danny reached over and gently raked them away. Jackie stood on tip toes and kissed him.

They went to the tow rope and knelt to adjust their boot bindings and put on their skis. Danny showed her how to press on the safety catch to lock her right boot into position. She repeated the procedure with her left boot. They were ready.

Tucking their poles under their arms, they grabbed hold of a fixed handle attached to the rope. The long rope loop ran through a bullwheel, or pulley, at the bottom of the slope, where the engine house lay, powered by a single engine. The tow ran east up the fall line and toward a warming hut. The tow had been used for as long as Danny could remember, and it would be 1946 before chair lifts were installed.

Still standing, Danny and Jackie held on and were pulled along, climbing up into the mountain. The snow was smooth and clean, and as they rose higher, Jackie felt an old familiar thrill, remembering skiing trips with her parents in Switzerland and Colorado. It was on those trips that she'd connected most with her father, a stern but often an affectionate man, who had doted on her when she was a little girl. He'd become less doting when she'd decided not to go to law school or join the military.

She hadn't been skiing in over two years, and she breathed in the cold, fresh, bracing air, feeling newly alive and happy.

"You said you were an experienced skier?" Danny asked.

"Yes. I started skiing when I was a little girl."

When they arrived, Jackie surveyed the area. Skiing took place on a single open slope. She guessed the vertical was 200 feet; possibly 300. The slope was quite wide— maybe a couple of hundred yards.

"It can ice up easily, so be careful," Danny said. They skied over to the old abandoned engine shack, tugged at and adjusted their mittens, and lowered their goggles.

They started across a flat plateau, about 150 yards across, skirting the edge of tall pines, heavy with snow. Danny was using the sliding forward stride he'd learned as a boy from Aksel Christensen, a man who'd settled in the area from Scandinavia many years ago. Danny moved quickly and, when he glanced back, he saw that Jackie was right behind him. Impressed, he smiled, and slowed down to ski beside her. He gave her a thumbs up.

They traversed the eastern side of the mountain and then started down. Jackie was filled with a fierce delight as they swept down the slope, trees whispering past them as they moved at a swift, thrilling speed.

They arrived at a small plateau that tilted upwards and came to an abrupt sliding stop on the ridge.

"How was that?" Danny asked, face alive with delight.

"That was awesome," she said, breathless. "Really freakin' awesome!"

Danny looked at her, strangely. "Where do you come up with words like that?"

She ignored him. "What next?" she asked, exhilarated.

On the other side of the ridge, the snow slope was almost vertical, falling away into a gray mist. Danny looked at her. "Are you game?"

Jackie peered over. "I can't see the bottom. Do you know what's down there?"

He shrugged. "I've skied it a couple of times. It's always a surprise."

She thought of his risky red hair. She thought of him jumping out of an airplane. She thought of last night and their kisses, and the thrill of sinking her tongue into his mouth. She loved the way he'd touched her neck and her breasts. She loved the smell of him and the feel of him. Then she thought, *Can I ski down that friggin' hill?*

She screwed up her courage, shoulders back. "Okay, Danny Boy, let's do it!"

They heard the clicking buzz of an airplane engine, and they shaded their eyes, gazing up, searching for it.

"That's Jeff!" Danny said. "I'm sure that's Jeff."

But they couldn't see the airplane.

Danny turned toward the slope, and went straight over the edge of the near vertical drop.

Jackie hesitated, suddenly wondering what would happen if she was killed. Would she wind up dead in her time, or dead in 1943? She took a deep breath, crouched, brought her skies together and plunged forward. She was immediately engulfed in the mist and disappeared.

CHAPTER 17

Megan, Jackie, Danny and Jeff were all seated around Aunt Betty's dining room table. She'd insisted on cooking them dinner and serving it herself. She stood over the table, hands folded, watching them, pleased and content that they ate voraciously. The baked ham, mashed potatoes, peas and freshly baked biscuits all evaporated before Aunt Betty's pleased eyes.

"I've never seen young people eat so much, so fast," she said. "You'll all be gone off to war soon, fighting for all of us. This is the least I can do, especially at Christmas. I just hope that we can all be here next Christmas, sitting around that Christmas tree out there. That's my prayer for all of us. Peace on Earth and good will toward men."

"Hear, hear," Jeff and Danny said.

They all toasted with their water glasses.

"This is so good," Danny said, reaching for another biscuit.

"You've really out done yourself this time, Aunt Betty," Jeff said, slicing into his second helping of ham. "Really cooked up a feast."

Elyse Douglas

Megan and Jackie were a little more contained, although Jackie had never tasted better biscuits or mashed potatoes.

"You are an excellent chef," Jackie said.

"I wish I could cook like this," Megan said.

"Well, you'd better learn how, for when you marry that special man," Aunt Betty said. "You'll have to cook and clean and make sure your man is taken care of. You want to make sure he is happy in every way. That's the job of all good wives: to make sure their man has anything and everything he wants, whenever he wants it."

Jackie passed Megan a glance of repulsion. Megan rolled her eyes.

"Isn't that right, Jeff?" Aunt Betty asked.

"Of course," he said, winking at Megan.

Danny looked at Jackie and beamed. Jackie could only manage a sneer. "And who's going to take care of the wives?" Jackie asked. "Who's going to make sure we have everything we want?"

Aunt Betty stared at her, perplexed.

Danny and Jeff stopped eating.

Megan swallowed down some peas. She liked Jackie's chutzpah. "Yeah, why can't we have anything and everything we want? Who's going to take care of us, the wives?"

Jeff chewed, thoughtfully. "I will," he said, grinning. "Yeah, I will."

Danny looked at Jeff, admiringly. "Yeah, me too. I say, we'll be a team."

Aunt Betty said, "Well, I never."

Jackie brightened. Megan sat up a little straighter.

"I like that," Jackie said. "I like teamwork. I've always been a team player. That's what Megan and I are. We're team players, aren't we, Megan?"

180

"We certainly are."

Jeff looked pleased. "So are Danny Boy and I, aren't we, Danny Boy?"

"Yeah. Sure, why not?"

Aunt Betty threw up her hands in exasperation. "I just can't get used to all this modern thinking."

She withdrew to the kitchen.

After dinner, they sat in the living room, sipping coffee and finishing off the chocolate cake Aunt Betty had baked, with the sugar and butter ration stamps she'd saved.

When Megan and Jackie insisted on cleaning up afterwards, Aunt Betty protested but finally agreed. Danny and Jeff shot up and went into the kitchen to help.

"Let's do some KP, Jeff," Danny said, rolling up his sleeves.

Jeff began stacking the dishes while Megan ran water into the sink and Jackie wiped the table and the counters.

"What's KP?" Megan asked.

"Kitchen Police," Jeff said. "I've peeled enough potatoes to feed an Army."

Danny laughed. "Good one, Jeff. Good one."

Jeff moved in close to Megan. She smelled his musky cologne. He leaned over and kissed her nose. "You're beautiful," he said, softly.

Megan melted a little, feeling a little drunk with desire.

Suddenly finding herself alone, Aunt Betty sat down in the lumpy chair, smiling to herself. It was comforting to hear the sound of laughter coming from the kitchen. She would miss them all when they left. Her heart sank a little at the thought of the boys fighting evil so far away from home. She picked up her knitting and whispered a prayer that the boys would come home safe and healthy, and that the girls, those nice girls, would find happiness.

At 8:30, the boys drove away, with the promise of seeing the girls the next day at 10 am, for a sleigh ride. Megan and Jackie stood on the front steps waving goodbye as the car's red tail lights disappeared around the corner. The boys' kisses were still fresh and warm on the girls' lips. Megan fought tears and heartbreak, already feeling the ache of impending separation that was to come.

Jackie fought the impulse to call out to Danny and run after him, as well as the impulse to run as fast as she could to the covered bridge and dash across it, begging God to take her back to her own time, away from the struggle and confusion of passion.

The girls were cold, standing outside, even with their coats on. They folded their arms tightly against themselves, both for warmth and to help contain their emotion.

"What now?" Megan asked.

Jackie hesitated. "Now, we go try to find our car at Burt's Pawn Shop. Now we try to get back home."

But Jackie didn't move. Neither girl did.

"I don't want to go back, Jackie," Megan said, softly. "I don't."

Jackie turned to her, fighting the impulse to anger. "Megan, don't be stupid."

"I'm not stupid."

"You're not stupid, but you're acting stupid."

"Because I want to stay? Because I love Jeff?"

"How can you be in love with him? It's only been two days, Megan. Two days. You don't really know anything about him."

"I know I love him. I know I've never been in love before. Never even close."

"Are you doing some scene from a musical now?"

"No!" Megan said, sharply. "And that's a mean and nasty thing to say."

"Megan, you've got to think this thing through. We are out of time and place. We don't belong here."

"Then why are we here? Tell me that."

"I don't know."

"Okay, so then maybe we're supposed to be here, because we were meant to fall in love with these guys, and we couldn't do it in our own time."

Jackie held up a protesting hand. "I'm not going to Never, Never Land with you, Megan."

"Don't you feel anything for Danny?"

"Of course I do, and you know I do. He's a great guy. A hot guy, all right? Yes, but he and Jeff are leaving, Megan. They're going off to war and they may never come back. We've been through all this."

"I know, I know."

Jackie dropped her arms and shoved her hands into her coat pockets.

Megan stared up into the sky, exhausted by thought. "So I'll take my chances. I'll be like every other woman who falls in love with a guy just before he goes off to war. It happens all the time. It happens in our time. It happened a lot in World War II. So I'll wait for him. I'll be here for him. I'll write to him."

Jackie turned away and walked to the other side of the porch. She was shivering from the chill. She looked up into the sky at the mass of glittering stars. A near-full white moon was rising over some distant trees. It was a lovely night. She turned and started back to Megan, who was standing still and somber, deep in thought, her arms still wrapped about her.

"Megan... I think we know that we both have to go

back, or we both have to stay. I don't know for sure, of course, but since we both came together, I'm betting we'll have to leave together, or it won't work."

Megan's eyes lingered on Jackie. "You don't know that for sure."

Jackie shrugged. "No, I don't. But it makes sense."

"Nothing makes sense, Jackie. Nothing. None of this, and I feel so lost and confused. We can't even talk to anyone about it, including Jeff and Danny, because no one is going to believe us."

"I can't just stay here and do nothing, Megan. I have to try to find that car and try to get back home. Sure, if I let myself, I could easily fall in love with Danny, but I'm not going to let that happen. I feel, in my heart, that my life should be lived in my own time, not here in the past. And who knows what would happen to history if we stayed here? We might accidentally screw up the entire natural course of human events."

"Oh, who cares," Megan said. "Maybe the entire natural course of human events needs to be changed. It's not like the world is a perfect paradise or anything. Maybe we'd help it by staying here."

"We're losing our focus again, Megan, and anyway, you know what I mean."

Megan turned away.

Jackie went to the door and opened it. Megan's voice stopped her.

"I'll help you, Jackie. I'll do everything I can to help you get back. But I'm still not sure I'll go back with you, if the opportunity comes."

Jackie kept her back to Megan for a time, then she withdrew inside.

An hour later, they were sneaking along the silent back streets, two shadows, advancing cautiously toward the edge of town. Jackie held a crow bar at her side, Megan a flashlight, switched off, both items found in Aunt Betty's garage. They made a right turn, kept to the narrow sidewalk and moved toward Main Street.

From Main Street, they edged along past the little red-bricked post office, their eyes taking in the silhouette of Burt's Pawn Shop, just ahead across the railroad tracks.

They heard the haunting moan of a train coming from somewhere in the night, and as they continued on, the blaring sound of the horn drew closer. The girls would have to cross the railroad tracks to get to Burt's, so they found shadowy shelter near the post office and waited. The train came thundering through town, a whoosh of air billowing their hair as it shot past them, its wheels clacking heavily across the tracks.

The girls gathered themselves and started off, scurrying across the tracks, heads down, making a dash for the pawn shop. They arrived at the entrance, then stopped and flattened their backs against the wall. They both felt intensively alive, despite their thrumming hearts. A slight wind rattled the bare-limbed trees, tall and dark above them.

Jackie crept to the window and peered in. There was a faint light coming from the back of the shop. She saw no movement, no sign of life. She turned back to Megan and, with vast enunciation of her lips, whispered, "No one there. Must be gone."

Megan jerked her head toward the garage. "Don't knock. Let's take a look in the garage," she whispered.

Jackie nodded. They peeled themselves away from the building, ducked and stole down the stairs to the side of the garage, stopping to hide in the deep shadows. Jackie searched about and saw a window. She pointed to it. Megan nodded.

Jackie raised up cautiously, but the window was covered by something. She couldn't see anything. She asked Megan for the flashlight. She switched it on and shined the beam into the window. She frowned and switched it off.

"It's no good. It's covered by a curtain or something. I can't see anything."

"What do you think?" Megan asked.

Jackie's mouth was crooked with a firm determination. "I'm going to pry the door open. That's the only way."

"Be careful," Megan whispered.

"You stay here and keep watch," Jackie said as she stepped around Megan, throwing watchful darting glances about. She edged to the front of the garage, heart racing. It had two warped wooden doors, joined together by a thick padlock. Jackie reached for it and jiggled it. Definitely locked. She studied the angle, the screws and the lock itself, calculating the best place to wedge the crowbar in to get good leverage, to pry the lock off at the base. *It should be easy*, she thought. The wood was old and probably rotten in places. Just as she was about to lift the crowbar, she heard a sound. She froze.

At that moment, the back light to the pawn shop flickered on and Burt Skall exited the back door, mumbling misery under his breath. He slammed the door behind him and tugged on the doorknob to ensure it had locked.

Megan had a clear view of him from where she stood. The heat of fear shot to her face. She broke for the front of the garage, anxiety making her breathe hard, white vapor rolling from her mouth.

"It's Burt!," she said in a loud whisper. "What do we do?"

Jackie glanced about. She pointed to the post office. They darted away, just as Burt passed the side of the garage, pausing at the entrance.

Winded, the girls hid behind a dark corner of the post office and watched Burt as he fished into his pocket for his keys. He wore an old overcoat, no gloves and no hat. He was bent and fumbling. Jackie thought he looked like an evil crooked finger.

Finally, he inserted the key into the padlock, turned and opened it. He removed the lock, released the hinge and dropped the shackle into the hinge loop. He opened the right garage door, struggling and cursing it as he wriggled, and shoved it open. The left door swung open with ease.

The girls peer sharply into the darkness, but couldn't see anything.

Burt disappeared inside.

At the first sound of the car engine, the girls stiffened, senses acutely awake. They waited for headlights, but there were none. The car slowly emerged from the tomb-like darkness. Megan gasped. Jackie cursed. It was their car. The red Ford Fusion sedan!

"That son of a bitch!" Jackie said.

"Shhh," Megan said.

Burt stopped the car, got out and shut the two garage doors.

"The hell with this," Jackie said.

She charged toward the pawn shop, shooting across the railroad tracks, just as Burt slid behind the wheel. He gunned the engine, turned left and shot away down a dark country road, with Jackie sprinting and cursing after him.

CHAPTER 18

Megan and Jackie were wide awake by 7am on December 24, 1943. Jackie's right arm lay across her eyes, and Megan was staring at the ceiling.

"I didn't know that car was so red," Megan said. "I mean, even in the dark, that damned thing is red, red, red."

"That doesn't help, Megan."

"No wonder Mitch ran like hell. After seeing all the old cars around here for the last couple of days, it even shocked me how futuristic and how red that car is."

"That's not helping, Megan," Jackie repeated.

"Jackie," Megan said, wearily, "We have spent most of the night running through every possible course of action we can take. We've got nothing. Burt has probably driven our car to some town a hundred miles away, and sold it to the highest bidder."

"We don't know that."

"What, then? What?"

"I don't know, but I'm going to kick the shit out of that greedy old bastard as soon as he gets back to town."

.

"That's not helping, Jackie," Megan said.

"Megan, please shut up and think."

"I am thought out, Jackie. I've got nothing."

"Okay, think about it this way. If this was a musical or a play, what would we do next?"

Megan rolled to her side, looking at Jackie, suddenly excited. "Now that's an interesting thought. What would we do next? Yes. Well, at this point in the show, we'd both probably sing a sad ballad about how sad and hopeless we feel. Maybe you and I would dance together, something balletic and whimsical, showing how we've become good friends despite all our difficulties. I'd wear my hair up, like a ballerina, and maybe you'd have your hair..."

Jackie broke in. "... I don't care about my hair, Megan. Action. What would the action be?"

Megan flopped over to her back, rocking the bed. "Okay, this would be the action. We would go see Mitch and ask him if he knows where Burt took the car. Mitch would probably sing a song here."

"Forget the singing, Megan, and stick to the plot."

"Okay, so Mitch tells us where the car is."

"I like that," Jackie said, lifting the arm from her eyes.

Megan frowned. "But then, on the other hand, maybe he doesn't."

"Why?"

"Because Mitch is a friend of Herman, the car garage owner, and he doesn't want to rat on him. Herman has the car and has found Burt a buyer. And the buyer is some evil jerk."

"What's in it for Herman?"

"Money. Herman gets half the money Burt collects."

"How does that help us?"

Megan pondered. "I don't know. Maybe we should go

talk to Herman?"

"No way," Jackie said. "He'd tell Danny and then he'd tell Jeff and then the whole thing would blow up in our faces."

So they lay there, brains working, straining for any new and original thought that would help them.

They were dressing at 8 o'clock, when there was a knock on their door.

"Yes," Megan called.

"It's Aunt Betty. You're going to miss breakfast, and Mitch Spivey's downstairs. He says he's just got to talk to you."

Jackie looked at Megan with new hope. "Come on."

Downstairs, Mitch stood by the front door, pacing restlessly. When he saw them descend the stairs, he stopped. His winter coat was too large, and it nearly swallowed him. His face was pale, his expression fearful.

"What is it, Mitch?" Jackie asked.

Mitch looked about, making sure no one else was around. Aunt Betty was in the kitchen and Arthur was at the dining table, his face covered by the paper.

Mitch whispered. "Burt took the car and drove it away last night."

Jackie sank, sighing. "I know that, Mitch. We watched it drive away."

"I made a delivery to him last night. I overheard him talking to someone on the phone."

Jackie and Megan leaned forward. "What did you hear, Mitch?"

"I heard him say he was going to take the car to Wicker's Airfield."

"Where's Wicker's Airfield?" Jackie asked. "Is it close to..."

Megan cut in. "I know where it is. Jeff's plane is there,

parked in a hangar."

"Are you sure?"

"Of course I'm sure."

Mitch spoke up. "Burt said it was too dangerous to leave it at the garage by the pawn shop. Burt told the guy he'd better come soon, or he'd give it to someone else. Then I heard him say he'd meet him at the airfield after dark on Christmas Eve."

"How do we get there?" Jackie asked.

"It's about four miles away," Megan said.

"Okay, let's go!" Jackie said.

Just as she pivoted, she stopped. "Mitch, wait here."

Jackie hurried up the stairs and into the room. She took 10 dollars from her purse and returned to Mitch, pushing it in his hand.

"Thanks, Mitch. Thanks a lot."

Megan took Jackie aside. "How much more money do we have?"

Jackie whispered, "Not much. Another reason we have to get out of here."

"There's one more thing," Mitch said.

Jackie and Megan returned to him, both holding their breath. "What?" they said in unison.

"I heard what Burt called the guy on the other end of the phone. Major."

"Major?" Megan asked.

"Yes," Jackie said, nibbling her lip. "Major, as in officer in Army Major. Burt must have contacted the military. Major, as in we're in major shit if we don't get that car back. Burt knows where the car came from. He knows it's ours. He's probably told this Major who we are. The Major will want to know where we came from and how we got that car."

"That's bad, isn't it?" Mitch said.

Jackie nodded. "Yeah, Mitch. That's bad."

"Maybe not," Megan said. "Maybe he's greedy and he wants the car for himself. Maybe he doesn't care who we are, or where we, or the car, came from."

"Do you want to take that chance, Megan? Let's call Oscar and get over there."

Oscar was waiting in front of Aunt Betty's house 10 minutes later, when Megan and Jackie left the house and hurried down the walkway to the car. They climbed in and closed the door.

"Hello, ladies. Merry Christmas. Where to in such a Christmas hurry?"

Oscar knew where the airfield was and he drove the quiet meandering roads leisurely, while listening to *The Jack Benny Show* on his radio. The show's sponsor was Grape Nuts and Grape Nuts Flakes, and it co-starred performers Megan had never heard of: Phil Harris, Rochester and Don Wilson.

Megan and Jackie sat tensely, listening to a clear baritone voice proclaim *"Don't patronize black markets, and don't buy any food without giving out proper stamps."*

The show continued with comedy sketches and the big band sounds of jazzy clarinets, trumpets and trombones. There was more corny comedy, and then a tenor sang *O Come All ye Faithful.*

As soon as Oscar approached the airstrip, the girls leaned forward, shaken to see a sign was blocking the entrance. Oscar stopped the car and they all read:

PRIVATE PROPERTY
VIOLATORS WILL BE PROSECUTED!

Undaunted, Jackie left the car and moved the sign to one side. She waved Oscar in. He hesitated, lifting his hands, helplessly, his eyes moving and nervous.

"Oh, come on, Oscar."

He shook his head, and she walked over to his rolled-down window. "Megan was here yesterday. It's okay."

"I don't want any trouble. I got a speeding ticket from the Sheriff two days ago. He doesn't have any Christmas spirit."

Megan leaned over the seat. "Oscar, we've got to get in there. I'll explain it to the owner if he comes by. We'll give you 10 dollars extra."

Jackie nodded. "Please, Oscar."

He shook his head, again in resignation. "All right, get in."

Jackie scrambled into the backseat, and Oscar drove past the sign and up the narrow dirt road. They'd traveled about a hundred yards when Oscar hit the brakes. The girls shot forward, bracing themselves with their hands.

"What is it, Oscar?"

He pointed. "Look over there."

The girls looked out of the front windshield to see a big man about 50 yards ahead, cradling a shotgun.

"That's Tom Pike," Oscar said. "He's mean as a snake and he's got a shotgun. That's it. I'm moving on out of here."

Oscar slammed the car into reverse, turned his head around to see through the back windshield, and guided the car back down the road.

"I'll talk to him, Oscar," Jackie said. "I can talk to him," she pleaded.

"No you can't. Tom Pike won't listen. He's been hired by somebody to keep people away and he is mean. He'll shoot my car and then he'll try to shoot me, and it won't be the first time."

Back on the main road, Oscar motored back to town, glancing back apprehensively at Jackie and Megan through his rearview mirror. "What are you two girls up to?"

Defeated, they sat brooding, mentally searching for another way to get to that airstrip hangar.

Jackie inclined forward. "Take us to Burt's Pawn Shop, Oscar."

Megan reacted with dread. "Jackie, what are you going to do?"

"I'm going to kick his ass."

Oscar braked to a stop in front of the pawn shop. Jackie pushed out and turned back to Megan. "Are you coming?"

Megan shut her eyes as if to escape reality for a few seconds. "Yes."

"Do you want me to wait?" Oscar asked.

"Yes," Jackie said.

The girls entered the dimly lit room of the shop. Even though there were two windows, the light of day seemed to avoid the place. Jackie sought Burt, while Megan sought courage.

"Hello? Burt, are you there?"

The girls heard a low, hoarse grumble. "Who is it?"

Jackie still couldn't see him. "It's the two girls you stole the car from."

Jackie saw his head jut out from behind a wall. "What?" he said, with surprise.

Jackie folded her arms. "Yes, us. We want our car back."

Burt's face fell into a dark scowl. He stood, came from behind the wall and started for the grill. He stopped about a foot away, his eyes burning. "Do you now."

"That car is government property."

194

"Is it?"

"Yes, it is. If you return it, now, you won't be prosecuted."

He grinned, darkly. "Well, isn't that nice of you? Well, if I had it, which I don't, maybe I'd take you up on it. Maybe I wouldn't. Maybe I'd ask you where you got it and how much you want for it. Because I am a business man, after all."

"You know as well as I do that the car is at Wicker's Airfield. We were just up there."

He gave an innocent shrug. "I know nothing of the kind. I do know that unless you leave my shop right now, I'm going to call the Sheriff and tell him you tried to rob me. Maybe you don't know our good Sheriff Dougherty. He used to be in the military, in the Navy. He was wounded in 1942 during the Battle of Midway. He limps and he's very bitter. He might be interested in your story. Shall I call him?"

Megan came forward and whispered in Jackie's ear. "Let's get out of here. There's another way."

Jackie ignored her, her hard eyes fixed on Burt. "My father's a general."

Burt's neck stiffened. The air turned hostile.

"And mine was a thief and a drunkard. So what? Why don't you send him over? I know a few generals. I know a lot of military men. In fact, one will be arriving later on tonight to examine some of my merchandise."

Jackie knew she was beaten, but she couldn't let it go. "Maybe the Sheriff would be interested in seeing your merchandise right now. Maybe I should call him?"

Burt flashed a crooked gash of a grin. "Please do, Love. I know he'd love to talk to you, especially when I tell him how you tried to rob me last night. I'll even show him the broken glass, where you tried to break into my garage."

"Come on, Jackie, let's go," Megan said, taking her arm.

Jackie smiled, pleasantly, but her eyes were ablaze. "One way or the other, I'm going to get you, sir. One way or the other."

Burt laughed, but there was uneasiness in his eyes. "I'll wait with bated breath for that awful and inevitable day. Good day, ladies."

Back in the cab, Jackie was fuming.

"Where to?" Oscar asked.

"Home," Megan said.

"We're screwed," Jackie said. "I don't know what else to do. I wish I had my father's old service revolver. I'd go back and shoot Burt in the foot."

Megan lowered her voice. "There's only one thing we can do. Let me talk to Jeff."

"No, Megan. No way."

"Listen to me, Jackie. Do you want to get back home or not? We need his help. He knows this town and the people in it. He knows the owner of that airfield. He took flying lessons out there. We have to try it, Jackie. We've got nothing else and we're out of time. Some Major is flying in to take our car. You'll never get back if that happens. Once that car's gone, we are stuck here."

Jackie looked at her, thoughtfully. "Do you still want to stay?"

Megan nodded. "Yes."

Jackie turned away, gazing out the window as they entered the town, passing The General Store and Dot's Café. A light snow was falling, and she recalled Danny telling her that, according to *The Farmer's Almanac*, there would be a white Christmas.

"Then it doesn't matter anyway," Jackie said. "You

know the theory: we both have to leave. We have to leave exactly the way we came."

"We don't know that for sure," Megan said,

"We don't know anything for sure," Jackie said, "but if anything makes sense, and nothing does, then that at least makes some sense."

"I'll talk to Jeff."

Jackie wouldn't look at her. "What are you going to tell him? The truth?"

Megan slumped down in her seat. "I don't really know what I'm going to tell him."

CHAPTER 19

Megan and Jackie were sitting on Aunt Betty's living room couch when the boys rang the doorbell, promptly at 10 a.m. Megan got up to let them in. Jeff removed his hat and kissed her, as Danny stepped around them, took off his cap, met Jackie standing in the living room, and kissed her.

Danny pointed to the window. "See, we brought the snow. The trails at the base of the mountain will be perfect for a sleigh ride."

Jeff took Megan's arm and led her into the living room. Aunt Betty was in the kitchen. She had just put an apple pie in the oven, and the aroma was sweet and heavenly. A simple fire was burning in the fireplace, hissing and popping.

"Ladies," Jeff said, "Danny and I have been thinking. Here it is, almost Christmas Eve, and you haven't told us where you plan to be tonight. Will you be in town or on some secret mission?"

The girls weren't smiling.

"Well, anyway, with your permission, Danny," Jeff,

.

said, indicating to his friend. Danny nodded. "Danny and I are inviting you to come to our houses tonight to meet our folks. First my folks, and then we'll all go over to Danny's house to meet his folks. We'll have dinner, eat some pie, drink some punch that Dad makes, no booze I'm afraid, and sing some Christmas carols. We'll just hang around and enjoy each other's company. Now, how does that sound?"

Jackie and Megan were staring down into the rug.

Danny looked at Jeff, inquiringly, while Jeff scratched his nose.

"What did I say?" Jeff asked.

Megan looked at him, her expression grave. "I need to talk to you, Jeff."

The room chilled down, despite the fire. Danny and Jeff turned serious.

"What's the matter?" Jeff asked.

Jackie's eyes were still downcast. Danny reached out and gently lifted her chin. "Is something wrong, Jackie?"

Megan took Jeff's elbow and ushered him into the dining room.

"I don't like the looks of this," Danny said.

Jackie faced the fireplace, with Danny next to her. He was looking to the dining room, where Megan and Jeff stood near a window, speaking in private, hushed tones. Behind them, the falling snow had thickened, and he could see it sugar-coating trees and shrubs. His mood shifted from happiness to dread.

Megan didn't look at Jeff as she spoke. She didn't tell him about the time travel; that would have been too much. She told him that they had come with a car, an experimental futuristic car, that they were testing for the military. Jackie's general father was involved. Megan kept this purposely vague.

"Why you two?" Jeff asked. "Why did they choose you and not soldiers? Why wasn't this secret futuristic car tested in some secure area, far from the public eye?"

Megan was ready for all his questions. She'd thought them through, just as she always did when reading a script. "Men are away at war, Jeff, you know that. Women are doing a lot of the jobs men used to do. Anyway, it *was* a secure area, but things went wrong. There was a storm and we got lost."

Then Megan lied. "Then we were exhausted. That's when we found Aunt Betty's house. We hid the car, intending to leave before dawn. But the next morning it was gone."

Jeff listened, and the more Megan explained, the more his lips flattened to a straight line.

Megan concluded by telling him about Burt and what had happened at Wicker's Airfield, leaving out the part about the Major, who was coming to examine the car and perhaps take it away forever. She was afraid it would further complicate the issue. And they were running out of time.

She stared at Jeff, earnestly. "Jeff, we have got to get that car back. Will you help us?"

Jeff presented his face to the window, watching the heavy flakes of snow beginning to blur the world. He was quiet for a long time, and Megan began to despair.

Finally, he faced her, looking deeply into her eyes. He gave her an absent, dreary smile. "Megan, I wish I could say I believed you, but I don't. Some of your story may be true, but, for whatever reason, you're not telling me the whole truth and I suspect a lot of what you have told me is a blatant lie."

Feeling a sudden panic, Megan opened her mouth to speak, but Jeff cut her off. "But I can see that you're both in trouble. That's obvious. That's not a lie. And Danny Boy and I always suspected that you and Jackie were way out of your element. We knew something wasn't quite right. Maybe that was part of the attraction at first. You're like people from another world, another time and place."

Megan's pulse surged. They stared eye to eye. Was she losing him?

"Megan, I love you. I do. I think I fell in love with you the first time I saw you. What was it? I don't know. What did the poet say? John Donne I think. *Twice or thrice had I lov'd thee, Before I knew thy face or name.*'"

Megan's eyes misted over.

Jeff continued. "Megan, I have the feeling that if I help you, you'll leave me and I'll never see you again."

Again, Megan tried to speak, but Jeff placed his hand over her mouth. "No, Megan. I don't want to hear anymore. We've said enough. If help is what you want and need, then I'll help you. I'll do anything for you."

He gently retracted his hand and bent, kissing her tenderly. Tears streamed down Megan's face.

He stood tall, shoulders back, more formal. His voice deepened. "I only have one request, Megan."

Megan nodded. "Anything."

"Before you leave town in that car, I want us to spend the rest of the day together. I want to go on that sleigh ride with you. I want to laugh and pretend that we have forever. I want to pretend that you'll never leave and I'll never have to go off to war. Then tonight, on Christmas Eve, I want you to come to church with me."

"Church?" Megan asked.

"Yes. I want to ask for something, and I want you to be there when I ask it. Agreed?"

Megan nodded, still fighting tears. "Yes, of course."

At that moment, Megan knew she'd have to leave town with Jackie. She'd have to be in the car as it crossed the bridge; otherwise, Jackie would probably never get back home, and Megan couldn't let that happen. She couldn't live with that guilt for the rest of her life.

When Jeff left for the dining room and began talking to Danny, Megan tasted the salt of her tears, and she turned away, allowing herself a good cry. Hearing bits and pieces of the conversation, she could tell that Jackie had also told Danny about the car. She joined them in the dining room and, about fifteen minutes later, they had formed a plan to get the car.

"Well, I guess it's time to get started," Jeff said. "If all goes well, you girls will be on your way by this evening."

After the dying fall of his words, there was an uncomfortable interval of stillness as the four of them stared at each other.

Megan and Jackie went upstairs to pack, while Jeff made a phone call. Before they left the room, pulling their carry-ons, they paused to look back at the room, and both smiled ruefully.

"Believe it or not, Megan, I'm going to miss this room."

"Me too. But I won't miss sleeping with you," Megan added, trying for a humorous tone.

They descended the stairs, quietly, clutching their bags. The guys met them and took the carry-ons. They all glanced furtively toward the kitchen, where Aunt Betty was still occupied with baking.

Jackie gave Danny some money and asked him to give it to Aunt Betty, with their gratitude.

Outside, as snow dusted their shoulders, Jackie kept Megan back while Jeff and Danny opened the trunk and loaded the suitcases.

"Megan, we don't have time for a sleigh ride or a visit to a church. Once we get the car, we need to get out of here. When Burt finds out we've taken the car, he'll call the Sheriff, that Major, and God knows who else. Probably a few gangsters."

"I promised Jeff," Megan said. "Besides, I can't leave now. I just can't. Jeff's and Danny's plan will work. Don't worry."

Jackie stood unmoving, unblinking and unconvinced.

None of the four noticed that Rose was watching them from behind a tree, about 20 feet away. She was coming to help Aunt Betty bake and deliver Christmas cookies to friends and neighbors. As Jeff's car drove away, Rose emerged, her expression full of mischief.

Jeff drove out of town and turned left onto the rugged, pothole-ridden road that led to Hazel Combs' house. Three inches of snow already covered the ground, and a steady wind was blowing the snow into a frenzy.

Jackie and Danny sat close but didn't speak. Megan sat next to Jeff, her left hand resting on his right knee. They said little. When they stopped in front of Hazel's home, Jeff turned and gave Megan a reassuring glance.

"Don't worry, everything will work out."

Hazel was waiting by the front door, standing as erect as a soldier, waving them in, a long wiggle of smoke rising from her brick chimney. Jeff had called to ask for her help, and she'd readily agreed.

Megan and Jackie left the car and paused on the porch, waving at the guys, their frosty breath visible. Jeff and Danny waved back, then drove away toward the airfield. They circled the town, passing gentle white meadows, twisting around pine trees crusted with snow, finally progressing along a silent back road that took them past the

Holly Grove covered bridge. Jeff was taking the alternate road to the airfield, the road he'd often taken when Harry was teaching him to fly.

"Do you have that thing Jackie gave you—what did she call it? The remote?" Jeff asked.

Danny took it from his jacket pocket and held up the remote, with the car keys dangling from it. "Yep."

"And the directions on how to use it, if we have to?"

"Yes. I've memorized them. You know I've always had a good memory," Danny said.

"Yeah, but do me a favor. Repeat the procedure again, just for me."

"Okay. We can start the car with this little remote from as far away as 300 feet. I press this little lock image on the left to lock or unlock all the doors. Then I press the 2X image twice. Jackie said the outside lights will flash twice and then the car will start. She said a little red light will come on to let us know the car has started. Once inside, we insert the key and we're ready to go. If we don't need the remote, we just use the key."

Jeff shook his head. "This car I've got to see, Danny Boy."

Danny shook his head. "All I can say is, if the Army has things like this, we should have this war over within a few months."

"You said it, Danny."

At the airfield, Jeff turned right and stopped, as Danny got out and moved the NO TRESPASSING sign to one side and climbed back in. Jeff gunned the engine and the back tires skidded, then grabbed the road. They advanced, cutting white tracks in the new snow as they traveled along the airfield toward the hangar. As expected, they saw Tom Pike emerge from the shelter of the hangar, wearing a dark overcoat and broad-rimmed hat, with the shotgun resting threateningly over his right shoulder. At 52 years old, Tom was tall, fit and as grim as an undertaker. Jeff braked to a stop and Tom ambled over, his expression serious.

"Hello, Tom. Looks like we're going to get a white Christmas."

Tom was chewing a wad of tobacco and his left cheek bulged with it. "Didn't you see that sign at the entrance?" he said, not pleasantly.

"Sure, Tom, but I came over to make sure my Jenny is okay. What's the shotgun for? You're not going to try to shoot old Santa Claus down tonight, are you?"

There was no humor in Tom's face. He spit out a stream of tobacco. "You go check your machine and then get on out of here, Jeff."

"As a matter of fact, Tom, I also came to tell you that Millie wants you home just as soon as you can get there."

For the first time, Tom's face became animated with tension. "Millie? Where'd you see her?"

"At the General Store. I paid my respects and then I told her I was coming up here to look at my airplane. She told me to tell you to get on home. She seemed upset about something."

Millie Pike was a tall, solid woman, who'd never found any joke or humorous situation funny. She was a no-nonsense, emotionally volatile woman, who'd been known to conk Tom on the head with dishes, or anything else handy, if he irritated her. The whole town knew Tom was afraid of her. Most of the town was afraid of her, too.

"Well, what does she want?" he asked, distressed.

"Tom, you know Millie. She's a woman of few words. She just told me to send you home."

Angered, Tom spit tobacco into the white snow. "I

can't leave my post. I told her that. In the First War, I never left my post. Never, even under heavy fire. Hell, even when those Hun bastards tried to gas me. I told her Burt paid me to stand watch to make sure nobody gets anywhere near that hangar. Now she knew that."

"Does Harry's father know you're out here?" Jeff asked.

"He don't know and he don't care. But Millie has no call to bother me like this when I'm out here on a job."

Jeff grinned, sadly. "Sorry, Tom, I'm just the messenger. You do what you've got to do. Danny Boy and I are going to make sure old Jenny girl is tucked in safe from this storm."

Tom cursed. "I tell you, that woman's going to push me one too many times."

"You know how the song goes, Tom," Jeff said, and he sang. "*Bless 'em all, bless 'em all. The long and the short and the tall.*"

"Oh to hell with all that!" Tom fumed. "Burt said there's a man coming by this evening and Burt's supposed to meet him here."

"Oh, I'm sure you'll be back by then, Tom."

Burt sucked in an irritable breath. He spit tobacco again, as a thought struck. "Will you boys stay around and keep watch for me until I get back?"

Jeff counted to five. "Well, I guess so, Tom."

"I'd consider it a favor. I'd owe you one."

"All right, Tom. Sure thing," Jeff said.

Danny said, "You go ahead, Tom. Don't you worry about a thing. We are soldiers, after all."

Tom cheered up, and spit again. "Yeah, of course you are. Good boys. Good. Thank you."

Jeff switched off the car and he and Danny emerged, amused as they watched Tom stomp off toward his parked car. He yanked open his door and, as an after-thought, he turned and shouted.

"I can't pay you nothing."

"Don't you worry about that, Tom," Jeff said. "You just go on home to Millie."

The boys watched him get into his car, start it up and bump away down the side road and out of sight. Danny turned, shaking with laughter.

"Danny Boy, Tom's going to be one angry guy when he comes back," Jeff said.

"Then let's get this futuristic car up and going and get the hell out of here."

CHAPTER 20

Inside the damp, cold, dimly lit hangar, the Jenny sat tethered to the ground by two ropes. Next to the Jenny was Harry Wicker's XP-9. To the left side of the plane was a car, covered by a tarpaulin. From the look of it they could tell it wasn't Harry's old 1932 Chevy. The boys ventured over, feeling curious and apprehensive.

"Okay, Danny Boy, let's see what we've got here."

Jeff grabbed the lower edge of the tarpaulin and slung it back, peeling it from the car. The red Ford Fusion lay shining magnificently before them, a dazzling marvel—an alien ship from another planet.

Both men stood transfixed. Danny's jaw dropped. Jeff stood gaping, his right hand slowly rising to his cheek, as the rupture of reality stunned him. He closed his eyes, wiped his face and reopened his eyes. They widened in new astonishment.

Jeff slowly lifted a trembling arm and pointed. "Danny Boy. What the hell is that?"

Danny was silent, feeling his heart leaping, thudding in his chest. "Son of a bitch, Jeff. Son of a bitch. Have you ever seen anything like it?"

Jeff struggled to speak. "Only in some sci-fi magazine, Danny Boy."

They backed away, carefully, as if the car might strike out and hurt them.

"It's a car all right," Danny said, finally gathering the courage to advance, and, with an outstretched hand, he touched the right side panel. "But what the hell is it made of?"

"Look at that paint job," Jeff said. "And the design. What a design that is, Danny. The headlights, the bumper. Where did this thing come from?"

"Hell, I don't know, Jeff. It's like something from another world."

Jeff and Danny slowly circled it. Danny peered inside and was shocked anew. "Jeff, this is incredible. Look at the instrument panel, and the seats. Who the hell are these girls and how did they get this car?"

Jeff was troubled. "I don't know. I just don't know."

"We don't have the kind of stuff to build this, do we?" Danny asked. "I mean not even the military can build something like this, Jeff."

"I'd like to put some wings on it and fly it," Jeff said.

They stood in awe, moving forward, stepping back, scrutinizing and questioning. Finally Jeff looked at Danny seriously. "Obviously, we wouldn't want this car to get in the wrong hands."

"It already *has* gotten into the wrong hands, Jeff."

Jeff nodded. "Right. You've got to admire old Burt for being able to hot-wire this thing and drive it away. He's smart, and he's got guts, I'll give him that. But if I know Burt, and I do know Burt, he's probably got two or three gangsters on line to look at this thing, and he'll sell to the highest bidder. Let's get it out of here, Danny. Do you think you can drive it?"

"Oh, yeah. Let's see if it will start."

And Danny took the remote and followed the procedures. When the engine came to life, the guys broke into wide happy grins. "Listen to the sound of that, Jeff. Boy, would I love to get to that engine and tear it apart."

"No time for that, Danny. We can't drive this thing out there. If somebody sees us, we're done for. Let's wrangle something with this tarp, to cover all but the front and back windshields."

Danny killed the engine, while Jeff found his tool box in his locker. They went to work, cutting holes so Danny could see out of the front and back windshields. Jeff secured the ends to the bumpers with rope, and Danny used metal clamps for extra grip.

"Do you think it will hold in this wind?" Danny asked.

"It's the best we can do, so let's get going. Get in and follow me. I'll take every back road I know. Let's keep our fingers crossed."

Danny slid behind the wheel of the Ford, beads of sweat popping out on his forehead. He was overwhelmed, intimidated and thrilled all at the same time. He started the engine, gripped the steering wheel and, with stern concentration, he shifted into Drive, touched the gas pedal and rolled out of the hangar.

Jeff led the way down the side road, keeping Danny in his rearview mirror. Jeff laughed a little at the sight of the Ford. Covered in the dark brown tarpaulin, it looked like a camouflaged vehicle ready for combat. Snow blanketed it, almost immediately. No one passing it would give a second glance.

They ramped along back roads, jolted about, going a few miles out of their way to avoid civilization. They passed farms, sprawling houses and thick forests until they arrived back at Hazel Combs' house. She and the girls were waiting, anxiously, and Jackie was irritated anew that 1943 lacked cell phones and text messaging, denying her the ability to get a blow-by-blow update from the guys as they repossessed the car.

The girls were surprised to see the car covered by the dirty flapping tarpaulin, but ecstatic that the boys had pulled off the theft. Jackie clapped, jumping up and down. They had their car back. Now they had a chance to get back home. Megan lowered her head, happy and sad at the same time.

The girls clambered down the front stairs and followed the car to the back garage, where Hazel was standing to one side next to the open door. Jeff parked his car in the driveway and hurried over, as Danny drove the Ford Fusion into the two-car garage and shut it off.

Jackie met him as he emerged from the car, threw her arms around his neck and kissed him deeply.

Megan took Jeff's hand and squeezed it, looking at him lovingly. "Thank you," she said.

"Anytime," he said.

"I'm all yours," Megan said, intimately.

Jeff allowed his eyes to linger on her. He had a very large lump in his throat.

Hazel cleared her throat.

Jeff snapped out of it. "Yes, well. Danny, Jackie, come on, you two. Let's transfer the girls' suitcases into their car, lock this garage and get out of here."

Danny and Jeff went to work and, minutes later, they were all inside drinking coffee and munching on the star-shaped Christmas cookies Hazel had baked. They were restless and distracted and wanted to be on their way, but they'd stayed out of respect and gratitude for Hazel's help. Finally, Jeff stood, glancing down at his watch.

"We'd better go. When Tom gets back and finds us and the car gone, all hell will break loose."

They repeated their gratitude to Hazel as they started down the front porch to Jeff's car.

"We'll be back for the car no later than seven, Hazel," Jeff said.

"Don't you worry," Hazel said. "It will be here. Nobody's going to even think about coming out here."

With everyone inside the car, Jeff backed out of Hazel's driveway and pointed the car toward the high mountains, ghost-like in the falling snow. As the car climbed the narrow winding road, the white face of the day encircled them, isolating and exciting them.

Thirty minutes later, Jeff drove onto a secluded road and nudged the car along until a simple rustic cabin loomed out of the curtain of falling snow ahead. A deer sprinted into sight across the road, sniffed, sensed danger, and fled down a slope in big plunging strides, out of sight over a ridge.

Jeff turned the car into a little driveway, and twisted around to look at Danny and Jackie.

"It's all yours, kids. We'll be back at six. That gives you almost six hours."

Danny pushed the door open and they got out, slammed the door and scampered over to the front door. When they'd vanished inside, Jeff turned to Megan. "Our little cabin is just up the road."

"Whose cabins are they?" Megan asked, threading his arm with hers.

"They've been in our families for years."

Thirty minutes later, Jeff and Megan were inside their cabin, lying on a thick crimson rug before a comfortable fire, sipping wine. The cabin was simple: knotty pine walls, pine furniture, a modest kitchen and two bedrooms with brass beds covered with quilts.

"I used to come up here a lot when I was a boy. I learned to ski up here in winter, fished with my father in summer. There's a beautiful little pond not too far away. Summers were always too short."

Megan imagined what Holly Grove must be like in summer. She imagined covered bridges spanning sun-dappled rivers, tall ripe cornfields and grazing cows. She could picture a landscape punctuated by churches with tall steeples and 18th-century brick houses behind white picket fences.

She would never see any of it, of course. Because if they did get back to their time, all this would be gone. Just like Jeff and Danny would be gone. None of it would have ever happened.

"Sounds like you had a wonderful childhood," Megan said.

"I did."

"Do you have brothers, sisters?" she asked.

"A sister. She's married and moved to New Hampshire. Her husband's fighting somewhere in Italy, last we heard."

"Your parents?"

"My father's a minister."

Megan raised up on an elbow. "A minister?"

"That surprises you?"

"Yes. I don't think I've ever dated a minister's son."

"My father's a good man. Could be tough at times, but a good man. My mother plays the organ. He directs the choir and preaches the sermons. They're good people."

"I wouldn't have guessed you were a minister's son," Megan said.

Jeff laughed, "Do I seem like such an evil sinner?" he joked.

Megan felt the return of desire for him. She loved the sound of his voice, the smell of him, his sense of humor. She winked. "A little sin is good sometimes. Don't you think?"

"Well, let me put it this way. I haven't always been the perfect son. But enough about me. I want to know more about you. Tell me about your childhood and your parents."

"I have an older sister. She's an attorney."

Jeff arched an eyebrow. "A lawyer? That's unusual. I don't know any women lawyers. I've never heard of a lady lawyer."

"Yeah, well, it happens where I come from."

Jeff sat up and crossed his legs. His eyes bored into hers. "And where do you come from, Megan? Please tell me. Where in the hell do you come from?"

She looked down and away, avoiding his question. "My father's a crazy contractor and my mother's a crazy housewife. They produced me, a crazy daughter."

"I'm so glad they did," Jeff said, and then he uncrossed his legs and slid down next to her. As she lay on her back, he kissed her, allowing his mouth to explore her lips.

Megan felt their sleepy chemistry. She was drowsy with love for him and the romance of him, feeling as though she were dreaming while awake. How could she leave the best thing that had ever happened to her? How could she leave Jeff Grant, and never know what would happen to him? Would he survive the war? Would he fall in love with another girl and have kids and a home? Would he remember her after she was gone, or when he was flying bombing missions over Germany? She couldn't bear thinking about it. She was, at that moment, deliriously happy. She reached for him and began to unbutton his shirt.

"This isn't sin, Jeff. This is love, and I've never really been in love before."

Danny and Jackie were undressed within minutes after entering the cabin. Jackie seized him and teased him. He chased her, caressed her and kissed her pouty mouth, lifting her up from the buttocks to kiss her neck and the tops of her breasts. She wrapped her legs about his waist, crushing his lips with hers. Danny carried her into the bedroom and eased her down onto the bed.

It was the playful tangle of lovers, rolling, tickling and exploring. Hands found buttons and hooks and they were released; clothes were tugged at and flung away. When the cold touch of skin startled, their laughter was low and their love became urgent with heated sighs and little yelps of pleasure.

The clock was ticking, but all time had vanished. It wasn't 1943 or the 21st century. Time ceased to be relevant or even necessary in their safe isolation, swept away by love, longing and happiness. The lovers, like all lovers in all times, were lost in a fortunate timelessness, sheltered from the storms, ecstatic now, pushing back the painful thought that time and the real world would soon reappear, and they might never come together again.

CHAPTER 21

They drove back down the mountain in silence. The worst of the storm had passed, leaving an eerily still and frigid night, with random flakes crashing into the windshield.

Jackie's head lay softly on Danny's shoulder and he caressed her hair, his expression remote, eyes moving, heart full of wishes.

Megan sat close to Jeff, her arm entwined in his, as if to never let him go. Jeff glanced at her and smiled, patting her hand. "Sorry we didn't get to that sleigh ride."

"Another time," Megan said.

Her words seemed to further dampen their mood. There would be no other time and she knew it.

When Jeff spoke, his voice was flat. "Danny Boy, Megan and I are going to stop at the church."

"Yeah, I know, Jeff. You know I'm not the religious type. Jackie and I will wait in the car."

"We won't be long, Danny."

Jackie looked into Danny's sad eyes, feeling an exhausted sense of sorrow. She could hardly speak. "Don't be long, Megan. We've got to go."

There was an icy silence until they turned onto Saw Mill Road. Jeff and Danny were instantly alert, searching about in case they were being followed.

"See anything, Danny?" Jeff asked.

"No, but you know Burt's poking around someplace. Probably the Sheriff too."

"Let's keep a sharp lookout," Jeff said.

At that moment, they had a clear view of the lighted church spire, rising up through the bare, dark trees, and then the entire white church appeared, illuminated by a golden light. They heard the dull clang of the steeple bell, as they drove along a snakelike road and turned into the parking lot. Two men in heavy coats and hats were shoveling pathways, from the parking lot to the entrance of the church. Jeff parked to the far side of the church and killed the engine. They sat quietly, listening to the scrape of the snow shovels and the ringing bell.

Megan and Jackie studied the little country church, feeling a kind of holy emotion come over them.

"It's so picturesque," Megan said.

Jeff got out, rounded the car and opened the door for Megan. He took her hand and helped her out. He closed the door, and they walked to the side entrance of the church, opened the door and went in.

Megan took in the interior, plastered and painted in white and gray. She saw the box pews and the high pulpit, and was dazzled by candles and poinsettias arranged artfully near the altar. Megan saw that choristers were entering the choir loft, wearing white robes with crimson front banners.

"It's lovely," Megan whispered.

Jeff took her elbow and led her to the altar, to a tall,

brass, seven-branch candelabra. One of the long red tapered candles had gone out. Jeff looked at Megan and smiled.

"This is perfect," he whispered. "This candle was calling to me."

He found a long wooden matchstick and struck it. Megan observed him as he lit the candle, his serene eyes focused on the flame, his lips moving in a silent prayer. She had a flash of imagination—she and Jeff at the altar on their wedding day.

Jeff turned to her. "That should do it," he said.

They laced hands, and he led her along the right aisle to a back shadowy pew, where they eased down. In a hushed voice, Jeff said, "They're going to rehearse. The service starts at 8 o'clock."

The church bell slowly died away into the night, replaced by the inspiring sound of the organ. A middle-aged man, dressed in a dark suit and tie, with salt and pepper hair and black-framed glasses, appeared from a side door, mounted two stairs and stood tall before the choir, their choir books raised, faces attentive.

"That's my father," Jeff said. "Like I said, he conducts the choir sometimes, while my mother plays the organ. I wish you could meet them. I know they'd love you as much as I do."

Jeff's father raised his arm, preparing to direct the choir. On a downbeat, they began singing a heart-stirring version of *Silent Night*.

Jeff reached into his uniform jacket and took out a small, rectangular black box. He opened the lid and Megan centered her attention on it, her face aglow with surprise. It was a small, gold heart pendant necklace. Megan was overcome with emotion, tears filling her eyes. Jeff gently lifted it from the box and handed it to her. She held it with care, and then turned the pendant over to read an engraved message on the back.

To Megan, with love, Jeff

Megan sought words, but none came. Jeff looped the necklace around her neck and fastened it.

"It's a little Christmas present," Jeff said.

She kissed him softly, taking his hand and holding it in hers. "Thank you," she whispered. "I'll cherish it, always."

Megan closed her eyes and offered a prayer, a prayer for a miracle. It was Christmas, after all, and weren't miracles possible at Christmas, more than at any other time?

The carol was a kind of drug that uplifted her, and put her into a drowsy peace. Jeff's hand was firmly in hers, and she looked around the church in a sweet bewilderment. Why had she and Jackie come to this town? Was it to know what real and true love really is? She shut her eyes and prayed for Jeff. She prayed for his safe return, and for him to have a full, rich and happy life. She prayed like she'd never prayed before that if it were at all possible, she and Jeff would find a way, somehow, to meet again.

When she opened her eyes, she saw that Jeff was praying too, his eyes closed, his lips moving. His eyes finally fluttered open, and he looked at her tenderly.

"Megan... whatever happens to either of us, I want you to know something: We will find each other again. Do you believe that?"

Megan stared into his eyes. She couldn't find words.

"Maybe we'll be different and maybe things will have changed, but we will find each other again. Do you believe that?"

Megan cleared her throat. "Yes, Jeff, I believe that."

Outside in the car, Danny and Jackie were gently kissing. Jackie pulled away from him.

"How can I leave you, Danny?"

"Then don't leave me. Stay here. Wait for me. Hell, let's go inside that church right now and get married."

"You're crazy," Jackie said, her eyes twinkling at the thought.

Danny tugged a little square black box from inside his coat pocket. Jackie focused on it, curious.

"What's that?" she asked.

"A Christmas present," he said, handing her the box. "Go ahead, open it."

Jackie took the box and thumbed open the lid. Surprised, she put a hand to her chest. "Oh my God, Danny. It's a beautiful ring."

Danny pointed at it with pride. "It's sterling silver. And that's a pink sapphire."

"Yes... it's so gorgeous. So beautiful."

"Put it on. I hope it fits."

Jackie plucked it from the box and slid it over her 4th finger. It was a perfect fit. She threw her arms around Danny and kissed him, feeling a loosening of tension and a swell of love.

After they had disengaged and Jackie was admiring the ring, Danny stroked her hair. "We could have a great life together, Jackie. You know we could. We fit together, perfectly, in every way. From the first time we met, we knew we were right for each other."

She gave him a soul-torn glance. "I can't stay, Danny. I wish I could, and I wish I could tell you why, but I can't."

"Why? Tell me."

"You know some of it."

"No, I don't. You won't tell me. You keep telling me

I won't understand. Okay, tell me, and let's see if I'll understand."

"For one thing, it's the car. You know what could happen if they find it. You know what could happen if it gets in the wrong hands."

"The hell with the car. I'll blow the damned thing up. I'm an expert in demolition. I can blow bridges and buildings to hell and back, so I can certainly blow up a car."

"It's not just that, Danny."

"Jackie, just tell me!"

Jackie swallowed, conflicted, staring into Danny's hopeful eyes.

"All right, Danny. I'm going to tell you. You're not going to believe me, but I'm going to tell you the whole truth, right from the very beginning."

Danny sat up, ready.

Just then, the red sweep of a dome light seized his attention. "Damn! It's the Sheriff."

Jackie's head whipped around to see the Sheriff's car drive into the parking lot and stop, as if scanning the area. "Danny, go get Jeff and Megan. We've got to get out of here."

Danny ducked, shoved the door open and, crouching, hurried off to the side door of the church. He met a troubled Jeff and Megan, exiting.

"The Sheriff," Danny said.

Jeff surveyed the area. "Let's go."

Jeff took Megan's hand, and they walked briskly toward the car, as the Sheriff's car entered the parking lot.

"He's seen us, Jeff," Danny said.

"Yeah, get in. We'll make a break for it."

They got into the car, just as the Sheriff's car pulled in beside them. Jeff saw Burt Skall was sitting in the passenger's seat, his face twisted with anger. In the back seat was a stocky man, who was not wearing a military uniform. He looked menacingly ugly, with a broad blunt face and a stony gaze.

Sheriff Dougherty got out and limped around the back of his car over to Jeff's window. Burt pushed open his door and stood, an intimidating expression spreading across his face when he saw Megan and Jackie.

Sheriff Dougherty was 30, and he had put on weight since his discharge from the Navy. He had a comfortable belly under his opened overcoat. His wide-brimmed hat was cocked to the left. He carried a flashlight that he switched on as he approached, his expression hard and suspicious.

Jeff rolled down his window. "Merry Christmas, Sheriff Dougherty," Jeff said, affably.

Dougherty grumbled a reply that was his own version of Bah Humbug.

Then Burt spoke up, wagging a bony, threatening finger at them. "Where's my car? I know you two took it. I know how you lied to Tom Pike and sent him home so you could steal my car."

Jackie started to speak, ready to attack, but Danny nudged her, smiling pleasantly. She struggled to restrain herself.

Dougherty aimed a sharp finger at Burt. "Shut up, Burt, and let me do all the talking."

Dougherty aimed the beam of light into the car, sweeping the faces, allowing the shaft of white light to frame each face for a few seconds. Jackie's expression was obstinate, Megan's contrite. Danny grinned, and Jeff's expression was genial.

"Were you boys out at Wicker's Airfield this afternoon?"

"Yes, Sheriff," Jeff said. "Danny Boy and I went out there to make sure my Jenny, my airplane, was secure because of the storm."

"Did you see a car out there?"

"Sure. Sure we did, didn't we, Danny Boy?"

"You bet," Danny said.

Burt took a step forward. "See Sheriff, I told you. I told you they took it."

"Now I told you to shut up, Burt, and let me handle this," the Sheriff snapped.

He turned his attention back to Jeff. "What kind of car was it?"

"I guess it's the same one that's been out there for months now. The 1932 Chevy Coupe that Harry left before he went off to war. It's covered by that old tarp."

Burt exploded. "That's a damned lie and you know it, Jeff Grant! My car was out there and you know it."

Sheriff Dougherty whirled toward Burt, his face pinched in rage. "One more word from you, Burt, and I'm locking you up. You got that?"

Burt turned away, cursing under his breath.

The Sheriff fixed his sharp gaze back on Jeff. "Tom Pike said you lied to him about his wife, Millie, wanting him back at the house. Did you lie to him? Now, remember, Jeff, you're Preacher Grant's son, so don't lie to me."

"Danny and I were just having some fun, Sheriff. We're going off to war in a few days, so we were just having some fun. You know how it is, before you go off to war. You just want to have a little fun."

And Sheriff Dougherty did know how it was and, for a few seconds, as his eyes traveled back and forth from Megan to Jackie, his face registered fond memories, and he nearly smiled. But the memories quickly vanished when he recalled the brutality of combat, and the limp and the pain he'd carry for the rest of his life. His expression darkened, and his frosty breath came faster.

"All right, look, it's cold out here. Now Burt says that these two ladies tried to break into his place last night. That's one thing. I've also got an irritated gentleman sitting in my back seat who says Burt offered him some car, and Burt says you and Danny stole the car that was promised to that gentleman."

Jeff ventured a look past the Sheriff to see the gentleman. "Forgive me, Sheriff, but that guy doesn't look like much of a gentleman to me."

"I don't give a damn what you think, Jeff. Now, I'm going to get to the bottom of all this one way or the other, because this is my town and I know you and Danny have been up to something. Do you understand me?"

"Yes sir, Sheriff, I do understand."

"Good. Now I want you to follow me back to the station so we can get this whole thing sorted out. Okay?"

Jeff grinned, broadly. "Happy to, Sheriff. Happy to."

Megan tensed up. Jackie sucked in a deep breath of anxiety.

Burt glared at them, antagonistically, as his hunched body lowered into the car.

Jeff turned to the other three, in a frown of concentration. "What have you girls done?"

Megan folded her arms, looking away.

"Okay, this is it, girls," Jeff continued. "What's it going to be? Do you still want to leave town, or do we follow the Sheriff and figure a way out of this so we can all live happily ever after?"

Megan looked at Jackie for an answer. Her conflicted eyes were moving, calculating.

Danny took her hand. "Jackie?"

"What's it going to be?" Jeff said. "The Sheriff is pulling away. It's now or never."

Megan was staring at Jackie, pleading with her eyes.

Jackie was shivering as her eyes lingered on Danny's face. "I'm sorry, Danny. I wish I could explain everything to you. There are just too many unknowns, and I don't do well with unknowns. I've got a life somewhere else and, before I can make any kind of permanent decisions, I need to get back to that life. And we can't let Burt or that gangster get our car. Forgive me, Danny, but I've got to go."

Danny's disappointed eyes dropped. "Okay, go if you have to, but at least tell me you'll write. Even if you won't wait for me, at least tell me you'll write."

"I can't, Danny. I've told you that. It's impossible. I would write to you if I could, but I can't."

Danny's eyes went dull with pain, and Megan's shoulders slumped.

"That's it, then," Jeff said, switching on the engine and wrestling the car into gear. "Hang on, we'll make a break for it when we hit Saw Mill Road."

Jeff backed the car out, turned left, and followed the Sheriff's car toward Saw Mill Road.

"Here's the plan," Jeff said. "I'll get you close to Hazel's place so you can get out and hoof it up to her house. Meanwhile, I'll lead them off on a wild goose chase. That should give you the time to get away."

"Away to where?" Danny asked, sorrowfully.

"We're going back across the Holly Grove Bridge," Jackie said.

"What?" Danny exclaimed. "What are you talking about?"

"That bridge is a broken down death trap! You'll fall through the thing and be killed," Jeff added. "Take the

225

parallel road, out of town, turn left on Highway 23. That'll take you out."

"No, it's got to be the Holly Grove Bridge," Jackie insisted.

Danny adjusted his body to face Jackie. "Jackie, that's crazy. Just crazy."

"That's how we got here," Megan said. "And that's how we have to go back."

Jeff and Danny were greatly bewildered. Jeff glanced into the rearview mirror at Danny, and lifted his eyebrows. "There's something weird going on here, Danny Boy. But then, it's been weird from the first time we met these two."

Danny looked at Jackie, for clarification.

"Don't ask, Danny, there's no time."

They approached Saw Mill Road.

Megan squirmed, wishing there was a way she could stay behind, but she knew she couldn't.

"Hang on," Jeff said.

The Sheriff turned left. Jeff let the Sheriff's car move a good 20 yards away before he made a sharp turn right, slammed his foot down on the accelerator and shot away in the opposite direction. They sped along the two lane road, snow spinning from the wheels. Megan wrapped both her arms around Jeff's right arm. She closed her eyes, branding the feel of him, the love she had for him.

He glanced at her. "The only reason I'm letting you go is because I know I'll see you again."

Megan smiled, weakly. "Yes, darling. Of course you will." But she knew otherwise.

"I'll find you no matter how long it takes. That's a promise. That was the prayer I made tonight in my father's church. I will find you, Megan."

The car veered left onto an isolated road, and Jeff

worked the gears as he muscled it along through heavy snow, tires spinning, engine whining. Megan reached into her purse and drew out a sealed white letter envelope. On the front of it she had written Jeff's name.

"Get ready," Jeff said, pointing ahead. "I'm going to drop the three of you up by that rock. Hazel's house is about a quarter of a mile up that road. Danny can lead you there and help you with the car."

Megan held up the envelope. Jeff looked at it. "What's this?"

Megan looked into his eyes, so deeply that she could have been lost in them for hours. "Open it after we're gone, Jeff. Don't show it to anybody else. It explains everything, from the very beginning."

Jeff regarded her, tenderly, and he watched as she opened the glove compartment, laid it inside and shut the door.

Jeff hit the brakes. "That should make for interesting reading."

Megan's stomach knotted up. "I love you, Jeff."

He reached for her. Their kiss was long and passionate.

They disengaged, and Jeff's voice was filled with strain. "Go now, and what ever you do, don't drive across that damn broken-down bridge. Go!"

Megan embraced him a last time. "Be careful, Jeff. Promise me you'll be careful."

He nodded. "I'll see you again, Megan. That's a promise."

Danny, Jackie and Megan stood outside in 13 inches of snow, watching Jeff drive away. The engine was high and grinding, the back tires fishtailing, shooting snow, as the car finally zigzagged away down a hill and vanished.

Megan didn't try to stop the tears. She let them flow cold down her face. Danny took both girls' hands and led them along into the big dark night that was now heavy with stars. They trudged through trees, around snow drifts and protruding rocks, slipping, creating small avalanches of snow. They scaled a small knoll, bracing against a stiff wind, using fallen sturdy limbs as canes to pull themselves along, their faces and feet stinging from the cold. When Hazel's house came into view, they paused, catching their breath, feeling the finality and poignancy of the moment.

Jackie straightened. "Let's go, Megan. Let's go home."

In the distance, they heard the cry of the Sheriff's siren, but it was moving away from them. Then they heard the glaring moan of the train whistle as it raced toward town. The sounds heightened the stress and urgency. Jackie and Megan broke into a run, following Danny, just ahead.

Megan knocked on the front door while Danny and Jackie stopped at the garage. They managed a final embrace before Hazel emerged from the back door with Megan. Hazel hurried over, opened the lock and Danny swung the doors open.

From the porch light, some of the yellow glow spilled out onto the snow, dimly lighting the inside of the garage. Danny went to work, removing the tarp and metal clamps, while Jackie and Megan climbed inside.

Inside, the girls paused, suddenly still and alert. It was startling how the look and smell of the car swept them forward to their own time; to the airport; to the snowstorm; to the panic of being lost and of first driving into Holly Grove, Vermont in 1943. They felt fear and delight at the same time, as if they were about to be launched into space to land on some distant and unknown planet.

Jackie gave a little shake of her head, to clear it. She started the car. It turned over easily, purring, waiting. Megan got out and hugged Hazel, thanking her and wishing her well.

Hazel looked at Megan closely. "Where did you come from?"

Megan glanced down at her watch. It started to snow again, and flakes drifted down lazily around them. "I wish I had the time to tell you, Hazel. It would add an awesome chapter to your mother's book. I can tell you that we came from the future."

Hazel searched Megan's eyes. "Is it a better time? Have things gotten better in the future? Is it a better world?"

Jackie called out. "Come on, Megan! We've got to go."

Megan hugged Hazel again. "Yes, Hazel," she lied. "Things are better. Much better."

Hazel's eyes glittered with hope. "You go now, and God bless you."

Danny finished his work and climbed into the backseat, while Megan slipped into the passenger seat and fastened her seatbelt.

"Crazy things, these seatbelts," Danny said, examining his. "It's a good idea, really."

"Where are you going?" Jackie asked.

"I'm going with you, to make sure you don't try to cross that bridge and kill yourselves."

"No, Danny. You can't come with us."

Danny folded his arms, obstinate. "Okay, fine. Then you'll let me out before you cross. But one way or the other, I'm going with you."

Jackie shoved the car into gear and drove away. They crept along, carefully, until Danny directed them toward the snow-covered road that would lead them to Main Street.

"We could take a couple of side roads, but after the storm, we might get stuck going up some of the hills."

"Main Street is fine," Jackie said, her face set in rigid resolve.

They were at the far end of town when they turned onto Main Street, heading north, toward the covered bridge. In her rearview mirror, Jackie spotted headlights, advancing.

"A car behind us," she said, nervously.

Danny twisted around and peered out of the back windshield. The red dome light came on and the siren screamed.

"It's the Sheriff!"

"Dammit!" Jackie said.

"Hit the gas," Megan yelled.

And Jackie did.

The Ford darted away, gaining speed.

"Good God, this thing can really jump," Danny exclaimed. "You're pulling away from him."

But the red dome light kept sweeping the world.

"I'll stop near the bridge, Danny, and you'll get out."

Danny was silent.

"And if I don't?"

"You will, Danny," Jackie said. "You have to. Trust me. If you love me, you'll get out."

Danny didn't respond.

A car burst out from a hidden road ahead. Jackie swerved, sharply, just missing it. It was Jeff's car.

"What the hell was that!?" Megan shouted.

"It's Jeff," Danny yelled.

Jackie slowed down as the Sheriff's car drew closer. Megan and Danny looked around.

"Hurry, Jackie, the Sheriff's gaining on us," Megan said.

Jackie stomped the gas pedal and they rocketed off, past Jeff, who was waving them on. He whipped his car around and, just as the Sheriff sped by, Jeff raced after him.

"The bridge is just ahead," Danny said.

"Okay, I'm going to stop and you get out, Danny. Please. Do it!"

The shadow of the bridge loomed out of the darkness, and it seemed to hover like a ghostly object from another world. Jackie braked to a stop. She saw the stab of headlights in her rearview mirror, and the red dome light sweeping. The siren shrieked, and the Sheriff's car came on like a wild charging animal.

Jackie turned to Danny. "Come home safe, Danny Boy. Promise me you'll come home safe," Jackie said.

"I'll find you," Danny said, pointing at her. "You can count on that."

"I love you, Danny."

He nodded in resignation and left the car, slamming the door, as Jackie rolled down her window. He leaned in and gave her a long, last kiss. As he stood back, he pointed again. "I *will* find you. I will. Now go!"

Megan and Jackie turned their anxious attention toward the bridge.

"Let's do it, Jackie. Let's get the hell out of here before I jump out and run after Jeff."

Jackie gunned the engine, just as the Sheriff and Jeff arrived, skidding to a stop. They all boiled out of their cars and watched in shock and horror as the red Ford Fusion shot away, bursting through the three wooden barricades, bouncing heavily onto the bridge.

Danny ran forward with Jeff on his heels. The Sheriff

scrambled ahead, with Burt Skall and the gangster right behind.

They stared in alarm as the Ford Fusion retreated into the darkness of the bridge and disappeared into a black smoky haze. They expected to hear a loud resounding crash of metal and glass. They braced for it, the boys wincing, feeling helpless.

"No! No!" Burt yelled. "My car!" He cursed, and seemed to dwindle in size as the car vanished.

They all waited, transfixed. Finally, Danny and Jeff stepped down to the bridge and peered inside, searching. The Sheriff appeared with his flashlight. He switched it on and waved the shaft of light about, squinting looks up and down, but there was no trace of them. All was quiet, just the sound of the singing stream splashing across the rocks.

Jeff and Danny left the interior and scampered out and around the bridge to get a good view of the other side. But there was no sign of the car. The boys stood, watching, stricken with wonder.

Megan and Jackie had just disappeared.

CHAPTER 22

The world veered and tipped and spun away into a white, swirling mass of falling snow. The car bounced hard, and Jackie's and Megan's heads brushed the ceiling as it ramped and pitched, finally coming to rest on a deserted, snow-covered road.

Jackie stopped the car, breathless. Megan searched about with wild eyes, unaware that she was holding her breath. It was snowing heavily; the wind circling them, making the world chaotic and out of focus.

The girls looked at each other, faces taut with fear.

"That was one helluva bumpy ride," Megan said, her eyes startled and jumpy.

"Do you see the bridge?"

Megan twisted around. "No. I don't see it. Do you?"

"No. And I don't see anyone behind us."

"So the question is, where are we? And what year is it?" Megan asked.

They sat staring, waiting, wondering.

Suddenly, they heard a trumpet, and they both jumped. The trumpet played *Bolero*, along with the steady beat of an exotic drum.

"What the hell is that?" Jackie shouted.

Megan lit up. "Oh my God! It's my phone. That's my ringtone. *Bolero.*"

She hastily unzipped her purse, and paused, unsure and confused as she looked down at the pulsing alien thing from her own time. The trumpet wailed on and on.

"Answer it, Megan, for God's sake," Jackie said.

Megan snatched up the phone and looked at the caller ID. She answered it. "Dad... Dad is that you?"

"Yes! Your mother and I have been worried sick. I've been trying to call you for over an hour."

"Where are you, Dad?"

"We just got back home from the airport. Where have you been?"

"We got lost. Dad, what day is it?"

"What day is it? Have you been drinking or something? Were you in some kind of accident?"

"No, Dad. What day is it? Just tell me."

"It's Monday, December the 20th, for God's sake. What the hell's the matter with you?"

"This is Monday!? December the 20th?"

Jackie shot Megan a look of surprise.

"Of course it is. What's happened to you? We just spoke a little over an hour ago."

Megan stiffened, her face drained of expression.

"What?" Jackie asked, her hands up and open.

Megan covered the phone with her hand, as she looked at Jackie. "No time has passed. It's Monday, December 20th. It's the same night we first crossed the bridge."

Jackie shivered, shifting uneasily. "Well, that's weird. I mean, that's really freakin' weird."

"Megan, are you there?" Megan's father asked.

Megan quickly recovered. "Yes, yes, I'm here, Dad."

"What the hell happened? Tell me!"

Glancing at Jackie for encouragement, Megan quickly created the story which she and Jackie would repeat a dozen times in the coming days. A snowstorm. A wrong turn. No phone service.

While Megan answered her father's questions, Jackie reached for her phone. It lit up her weary face as she thumbed through her messages.

After Megan hung up, Jackie gave her a strange, foggy look. "I have 55 text messages, 45 emails and 30 voicemail messages. We're back at the races."

They heaved out deep sighs at the same time then lowered their phones and sat there, thinking, remembering. They felt relief, exhilaration and exhaustion. They sat there for a long time, even as the storm slowly died away and the wind subsided. They leaned back into their seats, eyes open, their heads pressed against the headrests, lost in memory and emotion.

Megan spoke at a near whisper. "Do you think they survived the war, Jackie?"

Jackie shut her wet eyes, remembering that wonderful afternoon with Danny, only this afternoon—over 70 years ago. The afternoon she'd fallen in love. She touched the ring, and she ached for him. What had she done? Why hadn't she had the courage to stay?

"I don't know, Megan. I guess we'll never know what happened to them."

"What do we do now?" Megan asked.

"What do we do now? What else? We go home."

"And then what?"

Jackie opened her eyes and rolled her head to look at her friend. "We forget everything, Megan, because it all happened a very long time ago, or it never happened at all. And no one, not our family, not our friends, nobody, will ever believe us. We're on our own. It's always going to be our little secret."

Megan was trying to control her obvious grief and sort out everything that had happened. "Maybe I'll do some research to see if the boys survived."

"Megan, even if Danny and Jeff survived the war, they are very old men by now or very dead men. Either way, I don't want to know. I never want to know."

Jackie put the car in gear and drove away, tentative at first, but eventually speeding up, as habit took over. They found the highway and turned on the radio, moving awkwardly with the music, struggling to recapture their former selves. Twenty miles outside of Portland, Megan turned to Jackie.

"Do you mind if I turn it off?" she asked, her finger on the off switch.

"No. I keep hearing the Buddy Loren Swing Orchestra, anyway."

They sat staring at the highway, overcome with memories.

Megan finally broke the silence. "Will you do me a favor, Jackie?"

Jackie looked at her. "Sure."

Megan gave her a little smile, suddenly feeling peculiar and distant from her. Their friendship had been defined solely by their experiences in 1943. Without Jeff and Danny, without the urgency of their struggle to return to the present, their relationship was foreign and mostly unknown.

"Any chance you could meet me on New Year's Eve?" Megan asked. "Just the two of us. I'd like to remember Jeff and Danny. I'd like to offer them a toast."

Jackie felt a sense of steady fear and confusion as she remembered the past and anticipated the future. "Let's do it. It's a great idea."

"I feel so lost leaving Jeff like that. I just feel lost."

"Me too. And what am I going to do about Eric, Megan? After Danny... well..." her voice trailed off.

"Is it a date then? New Year's Eve?"

"Yeah, it's a date."

They drove on in silence until the lights of Portland came into view. They had returned home, back to their own time. Megan stared ahead numbly, her brain noisy with questions and memory. Jackie felt the empty stillness of the lonely, as she savored Danny Boy's final kiss. She turned to her friend.

"Merry Christmas, Megan."

Megan managed a smile. "Yeah... Merry Christmas."

EPILOGUE

It was clear and cold in New York City on New Year's Eve. The City was pulsing with anticipation and celebration. At 10 o'clock, Megan and Jackie met at The Capital Grille. An elegantly dressed hostess led them to a quiet table. Megan ran her hand across the white tablecloth and Jackie examined the little lamp with its golden shade. Such a contrast to Dot's Café.

They studied the menu and ordered a bottle of California Cabernet, lamb chops and a sirloin steak. After the wine was poured, they lifted their glasses and touched. The glasses rang like little bells.

"To the boys," they said in unison.

"To wherever they may be," Megan said.

"I'll drink to that," Jackie said, and they clinked again.

They took long, thoughtful sips.

Jackie and Megan had spoken several times since their return to the present. They'd talked about Aunt Betty and Rose, about Burt and Hazel. They'd shared stories about Christmas and their families, and about the highs and lows of re-entering their lives in New York City.

Inevitably, though, the conversation always wandered back to Jeff and Danny and what might have happened to them.

Jackie reached for her wineglass and guided it gently to her lips. "Do you know what happened when I broke it off with Eric?"

"No, what?" Megan said.

"It really pissed me off. He didn't seem all that upset about it, but he wanted the necklace back."

"What did you tell him?" Megan asked.

"I told him I lost it. That really pissed him off. It made me feel better though. Do you know what I realized? Danny was twice the man Eric is. He was thoughtful and nice, and he never would have asked for the necklace back, not that I give a damn one way or the other about the necklace. And Danny Boy would have never let me go. Never." She got quiet. "No, Danny Boy would have come with us, if I had let him. He would have followed me anywhere."

Jackie sat in memory, her red lips pursed. She was wearing an elegant long black satin dress with spaghetti shoulder straps and black heels. Her jet black hair gleamed in the soft overhead light, and she wore the silver ring that Danny had given her. She twisted it around her finger.

"Just think, Megan, I was actually going to marry Eric. Imagine that? And then came 1943 and Danny."

The gold necklace Jeff had given Megan was draped about her long graceful neck. She touched the pendant tenderly. She wore a red dress with a plunging neckline, and her hair was piled up on top of her head in a style similar to the one she'd worn in Holly Grove.

"I really fell hard for Jeff. And it happened so fast."

"It's funny how when you really fall in love, all the other relationships you thought were so wonderful just seem so pathetically boring and ordinary," Jackie said.

"I just can't get him out of my mind. Everywhere I look, I think I see him. The other day, I followed this guy for half a block before he finally turned around. It wasn't Jeff, of course. It wasn't Jeff at all."

"I've seen Danny at least five times. Not Danny, of course. How could it be? But guys I thought were Danny."

They sipped the wine, lost in their own thoughts.

"Remember the last dinner we had at Aunt Betty's?" Jackie asked. "Remember how good her mashed potatoes were, and that ham?"

"Oh, yeah. I wish we could have worn these dresses for the guys that night. I would have loved to see their faces."

Jackie grinned. "I'd love to have seen Aunt Betty's face. God, she would have come at us with a butcher knife."

Megan laughed, swirling the glass of wine in small circles. "Yeah, but she was a sweet, sweet woman, wasn't she, Jackie? I wish we could have said goodbye to her. I wish we could send her a thank you note or something."

"Yeah, me too. She was so good to us."

A tall waiter approached, deposited their dinners and withdrew. The girls ate quietly and grew reflective.

"It was a nice little town," Megan said.

"Yeah. Nice. And nice people."

"Yeah. And the guys were something, weren't they?"

Jackie's voice was small and sad. "Something. Yeah."

They sipped their wine in silence. Megan licked the corner of her lips, savoring the flavor and the memories of Jeff's kisses. She recalled how he traced her lips with his finger.

"When do you start rehearsals?" Jackie asked.

"In a week. One of these days, I'm going to get the leading role. One of these days I'm going to actually have my name up in lights."

"I'm coming to see you anyway," Jackie said. "And I'll bring all my family and friends. I'm going to point at you and say, guess what, that girl snores louder than a big black bear."

They both laughed so loudly that people at tables nearby glanced over.

After the main course, they sipped cappuccinos and shared a chocolate dessert.

"I've been doing a lot of reading about World War II," Megan said. "I read about the Airborne and about the air war in Europe. The casualties were bad, Jackie. A lot of boys were killed over there. I'm sure Danny fought during D-Day. Lots of the B-17 pilots were shot down, or they wound up in prison camps. Many were killed."

"Let's not go there, Megan. It's too hard. It's too depressing to think about those young and beautiful boys being killed, or even being old. It just hurts too much."

"Yeah... but I just can't get Jeff out of my mind."

"I know. Danny was the hottest man I ever knew. I couldn't keep my hands off him."

Megan licked her dry lips. "There's something else, Jackie. I *Googled* the Holly Grove Bridge."

"And?"

"It was originally built in 1886." She raised an eyebrow. "And guess what?"

Jackie drained the last of her cappuccino. "Ever the drama queen, Megan. So tell me," Jackie said.

Megan's eyes were eager and restless. "I found out that an astrologer and occultist named Phineas Monroe lived in that area of Vermont. Folk lore has it that he often used the bridge as a kind of time tunnel."

Jackie's eyes opened with interest. "Really... And?"

"And there's more."

"Okay, Megan, so stop the drama and tell me."

Megan held up her hand. "Patience, Jackie. Patience."

Jackie drummed her fingers on the table.

"I found some excerpts from Martha Comb's book, *True Weird and Unexplained Stories of Vermont.*"

Jackie sat up. "Are you kidding me!? So Hazel got her mother's book published?"

"Yes, a small publisher in Vermont published it in 1947, with a preface and a chapter by Hazel."

"That is so cool, Megan Did you order a copy?"

"It's out of print. I'm still trying to find a copy, but so far, no luck. Anyway, I was able to find parts of the book quoted in articles on the internet. So listen to this."

Megan leaned forward, lowering her voice to a near whisper as she glanced about, to make sure no one was listening. "*We* are mentioned in the book."

Jackie stared, incredulous. "What!?"

Megan nodded. "Yes. You, me. *We!*"

Jackie's blinking eyes traveled the room, processing the information. "That's unbelievable. What did Hazel say about us?"

"It's wild.... only a short segment. I printed it out for you."

Megan reached for her purse, opened it, and drew out the folded piece of paper. She handed it to an anxious Jackie, who unfolded it and read:

The young women came from the future, another time and place. They said that in their time, there were no more wars, no disease and no hunger. They spoke a strange language and wore strange, revealing clothes. There was a peculiarity about them, and an aura of mystery.

One sensed that they had the ability to read minds and travel to distant stars. When they finally departed in their red rocket ship, they bade me goodbye with hugs and kisses. Then they shot off into the sky, a streak of golden light, seeking the distant star of their homeland.

Jackie looked up. She brought a glass of water to her lips and sipped thoughtfully. "Wow! Who knew Hazel had such a wild imagination?" She handed the paper back to Megan. "Were we so peculiar? Were our clothes that revealing?"

"I thought we blended in pretty well," Megan said. "I wish I *could* read minds and travel to distant stars."

Jackie shrugged. "Well, anyway, I like the *aura of mystery* comment."

"Hazel died in 1958," Megan said. "I wasn't able to find out whether her husband and son survived the war."

It was a very long moment before they surfaced from their private thoughts and asked for the check.

Outside, wrapped in cashmere coats, they strolled leisurely toward the crowds at Times Square. The cold air felt good and, for a while, they walked arm in arm, two good friends who'd been through a lot together.

They stood on the periphery of the jumping, screaming crowds, finally screaming themselves when the giant crystal sphere dropped, bringing in the new year. They hugged and wished each other happiness, success and love.

Music thumped and pounded and people streamed by, high on celebration, dancing and singing. Megan and

Jackie did their own version of The East Coast Swing. Jackie nearly fell off her heels as they whirled about in delight, showered by confetti that fell like snow.

Later, as the crowds were dwindling, and the music fell into a soft ballad, Louis Armstrong singing the plaintive *Wonderful World*, they ambled along Broadway and 44th Street.

Megan laughed and pointed. "Look over there, Jackie. I'm doing it again. I'm seeing things."

"What?" Jackie asked.

"Over there," she pointed. "Look at that shiny old car parked at the curb. It looks like one from Holly Grove."

"Yeah, so? There are a bunch of people crowded around it."

Megan stood on tiptoes, craning her neck. "I see a guy, Jackie. I mean, I see a guy that looks like Jeff."

Jackie glanced at Megan doubtfully. "Come on, Megan, let's just not go there."

Megan broke away, picking her way through the gathering crowds. Jackie heaved out a sigh and followed.

"Wait up, Megan!"

Megan moved purposefully, her heels clicking across the pavement, her eyes wide and searching. When she was about 20 feet away, she stopped short, gulping in a startled breath.

Leaning back against the side of the old car, with his arms folded across his chest, was a tall handsome man wearing a vintage dark overcoat, his dark hair oiled and gleaming under the street lights.

Next to him, arms folded and searching the crowd, was a second man dressed in a chocolate brown overcoat, his red hair bootcamp short.

Jackie arrived, saw the two men and froze, staring in wonder. "No way. It can't be. It's impossible. We're seeing things."

The two men were glancing about, taking in the surrounding spectacle, caught by the excitement.

Megan and Jackie realized that something didn't seem right. It was as if they were standing in between two worlds. Time seemed to stop.

When the two men spotted the girls, both pushed away from the car and straightened, sharp gleams of surprise and recognition in their eyes.

"It's Jeff," Megan said, her voice tight in her throat.

"It's Danny," Jackie said, with a blank, entranced expression.

Jackie and Megan exchanged bewildered glances and then watched, breathless, as the two men approached.

A light snow began to fall and, in the distance over the Hudson River, the bright flash of electric red and green fireworks exploded into the sky. The men stopped a few feet away, smiling warmly, their hands pushed deeply into their overcoat pockets.

Jackie stared at Danny, confused and skeptical.

Megan couldn't pull her eyes from Jeff.

The ladies stood awkwardly, nervous and hopeful.

"Hello, there," Jeff said. "We were looking for you two, right, Danny?"

Danny cocked his head right, holding Jackie in his eyes. "Yeah, Jeff. Didn't I say that we'd find them at Times Square on New Year's Eve? I mean, where else would two beautiful girls be on this night of nights?"

Jackie and Megan offered sweet, worried smiles, still not convinced of what they were seeing.

Jeff said, "I hope you were looking for us and not two other lucky guys,"

Megan finally found her voice. "Jeff?"

He grinned broadly, spreading his hands. "Yep. It's me. In the flesh."

Megan studied him: the smile, the eyes. The same—exactly the same as Jeff's. But there was one change. He had a two-inch scar on the right side of his face.

"Hello, Jackie," Danny said. "It's our first time in New York. We hoped you'd show us around."

"But how? How did you…"

Jeff cut her off. "Before we left for war, Danny and I asked the town board not to tear down the bridge until after we returned."

Danny shrugged. "To our disbelief, they agreed. Of course, I don't think they thought we'd ever return home. But we fooled them, didn't we? We did."

He slapped his left leg. "I took a bullet in the leg and I walk with a bit of a limp, but the doctors said that in time, it might go away, and I'll be able to play shortstop again."

Jeff moved closer to Megan. "On December 28, 1945, Danny and I piled into this old Oldsmobile and shot across the bridge. I bet we were the last car that will ever cross that broken-down thing. It disintegrated all around us, but we made it, and here we are."

Jeff's eyes narrowed on Megan, as if he was seeing her for the first time. "I missed you, Megan."

Megan smiled, feeling strange and off-balance, feeling a swelling of love that warmed her in the cold night.

"Our wish was granted," Megan said, as her words puffed out into the winter air. She let tears spill down her face. "Remember the lighted candle? The wish we made came true."

Jeff shrugged. "It would seem so."

Danny took a step toward Jackie. Her mind was still scrambled, and she was still struggling to work the whole impossible thing out. She gave up when Danny held out his hand. She didn't hesitate. She took it, feeling an electric thrill.

"Would you two ladies like to walk with us to get a better view of the fireworks?" Danny asked.

Jeff gave Megan a hopeful smile.

Megan's eyes met Jeff's, and there it was again, that wonderful, indescribable attraction.

Megan watched snowflakes glaze Jeff's hair and shoulders. She inhaled a deep breath and let it out slowly, a new joy rising in her chest. She went to him, went to tiptoes and kissed his scar. Jeff put an arm around her waist, and she nestled in close to him

He kissed her nose. "Happy New Year, Megan."

And then he kissed her warmly and tenderly.

Danny leaned in for a kiss, and Jackie gazed into his marvelous and mischievous eyes. She curved her shoulders forward and eeled into him, her face close, her body warm, her breath sweet, lips moist. It was a long, private and exciting kiss.

Jeff and Megan locked arms and started off, their bodies inching closer as they started down West 44th Street.

Jackie and Danny followed, and as they strolled, their love fully reawakened. Soon, they were walking arm in arm and laughing, as if no time at all had passed.

A photographer, scanning the crowd for interesting shots, was captivated by the romantic scene. He darted over, crouched and snapped their picture as the couples wandered under street lights and falling snow. Above them a burst of red and white fireworks shattered into shimmering pieces, lighting up the night sky.

The photographer snapped away, capturing movement and color—and the resurgence of love.

When he was finished, he stood smiling. He watched confetti and snowflakes dance and swirl in a soft wind across the quiet empty street, as Jackie and Danny and Megan and Jeff drifted away under the glittering sky.

Thank You

Thank you for taking the time to read *The Christmas Town*. If you enjoyed it, please consider telling your friends or posting a short review. Word of mouth is an author's best friend and it is much appreciated.

Thank you,
Elyse Douglas

Other novels by Elyse Douglas that you might enjoy:

The Christmas Eve Letter *A Time Travel Novel (Book 1)*
The Christmas Eve Daughter *A Time Travel Novel (Book 2*)
The Summer Letters
The Other Side of Summer
The Christmas Diary
The Christmas Women
Christmas for Juliet
Christmas Ever After
The Christmas Town *A Time Travel Novel*

www.elysedouglas.com

Printed in Poland
by Amazon Fulfillment
Poland Sp. z o.o., Wrocław

56877779R00153